A young woman with unknown psychic powers begins a terrifying journey into the arcane to discover the identity of the mysterious stranger invading her dreams ...

Rian staggered up, but fell again. She thought she was going to pass out. Strange images passed through her mind ... the man in her dreams giving her the herbs, and then, her rescue by the ladies in the boat. They had once before saved her from this demon.

She tried to say the words, but they wouldn't come. All she could think of were the ladies in the boat ... and the lake. Were they the same? One of them was saying softly, "Say the words, Rian, and think of us. We are your kin. Try!"

The faery women continued to urge her softly, gently. Finally Rian, in her altered state, began to say the words again in her mind and whisper them softly. She wondered, is this what it feels like to die? Everything was getting darker and darker, and Rian felt as though she were sinking down ... down ... down into the waters. And then ... there was nothing.

The Rag
Bone Man

ABOUT THE AUTHOR

Charlotte Lawrence lives northwest of Baltimore, Maryland with her husband, youngest son, and four dogs. She owns and operates a Metaphysical/New-Age book store called Renaissance Books and leads metaphysical seminars. This is Charlotte's first novel. Previously, she was a professional musician, composer, and teacher.

HOW TO WRITE THE AUTHOR

If you wish to contact the author or would like more information about this book, please write to the author in care of Llewellyn Worldwide and we will forward your request. Both the author and publisher appreciate hearing from you and learning of your enjoyment of this book and how it has helped you. Llewellyn Worldwide cannot guarantee that every letter written to the author can be answered, but all will be forwarded. Please write to:

Charlotte Lawrence
c/o Llewellyn Worldwide
P.O. Box 64383-412,
St. Paul, MN 55614-0383, USA

Please enclose a self-addressed, stamped envelope for reply, or $1.00 to cover costs. If outside U.S.A., enclose international postal reply coupon.

Llewellyn's Psi-Fi Series

The Rag Bone Man

Part One of the Merrywell Trilogy

Charlotte Lawrence

1994
Llewellyn Publications
St. Paul, Minnesota 55164-0383 U.S.A

Cover Art by Hrana Janto

Cataloging-in-Publication Data
Lawrence, Charlotte
        The rag bone man / Charlotte Lawrence
            p.   cm — (Llewellyn's psi-fi series)
        ISBN 1-56718-412-X
        1. Young women—Maryland—Fiction. 2. Psychics—Maryland—Fiction. I. Title. II Series
PS 3562.A9114R34   1994   94-26188
813' .54—dc20   CIP

Llewellyn Publications
A Division of Llewellyn Worldwide, Ltd.
P.O. Box 64383, St. Paul, Minnesota, 55164-0383

This is a work of fiction. All the characters and events portrayed in this book are fictitious, and any resemblance to real people or events is purely coincidental.

About Llewellyn's Psi-Fi Series

Supernatural tales of magic
Magical tales of the supernatural

Guaranteed to send a chill up your spine, these tales are based on real metaphysical practices such as ritual magic ... seances ... astral projection ... ESP ... psychokinesis ... out-of-body travel ... shapeshifting ... crystals ... psionics ... and much more. You can be assured that the methods described in these books are *authentic* and *accurate*—whether the characters are attempting to fight off a psychic attacker, tame a murderous power trapped in a haunted house, or foil a sinister plot against the United States.

Our authors are actual practitioners—some are even world-recognized experts in the field. Read any book in the Psi-Fi Series, and you'll see psychic practices in a whole new light (or you just may want to leave the light on!)

Llewellyn, publisher of occult non-fiction since 1901, is proud to bring you this exciting and educational line of occult fiction.

Occult Fiction at its Bone-Chilling Best

I dedicate this book to Simone, Sherry, Angela, Morgai, Rennie, and my daughter Laura, who read this tale in serial form. I'm sure without their encouraging, "What's gonna happen next?" - this book might never have been completed.

To my husband, Tim, who remained supportive during my repeated absences from our bookstore, not to mention my all-night marathons at the word processor.

ACKNOWLEDGMENTS

Special acknowledgments to Simone for letting me bounce ideas off her so often, and who nursed it (and me) along; to Angie for her enthusiasm...and for calling my attention to the fact that magickal terminology was not a universal language; and finally to Rennie for his very helpful critiques and literary advice. I also wish to express my appreciation to Tama, for taking the time out to scan the hard copy to a disk and transferring it to my wonderful new P.C.; and to Eric for procuring this modern, magickal tool of art, and installing it!

My very deep appreciation to Nancy Mostad of Llewellyn for her support, advice and optimism.

Most of all, I thank the town that I patterned this book after for being every bit as enchanting as I described it.

For other reading on the Ladies of the Lake, I suggest *Ladies of the Lake,* by Caitlin and John Matthews, *The Books of Goddesses and Heroines,* by Patricia Monahan, and *The Women's Encyclopoedia of Myths and Secrets,* by Barbara Walker.

To Tennyson, Alfred, Lord: "Lady of Shallott" (p.164)

******

Forthcoming books in this series

Holographic Dollhouse
Part Two of the Merrywell Trilogy

CHAPTER 1

The Rag Bone Man

The stranger huddled in the early evening rainstorm, his meager possessions protected by a makeshift covering of dead dogwood branches. A simple fire he had started to escape the chill in the air had already succumbed to the storm.

Nothing could be heard but the torrential rain interrupted by loud claps of thunder and flashes of bright lightning. He pulled an old, floppy beret down over his ears and tried to crawl under the branches with his things, but it wasn't dense enough to protect him. Rummaging through an old canvas bag, he pulled out a thin denim jacket and put it on, but the rain soaked him anyway.

"Damn rain," he muttered. "Damn!"

After ten minutes, the rain slowed to a steady drizzle. The tall oaks served as protection from this phase of the storm.

When the rain finally stopped, he fumbled around for some matches, but there was no dry wood to rekindle a fire. He checked the inside of his bag. *Good, it was dry.*

The woods came alive again with the sounds of humming and buzzing. The stranger picked up his

1

belongings and found a little, grassy clearing where the summer sun was shinning through the trees. He looked up. From its position in the sky, he judged sunset would come in about two hours. *Still time,* he thought. He took off his clothes, hung them on a tree branch to dry, and stretched out in the sunlight.

A little later, he moved back into the security of the woods. He retrieved a small leather pouch from his canvas bag and took out some matches, herbs, and sandalwood chips. Then, he dug a shallow hole in the ground with a stick and poured some sand from a small plastic bag into the damp hole. He pulled out a roll of dry charcoal, lit it, and placed it in the sand. After it lit, he carefully mixed the herbs together with the sandalwood in the palm of his hands. As he did, he concentrated. He placed the herbal mixture on the smoking coal and began muttering a short rhyme over and over. He continued until he saw in his mind's eye a dark-haired young woman in a store. He mentally gave her the herbal mixture, but suddenly she disappeared from his image.

Damn! ... Too late. Goddamn storm ... threw my timing off!

He tried again anyway, unsuccessfully. She was already out of his reach, far below where he wanted her to be.

Cursing and muttering, he packed up all his things and began rummaging through his bag. He became alarmed. Furiously, he continued searching. It was gone. The book he needed was gone!

He looked around. It must have fallen out of his pack.

Damn! ... All this damn rain!

He went back to the tree-branch, yanked down his

clothes and got dressed. The sun was beginning to set and he took a small flashlight out of his bag and started carefully retracing his steps.

The farther he walked, the closer he moved towards The Apothecary.

She's got it, he thought.

He walked up the steps to the front door of the shop, looked in the window, and saw the girl reading a book, but the sign on the door said CLOSED.

Good! She's there.

In the darkness, he watched her through the window. Suddenly, the porch light came on. He moved quickly over to the door and knocked. The girl stared at him for a moment, then waved him off.

He decided it might be a mistake to make himself conspicuous right now. It would be safer to come back another time. She called out something about the store opening tomorrow morning.

The stranger left, muttering angrily as he walked down the street and disappeared into the nearby state park.

❈ ❈ ❈ ❈

CHAPTER 2

The Merrywells

Rian flopped down on the bed, her long dark hair falling carelessly across her face. Reaching up, she pulled it back, and then slowly, stretched out her body.

She had a strange day at work, and driving home made her weary. Usually, she enjoyed traveling though Maryland's green countryside with its rolling hills and small farms. Today, however, there was a severe summer thunderstorm and cars were backed up for miles. Worse, her car kept stalling whenever she turned on the air conditioner.

Now the air smelled fresh, and the temperature had dropped at least fifteen degrees from the sweltering ninety-five of the past ten days. Rian dragged herself up from the bed, pulled off her clothes and turned on the shower. Then, she changed her mind and ran a bath.

She found a bottle of herbal oil from her own shop, and poured a small capful of the orange-amber scent into the tub. After testing the tepid water, she stepped in, stretched out and relaxed, her eyes closing slowly.

Rian dozed off for a few moments and had a strange dream. In it, she was sitting on the railing of a bridge that was unfamiliar to her. A weather beaten man with a dark haze around him walked up to her and offered her a pouch of herbs. He told her if she carried these, they would protect her and bring her good luck, but if she ever opened the pouch something terrible would happen to her.

Suddenly, the wind came up, and she was floating beneath the bridge in the cool dark water.

She felt no fear, only calm and safe as the water washed over her. She realized that a boat had come up along side. In it were two women, their faces shrouded. They wore gauzy robes or gowns—the kind you see in old mythology books.

They helped her up into the boat, which was extraordinarily easy, considering how drenched she was. Nothing was said as the faery-like creatures rowed the boat noiselessly along.

Rian thought she asked, *"Where are you taking me?"*

Almost immediately, Rian noticed an old, blue covered book laying in the bottom of the boat. At that moment she woke up.

The dream had startled her. Finding herself sleeping in the bathtub startled her also. She hurriedly finished her bath and got out.

Rian recognized the man in her dream. He was the customer that she believed left his book in the store earlier that day. Her thoughts drifted back ...

It was bout lunch time when he had silently entered the shop. Rian was eating at the counter as she often did. She barely noticed him come in, so he startled her when he walked out of one of the other rooms carrying a large, old, faded, bulging canvas bag. The man was dressed oddly. He looked weather-beaten, but strong. His beard was black and stubby and his hair was unkempt, hanging loose beneath a floppy black beret. His clothes were red and black.

As if the stranger could read her mind, he opened his bag and showed her the inside. It was filled with old books, manuscripts, pouches, and other assorted odds and ends. She couldn't help notice the inside smelled like mold.

"Didn't want you to get the wrong idea," he grinned, and Rian noticed he had several missing teeth.

It was his grin that unnerved her. He kept staring and grinning, and there was something overbearing and dark about his *persona*. It frightened her. She backed away.

"Like a couple ounces of your best sandalwood chips," he spoke.

Alone in the store with this man, she felt vulnerable leaving the front counter. "There's a scale and paper bags in the other room. You can weigh it out yourself," she told him.

He nodded, went into the room Rian pointed to, and later returned with a brown paper bag full of sandalwood chips. Rian gave him a price, and he paid, grinned and left. Rian felt relieved.

About an hour later, Rian discovered the book. It was laying on the floor near the sandalwood jar. She picked it up curiously and looked at it. *It wasn't one of hers; somebody must have left it.* Immediately after her thought, she associated it with the weird man, and put it behind the counter hoping he wouldn't return for it. As the day went on, her nervousness continued. She felt relieved when other customers were milling about. Although the stranger didn't return, the whole encounter made Rian feel uneasy.

She phoned her older brother Kevin. Together, they had started The Apothecary several years ago, and recently Kevin had opened a second shop near the Baltimore Harbor Place.

"Hey, Kev, are you very busy?"

"Umm... not as busy as I'd like to be. Are you?"

"No. I was just wondering ... Can you come over here this afternoon?"

"Why?"

She hesitated. "'Cause I miss having you around?"

"Uh-huh."

"I do...sometimes."

"Are you trying to tell me you want me to do the bookkeeping again?"

He had unwittingly supplied her with a good excuse.

"Kev, I tried, but you know it's not my long suit!"

Kevin said he'd be over.

Later in the afternoon, he stopped in. Anyone could see they were brother and sister. Kevin had the same dark hair and sensual eyes. He was extremely attractive, with the kind of boyish grin that women seemed to be drawn to. When Kevin opened the second shop down by the harbor, it left Rian with most of the responsibility for the first one. She was enthusiastic about the expansion, but soon found running the shop without Kevin more than she bargained for.

"Hi, Kev! What's happening?"

"We actually got busy today, but I thought it was O.K. to leave Kelly alone in the shop," he said, referring to a new clerk he had hired. "She's catching on fast. I think she'll work out very well."

"I'm glad to hear that, because I could really use some help around here. I just keep getting further and further behind in the books. Maybe I should get Dad to help me."

Kevin laughed. "Don't do that, for heavens sakes, unless you want him to take over!" Kevin winked at Rian as he went by her, on his way upstairs to the office.

Kevin, whom Rian had always thought of as a *right-brained* sort of person, seemed to have inherited his father's knack for business, but now that he worked at the new shop so much, he had asked her to try and keep up with the bookkeeping.

Rian balked. She preferred ordering the books, shopping for the herbs and gifts, and helping customers. She didn't feel confident with numbers. Kevin teased her about it occasionally, but, basically, he understood her reluctance and didn't press.

Just before six o'clock, Rian went upstairs to the office. Trying to hide her concern, she put the book on Kevin's desk. Kevin turned around and looked up at her.

Rian pointed to the book. "What do you make of it?" she said. "Look.. it's all *handwritten*."

Kevin looked down at the book, and turned it over in his hands, repeating the title. "The Merrywells?" He glanced through it for a minute.

"There are pages missing from the back," Kevin commented. "Looks like parts of recipes, and rhymes and stuff. Where'd you get it?"

"Some very, very weird guy left it here by mistake. He gave me the creeps."

Kevin noticed Rian seemed uneasy. "Is that why you wanted me to come over?"

"I guess it is," Rian admitted.

"It's pretty old; probably came from a used book store."

"Umm, maybe. But I've had this strange feeling about it all afternoon, as though it was left here for me to find."

Kevin laughed. "You mean, you think he wants *us* to sell it?"

"No. I didn't mean that."

"What is it then?" Kevin put the book back on the desk.

"I don't know … women's intuition … ask Viv. She knows all about that stuff!" Rian was teasing Kevin now.

"Shut up and leave me alone so I can straighten up this mess," Kevin responded trying to sound official.

Suddenly, Rian heard a rumble in the distance and looked out the window. It had started to rain lightly. "No problem," she said, clipping him playfully across the shoulder. It's almost six, and I'm out of here!"

"Will you be back? I'd like to try and explain this checkbook to you."

Rian heard a louder rumble and frowned. "Don't know. Right now I wanna try and get home before the storm hits. See ya!" With those remarks, Rian picked up her purse and the book, hurried down the stairs, and walked out into the rain.

※ ※ ※ ※

CHAPTER 3

Marty

After her bath, Rian slipped into one of those cool, cotton Indian dresses, and walked over to the window. The rain was slowing down. She stood in front of a mirror and brushed out her long, dark brown hair; and clipped it up with a barrette. Her mirror reflected a comely face, with exotic gray almond eyes. Some people told her she looked a little Asian. When she wore make-up, she turned heads.

She made herself a glass of herbal iced tea, flopped down in the soft chair beside her bed, and looked at the small faded blue book. As Rian sipped the iced tea, she began to unwind. She leafed through the pages of the book, observing the faded script, and noting the etched carousel on the hand-bound cloth cover.

It must be very old, she thought. Rian noticed that the book looked as though it had been well cared for, and the pages missing in the back didn't appear to be connected to the main part of the story. In fact, it appeared to be more a journal than a story.

The handwriting was carefully done and easy to read. Rian thought it written by a woman's hand. She had developed an interest in rare esoteric books since she and Kevin had opened their shop, and had begun saving them whenever one came her way. Rian definitely considered adding this one to her collection.

She wondered about the age of the book. There was no publication date in the front, just a page on which was briefly written *"to Morgan Ceibhfhionn."* The middle name, Rian could not even pronounce, but *Morgan* gave her a little jolt. It reminded her of her mother's younger sister, Marty, who long ago had changed her name to *Morgana.*

Morgana was thirteen years younger than Rian's mother, Elizabeth, lovely and slim, with the long dark hair of her mother and the same beautiful sensual gray eyes.

Marty, whose proper name was Marianne-Tamara, from her mother and maternal grandmother, had gone to college during the 1960's and had become one of the "flower children." *Make Love Not War* was the bumper sticker on the back of her car.

That she ever had time to earn her teaching degree was a mystery to Elizabeth.

In college, she led sit-ins, marched and picketed for women's rights, civil rights, and student rights, and, of course, against the Vietnam War. Her lover was killed there one month before the truce. It took Marty a long time and a lot of soul-searching to get over it. Everyone agreed that the loss had changed her forever.

Rian adored Marty. Everyone said they looked alike. Marty had her own ideas about things, but she was very patient and sensitive. As the years went by the two grew very close. Marty often took Rian camping. She knew all about herbs and plants.

On one such trip, Rian said, "You really worry mom. She thinks you've gotten in with some very weird people."

"Such as?"

"You know, sub-culture, love-ins!"

"Love-ins! That went out years ago! Does your mother say I'm into love-ins?"

"She mentioned it one time. Are you?"

"No. Of course not."

"Mom says you've changed your religion."

"Your mother doesn't understand me at all."

"I wonder what she'll think of your new boyfriend?" Marty's boyfriend, Robin, looked really cool to Rian. His appearance reminded her of a character from the musical *Hair*. She learned later that his real name was Uri Kessler.

When she first met him, Rian commented. "Do you always dress like that?"

"Only when introduced to a pretty girl like you." He winked and smiled warmly and Rian could see that beneath his curly brown beard, he was rather good-looking.

Rian grew accustomed to seeing Marty and Robin together, and she became interested in their unusual spiritual path, because there was so much emphasis on ecology and nature. And there was something else, something that really intrigued Rian. They followed a concept shared by many ancient cultures. They venerated a powerful feminine deity connected to the earth and the moon.

Once, Rian had asked her Aunt Marty, "Do you follow one of those gurus?"

"Marty laughed "No! ... Our guru is Mother Nature. Do you know anything about Native American ... Indian spirituality?"

"Not too much."

"Well, there are some similarities. You see, for me the Church is too patriarchal and too dogmatic. Most of the followers of the earlier 'matriarchal' religions were eradicated. Remember the inquisition?"

Rian frowned, but then countered. "But you still believe in God don't you?"

Well, it's more a matter of *connecting*. We see God as a poetic expression of the male force, connected to the sun and the life of plants and animals; living and dying and being reborn. The Goddess represents the mother — the earth, the moon, the birthgiver to the whole cosmos!

"But that sounds more like mythology than religion."

It is, partly. We do take our perceptions from nature and metaphor, but all religions have their roots in myths and allegories. Most modern theologians do not take all biblical writings' literally'."

❧❧

Gradually, Rian discovered that many of Marty's friends, who were artists, musicians, or poets, were also involved. Marty usually referred to their tradition as the Craft.

While Marty was attending graduate school, she moved in with Rian's family, and though she tried to be discreet around her sister, Rian saw her come home a few times carrying a costume. Once, there was paint on her face. "I've been to the most exciting Earth Ritual!" she explained to Rian happily.

Rian wanted very much to go a ritual, but Marty

didn't encourage her knowing how much her mother would object. Instead, she gave her some books on the subject.

The modern Craft, Rian read in one book, *revived some ancient Pagan concepts and combined them with modern psychology ... Rituals were often held outdoors in sacred groves or nature locales ... Some groups adapted a variety of different tribal practices ... venerated many different gods and goddesses connected with nature.*

The books only aroused Rian's curiosity. She longed to see it all for herself.

For some reason, Rian could never remember everything that happened that fateful night Marty and her mother had their final confrontation. She could only recall it was in the fall of the year after Marty had come home from one of her *ceremonies.*

Elizabeth had gone out of town, but had returned unexpectedly. When Marty walked into the house that night, she was still wearing a garland of dried autumn flowers in her hair and a wispy costume.

Elizabeth stared at her strangely, because Marty had never worn any of her costumes home before. That night, the two of them began to quarrel.

"Marty, what's going on? Where have you been?"

"I've been to a festival, that's all."

"What do you mean, *festival?* What kind of festival?" Marty then announced to her sister that she would prefer to be called *Morgana.* She told Elizabeth that she had been through an Initiation, and had taken a new name. Marty was very serious.

So was Elizabeth.

She sent Rian out of the room, but her daughter

overheard everything. She could still remember sitting at the top of the staircase, listening.

"What on earth do you mean?" Elizabeth asked when she thought she and Marty were alone. "Aren't you a Christian anymore? Have you converted? Don't you believe in God?"

"Listen Liz: leave me alone. This is none of your business."

"It is very much my business! You live here in this house. You influence my daughter! You two are very close ... which is fine, but I don't like this religion stuff. God knows, I'm no fanatic or anything. I tolerated the sit-ins and the marches during the war, because, even though I worried about you, I knew it was for a good cause ... and you had your reasons. But this stuff is weird. It's, it's *Satanic* or something!"

"Elizabeth, you don't know what you're talking about!"

"What is this Goddess stuff? I found it lying in your room. Are you in a coven? Do you practice *witchcraft*?"

"Elizabeth! You were looking through my things? I'm thirty-one years old! What the hell right do you have going through my stuff?"

"Because I'm worried about my daughter, that's why!"

"You can go to hell. I'd never hurt Rian."

"What's this?" Elizabeth was screaming.

"Its just a damn newsletter, that's all!"

"Oh sure, just a newsletter. '*The Pagan Path,*' What, in God's name, is that? You're a *pagan*? A *Satanist*!"

"No! Pagan means someone..."

"I know what it means, someone who worships the devil!" She slammed down the newsletter.

"Bullshit! It means someone who has reverence for nature! Why don't you read it?"

"I have reverence for nature, and I'm not a Pagan!"

"Well, that's all it is. It makes me feel happy, it makes me come alive. I don't know what else to say."

Elizabeth turned away from her sister and for a moment said nothing. Then, forming her words carefully, she said, "Marty, this living situation is intolerable for me. I don't understand any of your beliefs. I don't know what you're about anymore. The thing is, I can't accept any of this. It's not for me … for us. I really think you should move."

"This is my house, too!" Marty screamed.

Her statement stopped Elizabeth in her tracks. They were the third generation to inherit the beautiful Victorian house. Her grandfather John Reinhardt, had it built for her grandmother, Tamara Mooreland, before they got married, and more recently Elizabeth's husband, David McGuire, had modernized and restored it.

All sorts of stories circulated about the place. One of the most intriguing was that of a dollhouse, constructed by Marianne's great-grandfather, Gwyn Mooreland, before the big house was built. It was supposed to be an exact replica of the house they now lived in. Marianne had told everyone that the dollhouse was so meticulously crafted, it was once exhibited in an art museum.

Rian had heard that when her mother and aunt were young, Marianne told them strange stories about the dollhouse, and it's secrets, but Elizabeth said she had never seen it, and wondered if it ever existed at all except in her mother's imagination.

Elizabeth turned away from Marty for a moment.

She seemed to be trying to compose herself. At last she spoke quietly, but Rian could still hear an edge in her voice.

"Marty, if you wish to stay here ... then we will move out."

Marty was silent for a few minutes, deep in thought. Then she said sadly, "No, I'll go. It will be easier all around."

Three days later, Marty, now Morgana, packed her things. She told the family she and her boyfriend had decided to move to California, where people were more open-minded, and where communities such as theirs were thriving.

Before Marty left, she and Rian had a long talk about everything. Rian asked her about her initiation and her new name. "I took my name from the Celtic Goddess, Morgana," Marty told Rian. "She was one of the most powerful of all Celtic Goddesses, a strong and magickal woman. Even warriors feared her powers."

Rian sulked for weeks. Elizabeth apologized to Marty, and begged her not to go, but Marty left anyway. Elizabeth felt terribly guilty. Rian was angry with her mother for a long time.

A few months later, Morgana called and said that she and Robin had been married, or handfasted as she had called it. They were moving to San Francisco and planned to get involved with the anti-nuke movement.

Elizabeth said nothing after the phone call, but she grieved for the sister she could never understand.

About six months later, Morgana wrote. She told of the happiness she had found in her new home. Then, she wrote that she had found a teaching position, and Robin had taken a job writing for a newspaper that was primarily concerned with environmental issues. She also wrote that she was becoming politically active in feminist causes. Elizabeth was only relieved that Marty had found a real job.

The years following were a lot less fun without Marty-Morgana.

❋ ❋ ❋ ❋

CHAPTER 4

Millcott City

About four years later, Rian enrolled in a local university where she majored in arts and sciences. For a while, she seriously considered going into nursing, but at some point the more she researched, the more she became interested in herbs, alternative healing methods, and holistic medicine. Finally, she found a community college which offered a new course in 'Pharmaceutical Herbology,' and immediately signed up.

Rian and her brother, Kevin, had grown close. Sometimes when Rian talked to him, he reminded her of Marty. He was sensitive, considerate, and intelligent.

One day after Rian had come home from class, her mother told her sadly that her grandmother had died. Elizabeth's eyes were red from crying. She took the death of Marianne very hard, which surprised Rian a little, because she knew her mother was never very close to Marianne. Elizabeth was much more devoted to her father, J.T. Chambers. Rian was just a child when he was suddenly killed in a boating accident, but she could still remember her mother grieving about it for a very long time.

Marianne remarried a successful playwright less than a year after J.T.'s death. Elizabeth felt the entire affair premature and disrespectful, and after that treated Marianne coldly, cynically referring to her as the 'Merry Widow.'

Marty would argue. "Why can't you accept the fact that our mother has become an independent and exciting woman?"

Marty's reasoning only made Elizabeth become more hostile. But now that her mother was gone, she felt guilty and remorseful. Marianne had always seemed so young and vivacious, and had aged so gracefully, that Elizabeth had expected her to live for many more years.

When Marianne remarried, she took neither her new husband's name of Meriden, nor maintained her late husband's name of Chambers. Instead, she reclaimed her family name of Mooreland.

A week after the funeral, the family gathered in the offices of the family lawyer to hear the reading of Marianne's will. Rian sat next to her Aunt Marty, who had returned for the funeral of her mother. Marty still wished to be called Morgana.

There was a well of silence everywhere. Rian could still remember the sudden, harsh sound of the door opening to the inner office, when the lawyer entered the room. He was dressed in a dark business suit, and his manner seemed almost as serious as the funeral director. He offered his condolences, and then, after a brief consultation with Elizabeth, sat down at his desk and opened his attaché case.

"This will is essentially a simple one," he explained, taking out a folder full of papers. He opened a blue covered document, looked through it earnestly for a few moments, and then regarded the family. "It was Marianne's wish that all of the property investments she held be divided equally between her two daughters. However, the house on Willow Drive is bequeathed to her oldest daughter, Elizabeth Helene McGuire, 'who has always loved and cared for it.' Marianne's interest in her late father's construction company has been left to her son-in-law, David Benoïc McGuire, "who has managed it soundly and honestly."

"The cash investments, which I will discuss with you later in more detail, are to be divided between her daughter Marianne-Tamara, also known as Marty, and her only grandchildren, Kevin Ancel, and Rian Enide McGuire. He smiled briefly at the grandchildren, as Rian winced at the mention of her middle name.

"There are just a few other personal items," he continued.

The lawyer read on about Marianne's jewelry and china. He mentioned her carousel collection, which was bequeathed to Marty, an antique map collection which was bequeathed to Kevin, and the dollhouse everyone had heard about. He told Rian if it was ever found, her grandmother would like her to have it. Rian thought she detected an amusing tone in his voice when he mentioned that part.

Marty decided to leave the carousel collection intact in her mother's old room, where she felt it would be safer. As for the dollhouse, no one present at the reading had ever seen it.

The inheritance changed Rian's and Kevin's life. They decided to invest the money in some kind of business together. Rian would continue her studies for at least another year, but she would also work part-time.

After visiting with Marty for several days, Kevin and

Rian came up with the idea of opening a small, alternative book and health-food store.

To say that they were both excited about the idea was an understatement. For the next few months, they poured through everything they could find on the subject, and decided to start off with a small shop, selling natural vitamins, herbs, incenses, and aromatherapy oils.

They would also carry books on nutrition, herbs and holistic medicine. Rian took a course in homeopathy and massage, and Kevin took some classes in Shiatsu, and Tai Chi. Both became interested in yoga and meditation techniques. Rian was already studying about the medicinal benefits of herbs in college.

Elizabeth shook her head in disbelief. *It's happening again.*

Rian still lived at home, but was constantly being harassed by her mother. At nineteen, she considered moving out, but every time she did her mother promised to stop criticizing. Besides, she wanted to use as much of her inheritance as possible towards the development of her new venture.

Kevin had it easier. Five years older than Rian and already out of college, he shared a house with some other people.

"I don't know why you're investing in this shop," Rian's mother would argue. "Why don't you put your money in the bank and finish school?"

"Because this is what I want to do!"

Elizabeth sighed. "Sometimes you remind me so much of my mother."

"What's wrong with that? Grandmom was great!"

"Yes, she was. But she was also headstrong like you,

and... eccentric."

One day Rian finally told her mother, "Mom, I know you want me to live here, and right now, it would be better for me financially if I did, but the differences between us are becoming so unbearable! I really think I should move out."

"Rian, you're only nineteen!" Elizabeth was frightened. She had alienated her mother and her sister, she didn't want to drive Rian away too.

Rian finally made a bargain with her mother. She would stay and finish school if her father built her a private entrance to the house, so she could come and go as she pleased.

Rian's father did better than that. He built her a private apartment upstairs with a kitchen, bath, sitting room, bedroom, and separate entrance. The apartment had access to a little private upstairs porch which faced some woods and a garden below. Rian loved it.

The compromise worked. Elizabeth wisely kept quiet, hoping her daughter would marry a nice college boy with a future, and forget the silly health store business.

There was no question as to where Rian and Kevin wanted their shop. It had to be in Millcott City. The well-known, restored town just nestled there, totally out of place, and, Rian sometimes thought, 'out of touch' with the rest of the modern world. It was centrally located, between the large city of Baltimore and the newly-built modern town of Metro-Station.

Many of the stone buildings were more than two-hundred years old and lay over part of a great river, where years before it had been a busy shipping depot. Most of the buildings had been converted into shops.

Some had apartments upstairs.

Up the hill and around the bend from the town, an old mill was still operating. Because the tiny town was built into a little mountain, narrow streets ran up and down steep hills, and some of the buildings had walls of stone steps and granite in place of backyards.

In the winter after a snow fall, the town reminded Rian of a little Christmas garden. Shops sold exotic gifts, fantasy items, clothes, unusual jewelry, wonderful dolls, hand-made quilts, antiques, American Indian artifacts, crystals, pottery, and more.

The old railroad depot, which had once serviced freight and passengers alike along the east coast and west to Ohio, had been restored, and was now a museum. It brought many tourists to the town. Fine restaurants had opened up and down Main St., and that, too, added to the town's attraction.

Tourists often remarked that they felt something special here, and now and then someone would return and open a little shop, or rent an apartment above one of the stores.

After a few months Rian and Kevin found their first shop. It was located on the first two floors of an old, commercially converted stone house at the very end of Main Street. Although it was somewhat isolated from the more highly traveled parts of town, they loved it.

The rooms were small but beautiful, with restored polished wood floors and stone walls. It even had a fireplace. They hung out their shingle: *The Apothecary*.

Beyond their shop and around the corner was a parking lot. To the east of the store, a bridge took you either back into civilization, or into a large state park.

Books on acupuncture, massage, Shiatzu, vegetarian cuisine, and vitamin supplements lined the shelves in the front room. On the tables sat massage oils, incenses, leather pouches, crystals, jewelry, and other related gift items. The second floor rooms were used for office space, meditation classes, or workshops.

Over the past few years, Rian and Kevin had broadened their subjects to include many different spiritual paths such as yoga, Buddhism, women's issues, and mythology. And as they became more familiar with the New Age genre, they added books on inner-growth, popular psychology, and the teachings of many contemporary spiritual teachers of different esoteric traditions.

Cassettes playing new age and ethnic music hummed in the store and sold as fast as Rian could order them. Kevin, who had recently developed an interest in the arcane, added books on mystery schools, astrology, parapsychology, dreams, and metaphysics.

Some of the best selling items in the shop were Tarot cards. Rian and Kevin discovered there were over a hundred different decks, some painted by famous artists such as Salvador Dali. The decks interested Rian not so much because she believed they foretold the future, but because she liked the art and the archetypal pictures they contained.

For those who lived in or near the town, Millcott was popular because of its unusual atmosphere. Some of the residents were unusual, too.

Rian knew a few regular customers secretly camped out in the adjacent state park all year round, which she viewed as astonishing. Whether it was due to lack of funds or some other reason, she had no idea. Others were drifters, and a few just seemed to be living in another time, still dressing like flower children and hippies.

Of course many of the shopkeepers were artists and craftspeople, which explained the unusual ambiance of the town. Others were seemingly ordinary people, just running their small businesses. Rian called it the *Brigadoon* of her day.

❈ ❈ ❈ ❈

CHAPTER 5

Morgan

Rian came out of her reverie and looked out of the window. The summer storm had finally moved into the western Maryland mountains and the sun had broken through the few remaining clouds, casting long evening shadows across the garden below.

She made herself a pasta salad for supper, and while she was eating, picked up the book she'd found in the store. It almost seemed to beckon to her, but for some inexplicable reason, it also disturbed her. Finally, she gave in and began to read it.

The story was written in the first person by a woman who called herself Mere-Ama. It began with a Celtic family's journey from what would now be somewhere near Turkey, to the Norse country, and their final migration west to Wales. The time was around the fifth century. The story didn't seem very interesting at first, much of it involving tribal warfare, but Rian read on. After Mere-Ama arrived in Wales, she joined the priestess community of the Ladies of the Lake.

As the journal continued, Mere-Ama's name periodically changed from Morgan to Morcant and Miranda,

Margante to Argante, depending on what role she assumed. The story, or diary, seemed to be connected to one or more of the Arthurian legends. It talked about Faerie and Annwn, another name for Avalon, the Otherworld of the Celts; and of course, like many fantasy books, it spoke of visions and magick, especially the healing and rejuvenating magick of the lakes.

The story and various names puzzled and intrigued Rian. After reading a few more chapters, she finished eating and changed into a pair of jeans. Then, she scurried down the outside steps to the driveway, got into her car and rolled the car windows down. Driving back to the store, the air was refreshing and cool after the storm.

Rian arrived at the shop about twenty minutes later. It was still daylight, the long summer days lasting until nearly nine-thirty. She noticed Kevin's car was gone and the CLOSED sign was hanging from the inside of the door. *Guess he figured I wasn't coming back,* she thought. She unlocked the door with her key, and once inside, went over to the shelf marked mythology.

Rian took down some books on the Celts and read that many historians believed the Celtic race migrated to the British Isles from as far away as southeastern Europe. Once there, they connected their older myths and traditions to the land, lakes, and coastal waters of Britain and Ireland.

Rian looked up the name Morgan. Here she found a wealth of information, most of it connected to the Ladies of the Lake.

"*Mor*, she discovered meant *sea* in several Celtic languages. But in other languages it also meant *death*. Therefore, to the Celts, death and afterlife were both connected to *water*. Furthermore, Morgan is a name which still survives in Brittany today, where sea-sprites are called *morgans*.

Looking further, Rian discovered that the most famous lake-goddess was Morgan Le Fay. Rian remembered that name from reading the Arthurian legends. She was the sorceress and half-sister to King Arthur. She did in Arthur by tricking him into making love to her and begetting the dreaded Mordred — Arthur's infamous son and rival.

But these books revealed that those legends were added later during the Christian era, when trickery and misfortune were usually blamed on the powers, or sorcery, of women. In the earlier stories, the Ladies of the Lake were healers. They guarded the restorative powers of fountains and wells, transforming death into life within their healing cauldrons.

Rian read on. In Welsh myth, Morgan was said to be the Queen of Avalon, the underworld land of faery, connected to the magickal-lake stories. There, King Arthur was taken after he vanished from this world. In ancient Ireland, there was a trinity of goddesses of war and death. One was Queen Morrigan who was mentioned as a battle goddess and shapeshifter, and who took the form of a crow or raven. Most scholars agreed that *morgan* names meant *Great Queen*. Suddenly, Rian remembered what Marty had said about warriors being afraid of the powerful Morgana. *Is this who she was talking about?*

Le Fay, she read, was linked to *fate*, though other scholars connected it to faerie or sea-fay, merfeine or mermaids. *Ama*, she discovered, meant *muse* or *mother*.

Yet they all merged! Rian concluded it was because the Celts believed in reincarnation. Names like *morgan, faerie, ama* and the rest were all aspects of the same idea — the waters of rebirth. *Could it be,* she wondered, *that the lakes were a metaphor for the womb?*

Rian looked up *Ceibhfhionn,* pronounced *Schvonne,* and discovered she was an Irish Goddess of Inspiration who stood next to the Well of Knowledge. She constantly filled a vessel with its water and poured it out, without letting humans seeking wisdom, taste it. *Hmm, a wee bit selfish of her,* Rian mused.

Then she thought of the book, 'The Merrywells' ... *Well of Knowledge* ... *Mere-Ama* .... *Water-Mother. It all seemed connected.*

Preceding that legend, Rian discovered other names. Liban ... Meredith lake creatures and *well guardians.* The damsels of the wells courageously guarded the waters in the *pagan* grail. Unfortunately, they sometimes got raped or abducted, in which case they would withdraw their services. The loss of the grail was said to have caused the downfall of Arthur's kingdom.

In Celtic lore, these earlier myths of well guardians and restoring lakes always stemmed from the West, the coast of Britain and Ireland.

The names and aspects went on and on, one idea blending into another. Rian, fascinated, read for hours. Finally, she became tired, and it had grown dark outside. She put the books back on the shelf wondering why she had felt the need to look all this up tonight.

She turned the store lights off and the porch light on. Suddenly, Rian froze. In the window-pane she saw a face watching her. He was grinning, and she recognized him as the stranger with the missing teeth. Slowly, without moving, Rian's eyes moved towards the latch. It was still open. Rian felt paralyzed with fright.

He's come for his book, she thought, trying to stay rational.

Fortunately for Rian, the CLOSED sign faced the outside, but the stranger kept staring. He stopped grinning and knocked.

Rian stiffened. For a moment she couldn't think. Then, her mind began to function again. She pointed to the sign and said, "We're closed!" She wanted it to sound plural.

He kept staring. Finally he asked, "When will you be open?"

"We open at ten!" Rian managed, "Tomorrow morning."

"I will be back," he said as he turned and left.

Rian locked the door, and watched him from the window. He walked down the street and over the bridge. Rian watched a little while longer … .He didn't return. She opened the door slowly, looking both ways. Then, she ran out to her car and hopped in as fast as she could, quickly locking the doors. As she drove over the bridge, she looked around, but it was too dark to see anything.

Driving home, Rian wondered, *What is it about this man that frightens me so?* It seemed foolish in a way, but she couldn't help feeling there was something alien about him. Before and after she got out of her car, she glanced around again, and quickly ran up the steps to her apartment.

❉ ❉ ❉ ❉

CHAPTER 6

Richard

Rian locked the door securely behind her. She threw her shoulder bag and keys across the bed and slowly moved to the windows. The garden below was partially lit by a few outdoor lamps her father had placed around the house. Carefully cracking the curtains, she peeped out of each one for several minutes, but saw nothing unusual.

She made herself a cup of herbal tea and still sipping it, pulled the curtain aside again to look out the window. Then, finally satisfied, she slumped down in the chair beside her bed, and allowed herself to relax.

It was times like this that she missed Richard. They had dated for three years. Her mother was crazy about him. Tall and handsome with a secure career ahead of him, he was everything a mother could want for her daughter.

He had graduated from medical school while they were dating and was specializing in radiology. Gentle, intelligent, good family, but Rian and he had little in common.

Richard loved sports; Rian loved books. Richard was left-brained and logical, Rian right-brained and emotional. Richard was scientific, Rian holistic. Richard liked to hunt and fish. Rian was an animal protectionist.

When Richard got excited about a deer he'd brought down, Rian had no desire to be with him for a while.

Richard was conservative; Rian was liberal. Richard wanted to get married and start a family. Rian wasn't ready. They broke up.

Still, Richard had been comfortable and dependable. He was committed to his medical career, his computers, and healing people, but sometimes he made fun of the acupuncturists and holistic healers that Rian hung around with.

Now, however, she longed to call him ... to spend the night with him one more time.

Rian suddenly realized how lonely she had been without Richard, and then, just as suddenly, she felt she was going to have a bad panic attack. She hadn't experienced one for at least a year, but she could feel it coming on.

She began sweating, and shaking. Her head ached and she couldn't think, except she was sure she was going to die.

The room was spinning, and she clutched the bed as she fell to the floor in tears. Somehow, through the confusion and fog, she remembered her therapy. She began to breathe more slowly, trying not to hyper-ventilate anymore than possible. She breathed in and out through her belly and closed her eyes.

When she felt a little stronger she got up and rummaged around through some drawers until she found her panic attack cassette. Fumbling, she got it in the tape recorder and turned it on. Sitting on the floor, which felt more secure, she listened to the reassuring instructions on the tape. Gradually, she calmed down.

Thank God it didn't hit in the car, she thought. Rian

kept a spare tape in the car, just in case. Once she had a panic attack so bad while driving, she felt she would drive her car off an embankment. After that, she made an appointment with a therapist and got into a support group for her malady. It was helpful and reassuring to discover that other people suffered from such things.

It was in just such a group that she met Richard. It was the only weakness she supposed he had.

"That's why I went into radiology, instead of surgery," he laughed when they met. "Wouldn't do to have an attack when you've got somebody's gall bladder in your hands!" They both laughed and went out for a snack.

"How long have you been having them?" Rian asked.

"Oh, ever since I was in high school, I guess. The first time, it scared the hell out of me. I thought I was really ill. Then it happened a few days later, so I told my parents. They took me to a doctor, and he ran all sorts of tests, but everything was negative. I didn't get another one for months, then there it was in the locker room after a game."

"God, what'ya do?"

"Got out of there fast. Broke a date. Didn't even show up. Told everybody I was sick."

"So what happened?"

"More tests. All negative."

"How did you find out what it was?"

"Well my doctor suspected it, but my parents didn't want to believe that their son could have any mental problems."

"It's not a mental problem!"

"Well it is ... kind of. Not everybody has panic attacks."

"Not everybody has allergies either."

He shrugged. "Well, finally I got some therapy, and it really helped."

"Did you see a shrink?"

"Yeah, for a couple months, and she told me to join this group."

"Do you come regularly?"

"I used to. The tapes and support group helped a lot."

"How long have you been coming?"

"I'm not a patient anymore. I counsel other people. After a while, I learned how to control … how to handle them."

"Really?"

"Sure. It's not a big deal."

"To me it is. It terrifies me."

"I know, but you'll see. After a few meetings you'll begin to understand what you can do when it happens."

And Rian did. She got the attacks under control and found a boyfriend all at the same time. But now it was over. Three years of dating, lovemaking and fun, and she had ended it. Last she heard, Richard was engaged.

❄❄❄❄

CHAPTER 7

The Queen of Cups

Rian phoned Kevin that night, and told him that she would not open the store by herself. He agreed to come in and work for her that night.

She finally fell asleep and dreamed that she and a young man, she assumed was Richard, were on the beach together ... or maybe it was a boat. The dream had a slippery sensation about it. Then she saw a shrouded blue woman who seemed to be part of the sea itself. Later, Rian would recall this dream, but just now she drifted off into tranquillity.

Rian went in late the next morning on purpose. She remembered the stranger, but forgot to bring his book.

"Damn! That means he'll be back."

"He's probably some wino, Ri," Kevin assured her. "I'm sure he won't."

"He'll return for that book."

"Did you read it?"

"Just a few chapters. It was some kind of fantasy book about the Ladies of the Lake."

Kevin started towards the door.

"No, wait!"

"You really are scared. I've never known you to be

afraid of being alone here before!"

"I can't explain it ... I'm just afraid of him."

"O.K .... . Viv is off work today. Why don't I ask her if she can come over and keep you company."

Rian hesitated.

⁂

Once a week, a tall, slender woman with long, straight, auburn hair came in and read tarot cards for customers. She wasn't pretty in the usual sense of the word, but there was a certain aura about her, a charisma.

Rian found her mannerisms a bit too mystical at times, but couldn't deny that her readings were usually on the mark.

Soon after they met, Kevin began dating her. She called herself Viviene, though that was not her real name. Rian and Kevin wondered if she followed a metaphysical path similar to the one Marty-Morgana had been initiated into years before. Morgana had called it The Craft of the Wise.

Viviene admitted being familiar with such a path, but she simply called it *The Craft*. "It's a path of poetry and metaphor, not dogma," Viviene told them, but that was all she ever said about it.

"Do you ever fool around with magick and the supernatural?" Rian asked her one day.

Viviene answered, "Everything is natural. I don't believe in the supernatural. Magick is simply the art of training your mind to work with the natural flow."

"How did you get into this?"

"I've always been this way I think. A little psychic ... into magickal books and fantasy."

"But you just said that you didn't believe in the

supernatural!"

"Well, there are many things that cannot be explained in ordinary terms, but that doesn't mean they are not naturally caused."

Rian became thoughtful for a moment. "Does that mean that you think your mind can make things happen?"

"Well, you're into holistic healing, aren't you?"

"I believe it has great value."

"Isn't a lot of that mind over matter? I mean by changing your thought patterns you can heal your body?"

"I suppose ... But that's a little different. Some people become ill because of stress or fear."

"Of course, and that proves my point. The mind is very powerful. Not only can it help you heal yourself, it can also make you sick."

Rian countered, "But that's because stress and fear changes your body's natural mechanisms, its immune system, and prevents it from working properly!"

"Exactly."

"But you believe ..."

"Belief is so dogmatic don't you think? I prefer *perceive*."

"O.K., you perceive ... if I understand you correctly, that magick can cause things outside yourself to happen or not happen. Right?"

"Lets just say that I feel we are all a part of the natural cosmos, and that everything is interconnected. If my mind can heal me, it may also connect with other forces, which, though they may be outside of me personally, are nevertheless connected to me."

Rian conceded. She wasn't sure if she accepted this theory, but she was open-minded enough to speculate.

Anyway, she didn't feel knowledgeable enough about metaphysics to debate.

She did ask Viviene if she was *Pagan*.

"Why do you ask?"

"Because you remind me of my Aunt Marty. She had some of the same beliefs ... or perceptions you do, and that's what she called herself."

Viviene didn't reply. It was Viviene's way when she wanted to shroud herself in mystery. Rian could never understand it.

Once, a man came in to have his cards read. Viviene seemed to know him. They chatted for a few minutes, and then Viviene took him to the second floor where she usually read cards privately.

A few minutes later, Rian heard an argument going on upstairs. The man raised his voice louder and louder. Then she heard him call out, "You're a fraud! Always have been, always will be!"

Rian felt uneasy. This had never happened before! Viviene came out and pulled herself up tall. She looked menacing, powerful. She told the customer to leave. "We cannot have this sort of thing here!" she said angrily.

The man left, and as he did, he threw some kind of trinket at her. Then he walked out of the store and slammed the door behind him.

"What was all that about?" Rian asked.

"Nothing ... I can't talk about it."

"But Viv, this is a *business!* What happened?"

"Its my ... *group*, Rian. I just can't discuss it with anyone. Look, I'm really sorry about this. I never thought he would behave like that."

"You mean you knew he was coming?"

"Yes."

Rian just shrugged. "God, I hope we don't see him again."

"You have my word; we won't."

About a half-hour later, there was a phone call for Viviene. She spoke very quietly as if she didn't want Rian to hear, glancing up from time to time to see if Rian was watching. But even though her voice was quiet, Rian sensed an urgency in her manner.

Rian knew that Viviene was involved in some sort of magickal lodge or metaphysical group, but she always acted very secretive about it. That was the side of Viviene that Rian didn't trust. She often wondered what Kevin saw in her.

When Viviene got off the phone, she looked extremely irritated, and told Rian she had to leave. The only other comment she made was, "This is just outrageous!" Then bitterly she added. "There are certain kinds of people who should just never get involved in magick. It only makes them crazy."

Viviene walked out the door without saying goodbye, leaving Rian to explain her broken appointments.

❋

Ever since that day almost a year ago Rian avoided getting too close to Viviene, but now she would be more than glad to have her company.

Kevin called Viviene, and she said she would come over. Rian was relieved. A few minutes later, Kevin started to leave.

"Can you wait until Viv gets here? Please?"

Kevin looked at her strangely. "Do you want me to call the police? I mean, did he threaten you in any way?"

"No ... he didn't threaten me ... I just feel threatened by him. You know?"

"Well, I can certainly see you're frightened. I'll stay."

"I really appreciate this. I owe you."

About an hour later, Viviene arrived.

Rian explained the problem, and Viviene looked puzzled.

"Do you have the book?"

"No, I forgot it."

In Viviene's usual style, she appeared far away and mystical for a moment, and Rian wondered if this trait was real or put on.

After Kevin went upstairs, Viviene asked, "Mind if I throw the cards?"

"Well ... no. Why?"

"Just a hunch. I've never seen you like this before."

Viviene sat down at a small table and took out her tarot deck. She had several. Some she read for others, and one she reserved for herself. This time she took out her personal tarot.

She laid them out in a pattern and then studied them for a while.

"Well," said Rian, "what is it?"

"O.K. ... I asked a question ... for myself." Viviene hesitated. "I needed to know if I should get involved in this. There are times when I sense I shouldn't read for somebody, that they need to work things out on their own. With your situation I had mixed feelings, so I asked."

"And?"

Viviene put her personal cards away as Rian looked on curiously. Then she took out another deck. "Shuffle and think of your question," Viviene instructed.

Rian had seen this procedure many times though it was a first for her. She sat down across from Viviene, shuffled the cards and thought of the man, then handed the cards back to Viviene.

The pictures on the cards were very interesting to Rian, though she didn't understand them. She knew that they were archetypes with inner meanings, but beyond that she had little knowledge.

Viviene began to study the cards. Finally, she spoke.

"What this says to me is that you are involved in some sort of ... I don't know, esoteric mystery, subconscious perhaps. Have you had any strange dreams lately?"

Rian always had difficulty remembering her dreams, but she did recall the one about the two women in the boat, and the stranger on the bridge.

"Well over all, the cards say that this stranger is trying to involve you in a magickal experience which has something to do with the feminine part of you, the intuitive part. See all these cups?" Viviene touched some of the cards.

"They are connected to water, and they represent emotions and intuition. But that Magician card inverted means the Trickster to me, and I think he represents the stranger that you fear."

"What do you mean by the Trickster?"

"Someone who can't be trusted, who throws you off balance. The magician is a powerful card, usually a man who knows how to manipulate all the forces of magick."

"So my feelings about this man are right.?"

"I would say yes ... definitely. And see these swords? They represent difficulties, even trauma ... and they surround him. He's bad news."

"What about the future?"

"The Page of Swords. Here I would interpret that as information. I think someone will reveal something important to you about your question in the very near future. "The card that really intrigues me is the Moon card over here." Viviene pointed to another card as Rian watched. "It's in your immediate past," Viviene continued.

The card had a large golden moon at the top, and from below two dogs howled up at it. A scorpion was crawling out of the water. It was inverted.

"What this card means to me is that there are slow changes going on in your psyche, and there is some possibility of deception."

"What can I do?"

"Well, my impression is that we are dealing with a secret or a riddle that must be unraveled."

Viviene paused and studied the cards for a moment. "I see you here represented as the Queen of Cups … the first card. That is you." She pointed to one of the cards.

"When's your birthday?"

"March third."

"You're a Pisces, a water sign. That fits. But crossing you," she pointed to another card that crossed the Queen of Cups, "is the eight of swords; someone who is traumatized and can't make a decision."

"Well, that's true."

"This card I mentioned before is at the root of the problem. It depicts the Magician. But he is inverted! It means that like it or not, he could be trouble."

Viviene continued to read the cards. She told Rian that because there were many Major Arcana, or trump cards, this reading was *karmic* in nature, that is, something she had to go through or a lesson that she must learn.

"The Hierophant is above you. He or she is the great esoteric teacher of all traditions. In this place, I would say that hanging over your head is the possibility of a spiritual transformation."

Viviene noticed Rian's blank expression and offered. "It could be from a past life."

"A past life? Oh, come on."

Viviene looked up. "Don't you believe in reincarnation?"

"Well, I don't really know. I try not to think about death if I can help it." Rian remembered last night.

Hearing Rian's pain, Viviene lightened up.

"In your environment I see the three of cups. That's good because it means your friends and family are supportive of you."

"And the final outcome is the Star card, which means that no matter what happens, things will probably work out well, and that hope springs eternal!" Viviene started laughing a little at her last remark.

"Thanks a lot. I'm really glad to hear that."

"Come on, Rian. We all have lessons to learn. Maybe yours is a lesson about reincarnation."

"The other day," Rian admitted, "I was reading a magazine article about time. In Sioux philosophy everything is a great circle — birth, life, death, even time."

"Yes, I think that way too.

"You do?"

"Yes. Would you like me to show you?"

"Sure."

"Do you have some string or cord?"

Rian looked at Viviene curiously. Then, she walked over to

the counter, reached underneath, and pulled out a spool of twine.

Viviene took scissors from a hook on the wall and cut the twine a few feet long. She slipped off her silver ring and put the cord through the ring.

"Hold one end," Viviene instructed. Rian held one end of the cord and Viviene held the other, pulling the cord out straight.

"Now, lets say that the present is this ring, and the cord is time. And the cord is labeled past on one end and future on the other. As the ring moves along the cord into the future, the past gets longer," Viviene moved the ring towards one end, "and the future gets shorter."

"But if time is circular," Viviene went on, "the past and future can be infinite and also equal. I don't think time is a straight forward phenomenon at all. I think its more like a river with swift streams, whirlpools, and counter-currents." She slipped the ring back and forth along the cord.

"That's interesting." Rian agreed, "It might explain deja-vu … or prophecy."

"Yes, and the pain of nostalgia. Couldn't that be the difficulty one might face when confronting his or her own personal time-frame?"

Viviene put the ring back on her finger and laid the twine on the counter.

"Think about the cosmos. Everything is circular or spiral." She made a spiraling gesture with her hand.

"Are you implying that many different dimensions might be going on … round and round at the same time?"

"Why not?"

Rian and Viviene talked about this principle for a

while, and Rian wondered if there was any scientific evidence for such an idea.

Then, her thoughts turned back to the tarot cards. Walking back to the table, Rian pointed to a card Viviene hadn't spoken of. It was at the bottom of a line. She asked "What about that card?"

They both sat down again.

"That's your inner image Rian; yourself. It is the High Priestess card. She speaks of cosmic memories; the Akashic Records, magick and dreams.

"So now, how does this all fit together?"

"Well, as I said before, I think all these water, these lunar, images are connected with something very intuitive and powerful, but not known to you at this time. I would further say that you have a great fear of uncovering this information. The Knight of Swords is in your hopes and fears position."

"In other words, the guy who left this book here is the Trickster, and I kind of know he's opened a Pandora's box, so that's why I am afraid?"

"Exactly. And you have good reason to be. He has the ability to manipulate you, particularly through your dreams.

"Does this have anything to do with his book?"

"I sense it does. Would you mind if I took a look at it sometime?"

"Come 'round the house and I'll show it to you."

As Viviene gathered up the cards, a shadow fell across her face.

Standing behind Rian was the stranger with the missing teeth.

❋❋❋❋

CHAPTER 8

Morgana

"I conjure thee, O Circle of Power, that thou b'est a meeting place of love and joy, a boundary between the world of men and the realms of the Mighty Ones; wherefore do I consecrate thee."

With those words, Morgana drew a pentagram at each quarter and lit a candle. The room was quiet. About nine people sat cross-legged and robed on a colorfully woven carpet, alternating men and women.

Another woman walked around the circle sprinkling some salt water saying: *"Water and earth, I purify thee, a place between the worlds to be."*

A man walked around the circle with a smoking smudge stick saying: *"Creatures of fire, this charge I lay, no evil in our presence stay."*

Robin rose up from his place next to Morgana and walked around the circle with an intricately carved knife. He drew an imaginary circle of light around the whole group saying: *"East, South, West and North; come and call our circle forth."*

Soft music was playing in the background during this part of the rite, and a full moon shined through a skylight. After Robin sat down, the music was turned off, and the group began to drum rhythmically, first slowly, then gradually faster. As they drummed, they chanted in tones that sounded Native American. They chanted to the trees, to the elements, and to the totem animals. They chanted to the Goddess of Life and Death and Her consort, the Horned One, the Lord of Plants and Animals. When they finished raising the power, each person placed a small white parchment in a small central cauldron which sat on a table in the middle of the circle.

Everyone directed their hands towards the smoking cauldron. When the ritual was finished, Morgana said, "Does anyone have anything special they want us to help them with?"

One woman said she needed a healing. She sat in the middle of the circle next to the table, and told the group that she had been having terrible headaches, and would like some help.

Morgana placed her hands just above the woman's head. Then she closed her eyes and visualized a healing white light from above coming through herself, through her arms and hands, and down into the woman. The group began chanting again. They visualized a white light surrounding the woman and bringing her peace and tranquillity, which they knew that she needed at this time in her life.

With this, the rite ended. The group thanked the gods and elementals for their help. A younger woman brought out a cake and some wine. Morgana and Robin blessed the food and everyone ate, laughed, and talked. After a little while, Morgana went to each quarter, and put out the candles. She dismissed the elementals, and thanked them for participating in the ritual.

Then, everybody joined hands and said together *"The Circle is open, but not broken. May the peace of the Goddess go in our hearts. Merry meet and merry part, and merry meet again!"*

The circle was over, and the atmosphere changed. Snacks were served and everyone relaxed and chatted. A few people went into Robin's office. He was working on an environmental article, which was going to appear in a local newspaper. A few others went out onto a little sunporch and talked with Morgana. About an hour later, everyone left.

Morgana was troubled. She wasn't sleeping well. Robin, who was now an assistant editor, was having serious financial problems, and Morgana was unhappy with her teaching position. But it was more than that. There was something … something bothering her that didn't have anything to do with these everyday problems.

For the past few weeks, she had been having a series of nightmares. They woke her up, and then she couldn't get back to sleep. One night, she dreamed of a drowning. She knew the person who was being pulled under. It was Rian.

Another time she dreamed that she saw Rian dead. She was lying in the woods wrapped in a blue shroud. When Morgana looked more closely, she noticed a book clutched in her hand. Then, the dream changed. A man stood facing the sea. His arms were raised, and he was calling out words she couldn't quite make out. Morgana confronted him. He challenged her and hissed through missing teeth.

Morgana woke up in a cold sweat. She sat up in bed and opened her eyes. For a moment, she felt confused, as though she were still in the dream, but gradually she came to herself, and then she began thinking of her niece. Though Rian was quite young when Morgana left Maryland, she still felt extremely close to her.

For some reason she thought of a funny conversation they once had when Marty had sneaked some pot into the house.

"Why do you burn incense all the time?" Rian had asked her.

"Oh ... so your mom won't smell my funny little cigarettes."

Rian giggled. "I know what you smoke ... It's pot, isn't it?"

"Won't tell on me, will you Rian?"

"Who me? Hey, this house is so big, mom will never smell it anyhow!"

"If she does, I'll tell her it's medicinal herbs."

Rian giggled again. "If grandmom heard you say that, she'd never believe it!"

Morgana smiled. "You're probably right. My mother might be from a different generation, but I've heard she was rather infamous in her day!"

"What's infamous mean?"

"Uh ... someone with an interesting reputation!"

The daydream faded, and Morgana came back to the present. She woke Robin and told him what she dreamed.

What she really needed was some reassurance. The dream had disturbed her so much she couldn't even explain it. Robin tried to be supportive. Morgana always seemed so sure of herself; it threw him to see how frightened she was. But sometimes her gifted psychic abilities confused her. When she couldn't figure out what was going on, she became frustrated and felt muddled. This was one of those times.

"Tomorrow, I'm going to talk to Dru. That is," she added a little sarcastically, "if I can find him."

"It can't hurt." Robin began massaging her neck.

Morgana closed her eyes. The neck massage felt good, but it didn't ease her apprehension. "I know something's going on with Rian, but I just can't get it clear. I really hate when that happens."

Robin left the room for a moment, and then came back with a cup of coffee. "Here, this'll help."

"I wonder if he still lives over on 36th Street?" Morgana began sipping the coffee. "Caffeine?"

"Yeah, thought you might want to get up."

Morgana put the mug down on her night stand.

"No, what I would like to do … is finish this dream."

Morgana had developed the ability of lucid dreaming. She wasn't always successful, but learning to control her dreams was an art which she had been developing for many years.

"Don't you have his phone number?"

"I think so, but it's been so long since I've seen him. He's probably moved."

"Yeah, but you know how it is. Ask around."

"Yes, I think I will." Morgana felt much better. She stretched her slender body across the bed and then curled up, her head relaxing on the pillow.

"I think I'll try to go back to sleep."

Morgana looked at the digital clock next to her bed.

It was nearly 6 A.M. The sun was up and shinning, and it looked like it would be a nice day. Robin went jogging.

Morgana fell asleep again. This time, she dreamed that she saw Rian floating in water. At first she seemed fine. Her eyes were closed and she looked very peaceful, but Morgana sensed something was wrong.

Morgana used her years of training and willed herself to change. She was suddenly high above the ground, black feathers covering her body. She knew her totem well, and trusted Her implicitly.

Morgana took charge. She flew down into the woods where before she had seen Rian dead, instinctively seeking her prey. Then, Morgana saw the man again, but this time she knew he wouldn't be able to see her. When she shapeshifted into a crow she could also *veil* herself.

She perched on a tree limb above the man.

He was burning herbs, and he was thinking of Rian. But Morgana still couldn't understand the connection. Gradually it became clear, as though she were slowly focusing an image with a camera lens. It became clear so unexpectedly that it made the feathers on the back of her neck stand up.

For now, she recognized the stranger even in his disguise. He was real, and he could be very dangerous to Rian if she was unprepared. He was also very determined. Morgana sensed this man (or creature) had been sent to Rian by the *Awakener*.

✖✖✖✖

CHAPTER 9

Dru

Morgana stood in front of an old brick row house in a cheap, but arty part of the city. Here, painters, writers, and musicians shared the same neighborhood with winos, drug dealers, and a few other unsavory characters.

She hesitated for a moment and rang the bell. A few minutes later, a young girl dressed all in black answered the door. Morgana thought she couldn't be more than eighteen years old. Her hair was punked and streaked with several different shades of purple. The rest of it was very dark. *Probably dyed black,* Morgana thought. She wore heavy black eyeliner, but her skin looked fair enough to be a natural blond. Morgana noticed that her long painted fingernails matched the purple streaks in her hair. The girl smiled sweetly and asked if she could be of any help.

"I have an appointment with Dru."

The girl looked puzzled and a little spacy. "Dru? Humm.. There's nobody here by that name." She smiled again.

"But I spoke to him yesterday, and he gave me this address!"

A young man appeared at the door and looked out

at Morgana. He wore no shirt, but his body sported some fascinating tattoos. "Can I help you?"

The young girl spoke slowly. "She's looking for someone named Dru,"

"Dru?" The young man look blank. Then he seemed to remember something, "Oh yeah. Wait a minute." He turned around and called out.

"Hey, Ivy!"

Morgana heard a voice from upstairs answering, "Yes?"

"Can you come here a minute?"

"O.K."

He stood to the side of the door and said: "Sorry, come on in."

Morgana hesitated, and decided to wait outside.

A few minutes later, a beautiful young woman with long, bright red, wavy hair came quickly down the stairs and walked over to the door where Morgana waited. Her beauty stunned Morgana.

"Hi! I'm Ivy, sorry to keep you waiting."

"Oh, that's O.K. I'm looking for someone named Dru. Do you know where I can find him?"

Ivy laughed; her smile was breathtaking.

"Of course, he's been waiting for you. Morgana, right?"

"Yes."

"Please, come in."

Morgana, feeling a little better, stepped inside. She stood in a sparsely furnished room; the only furniture being a table and a few very old chairs. A television was playing, but nobody appeared to be watching, and then Morgana noticed a man sleeping in one of the chairs.

The unmistakable smell of marijuana was in the air.

Morgana didn't fool with drugs anymore. She'd seen too much.

"Excuse me," the young lady said to Morgana.

Ivy went over to the sleeping man in the chair and shook him. "Dru ... Wake up!"

Ivy shook him again. She looked over at Morgana and smiled. "Sorry." The man gradually woke up. "Dru, Morgana is here," Ivy whispered softly.

After a moment of silence, "Oh, O.K."

Dru slowly got out of his chair, stood up and turned around. When he saw Morgana, he smiled and walked slowly over to her, his hand outstretched.

"Morgana!"

Morgana was shocked by his appearance.

When she had last seen him, he looked entirely different. Dru had always been a colorful dresser with beautiful long dark-brown hair falling straight down his back. Often it was braided with beads. An avid health-food junkie; he always looked robust and tanned and had a mysterious smile on his face. Many thought he was part Native American, though he never confirmed nor denied it.

How he had changed! His hair had turned silver white, and was severely combed back, cropped just above his collar. He had grown a beard, also gray, but you could still see traces of brown in it. And how much older he looked! When Morgana had last seen him, which was quite a few years ago, she thought he was probably in his late thirties, though he kept himself so fit, it was hard to judge his age. Now, he looked like he had aged twenty years.

"Dru?"

Dru attempted to give Morgana a hug, but she felt

uncomfortable. He seemed a stranger to her now. She wished she hadn't come.

"Morgana, so good to see you again. You look great!"

Morgana felt speechless. How could she reply?

Sensing her embarrassment, Dru said, "I know ... I look terrible."

"Have you been sick?"

Dru nodded slowly. "You might ... say that."

Morgana had seen it before. But she had never expected it from Dru. He was always so disciplined. But it was unmistakable. This house, his appearance, the heavy smell of pot ... Dru was obviously on drugs.

She wanted to cry. He had been her mentor, her teacher. And he had detested drugs and red meat, all that sort of thing. And now, here it was. He, too, had succumbed to that deadly stuff.

"Morgana, don't be upset. It happens."

She just shook her head. "But you, Dru? Why?"

He walked her over to the couch and they sat down. Dru lit up a cigarette, inhaled deeply and then sighed. "It's a long story, and you've heard it all before ... I started experimenting, and I rationalized it to myself." He hesitated. "You know, for magickal purposes, of course."

Morgana nodded. "Of course."

He took another drag off the cigarette. Then he spoke very slowly, very carefully. "At first, I thought I had it completely under control ... Got into mushrooms." He laughed cynically. "That was quite a trip." Morgana thought he almost sounded nostalgic.

"But Dru, I thought you didn't approve of drugs. In

fact, you hated them!"

"I know … " He got up and started pacing slowly, not looking at her. "But when I started using mushrooms I really believed they were different; that they were a spiritual experience."

Morgana watched him closely.

"But then I started looking for more. Looking deeper. You know?"

Morgana was grateful he wasn't facing her. "So what'd you get into Dru, coke?" Her voice was filled with bitterness.

He turned around and confronted her. "Oh, no, **no**! Not that stuff! He paused a while, shrugged, and looked away again. "Back then we called them mind expanding drugs. You know … LSD … peyote … different colored pills … finally, even alcohol."

"Oh, Dru." Morgana was speechless.

"Don't you think I know? Believe me … " He shook his head. "Now I know how right I was about drugs back then, when everybody else was laughing at me."

Morgana looked around. Ivy had left them. She wondered what part she played in the picture.

He sat down again. "Look Morgana, that part of my life is over. I'm in recovery. I know I'm an addict, but I haven't touched drugs or alcohol in nearly eight months."

"That's good, Dru. That's good." But inside Morgana's heart sank. She'd known very few addicts who had recovered.

"Well, I can't take all the credit. Ivy has helped me a lot."

"How did you come to know her?"

"Ivy? She's my daughter!"

"Your daughter? I never knew you had any children!"

"Remember Silvia?"

"Silvia," Morgana went back to 1980 when she first came out to California. "No I don't think so."

"Well, she was my Priestess. I met her in sixty-eight. We were together for years."

"I don't remember her."

"Yeah, well … she moved to New York. Ivy is ours."

"Why did they go to New York?"

He shrugged. "We were having problems. Silvia wanted to work in New York. At the time we both thought it was for the best."

"So, when did you and Ivy reunite?"

"Ivy and Silvia both came out here about a year ago. Silvia went back to New York, and Ivy and I got reacquainted."

"And she helped you?"

"She saved me."

"That's great Dru; I'm proud of you."

"She's a beauty isn't she?" He was obviously very proud of his daughter."

"Oh, Dru, gorgeous!"

He crushed out his cigarette, and immediately lit up another one. Then he stood up and laughed a little. "I've nearly quit these, too," he said, holding up the cigarette." He smiled. "Ivy detests it when I smoke … but seeing you again … " He shrugged. "Made me a little nervous, you know?"

She nodded.

"Morgana, tell me, how can I help you?"

"Dru I'm not sure if you can … now."

Seeing her reluctance to confide in him anymore, he

looked sad. At one time, the old Dru had very special feelings for Morgana. When she first came out to California, he had seen in her the makings of a first-rate Priestess and psychic. He'd worked with her for several years and trained her in the mysteries.

Now, seeing her reluctance, he told her he was ashamed of himself, of everything he had let himself get into. For years he had hidden it, even from his closest friends.

After his addiction grew worse, Dru avoided seeing his friends, always telling them he was involved in some long-term esoteric venture. He didn't keep a permanent address. Finally, he simply disappeared. Only a few old friends knew how to get in touch with him. His condition had remained a secret from the world he once knew and led.

Now, he told Morgana, he was trying to come back. To take his position as an elder in the magickal community. He knew it would take time and great perseverance, but he truly believed he could control his addiction. And more importantly, he wanted to. He went to recovery meetings nearly every day, sometimes twice a day. He understood the difficulties, the hardships, but he treated it as a spiritual path and that helped. Most of all, Ivy supported him, and that helped him feel he had something to live for.

Dru seemed calmer and more relaxed now that he had told her everything. He put out his cigarette. "Look Morgana, you don't have to confide in me if you don't want to. I understand, really I do. But I've been clean eight months. No big deal, I know, but I think I can handle whatever it is you want to tell me. In a way, I'm stronger than before. I've had to lick this thing, and it's made me strong."

"Do you live here?" Morgana thought the atmosphere not very conducive to getting out of drugs.

He smiled. "No, of course not. Ivy has a little flat upstairs. She's an artist, and a good one. I thought it might be better to meet here than where I lived."

"Where do you live?"

Dru paused again. "In a half-way house."

Morgana felt ill. She didn't know what to say.

But even as Morgana had lost faith, Dru seemed to be gaining his. And the longer he chatted with her, the more self-assured he seemed to grow. Finally, he said: "It's O.K. It's a beginning. I'll probably be out on my own in a few more months. Ivy and I plan to get a place together for a while. And I've got a part-time job. Nothing stressful, but interesting. I like it." He smiled, and for a moment Morgana thought she caught a shadow of the old Dru.

She asked, "What do you do now?"

Back when Morgana had known Dru, he made a living giving workshops and classes. He was so good at leading encounter groups that Morgana had assumed his formal training was in psychology. He also frequently gave seminars on subjects such as blending the art of meditation with everyday life, or personal growth development. It was at such a lecture that Morgana had first met him. Yet, Morgana had no idea what sort of formal education he had.

She did know without any doubt that he was extremely intelligent, with a penetrating mind such as she had never known before or since. He had a huge library in the flat where she had spent most of her time with him. And Dru knew most anything you could think of about the arcane, magick and other esoteric subjects.

"Well," Dru answered, "believe it or not, I'm working in a metaphysical bookstore."

Dru's remark startled Morgana, but now she felt reluctant to reveal any of her fears about Rian to him. Instead, she only forced a smile and said. "Really? What a coincidence. My niece … has a store like that."

Dru became very quiet and looked at her more closely, yet it only took a split second for him to tune into her thoughts. Morgana recognized that familiar look in his eyes, but at the same time she also sensed a foreboding darkness.

"And that's why you're here isn't it?" he asked. "Your niece is in danger."

※※※※

CHAPTER 10

The Bargain

Rian stood up when she saw Viviene's face and turned around. Viviene had been sitting facing the doorway.

The stranger stood still....waiting.

Rian felt confused. Why hadn't she brought the stupid book? "Look," she began, "I forgot it. I mean, I just took it home to read, and forgot to bring it back. I'm really sorry."

The stranger was frustrated. He tried to cover up how disturbed he was, but it was obvious. *Damn!* he thought. He wasn't grinning.

Rian felt more intimidated by the second. "Look, I'll tell you what. My brother is here." She wanted him to know that. "I can drive home...I don't live far. I'll bring it back...O.K.?"

It was getting late for him to do the work. By planetary hours he needed to be at it in less than an hour. If he waited, he'd miss his chance.

Suddenly, the phone rang. Rian welcomed the reprieve. She excused herself, and went over to the counter to answer the phone. It was Morgana!

"Morgana! Hi! How are you?"

Morgana spoke quickly and quietly.

"Rian, are you all right?"

"Well, yes ... sort of. Why?"

"Listen very carefully. This may sound very strange to you, but I've been having some unusual dreams about you the last few weeks."

"You have?"

"Yes, and while I don't want to alarm you, I'd like you to be careful, especially of strangers."

Rian felt weak. The stranger was still standing nearby.

"One more thing. Have you recently acquired an old book with sort of faded blue color?"

Rian felt another panic attack coming on.

"Rian?"

"Morgana, can I call you back?"

"What's the matter?"

"I have to go now."

"Listen to me. Don't give away the book. It's important!"

Rian couldn't answer.

"Rian, listen to me. I think this may have gone further than I realized. I can tell by your silence that you know what I'm referring to!"

Suddenly, Morgana got the message. Sometimes she thought in such complex terms, she didn't see the simplest things.

Viviene, who was watching this whole affair, saw Rian beginning to shake. She also couldn't help overhearing Rian's telephone conversation. Hearing the name Morgana startled her. It was a Pagan name—a Craft name.

At the same time, she instinctively looked at the

stranger. She noticed that he was also startled by the name and began to look very uneasy. He started shifting from one foot to the other.

"Rian," Morgana said softly, "You can't talk right now can you?"

"That's right."

"He's there?"

"Yes."

"Listen. Don't worry. Everything's under control. Just think of a way to hang on to the book. Can you do that?"

"Don't know."

"O.K. I'll be helping you. Listen, do what you have to do. Offer him money if necessary. I think he'll take it."

Rian was shaking, "I have to go now."

"O.K."

Rian hung up the receiver. Without looking at the stranger, she turned around and went upstairs to her brother's office.

"Kevin, he's here...downstairs, and I forgot to bring his book."

Kevin stood up. "Well, just tell him to come back later."

"I tried." She shrugged. "But I don't think he's happy about it. And then all of a sudden Aunt Marty called! She must be psychic."

"Why?"

"Because she knows, don't ask me how, about the guy and that book! She said not to give it back to him...to offer him money for it if necessary. She said it was very important! Kevin, she really sounded worried."

"But Rian, it's his book. What's the big deal?"

"How should I know?"

"O.K. I'll try and handle it."

Kevin went downstairs, and for the first time confronted the stranger. *Rian is right*, Kevin thought. *He is definitely weird.*

"Look, we're really sorry. The truth is your book is missing. We found it laying around here yesterday and it was so old and everything, I think we just discarded it!"

The man was getting agitated. "No, you didn't. That girl said she took it home!"

"Well, she just said that because she feels bad that we lost your book. It was a mistake. Listen, I'll reimburse you for it, O.K.?"

"I need that book!" The man looked upset.

"Well, I'm very sorry. We don't have it."

Kevin took out $50 from the cash drawer. "Will this take care of it? I know it was probably very rare, and I can see it meant a lot to you."

The man stared hungrily at the money. "Couldn't replace it for $50."

Viviene spoke. "I'm sure we will make every attempt to recover it. In the mean time why not take the money? Possibly you can replace it."

The stranger looked over at Kevin. He seemed interested.

Viviene carefully watched the scene playing out. Then, her eyes caught Kevin's. They said, offer him more.

Kevin pulled a wallet out from his pocket and retrieved some money. "Here's another $20. It's my final offer." By now Kevin would do almost anything to get this guy out of Rian's life. Furthermore, he trusted

Marty's instincts and felt they should hang on to the book, whatever her reasons might be.

The stranger hesitated for a minute as though he were weighing something in his mind. He looked nervously from Kevin to Viviene, and then he noticed the tarot layout on the table. He stared at it for a few seconds silently. Then he reached out his hand and grabbed the money from Kevin, muttered something under his breath and walked towards the door.

Suddenly he turned around.

"If you find the book, I'll be back. I'll know!"

"But you've already sold it." Kevin said, "We've paid you!"

"No, I wouldn't do that. I wouldn't sell it. It's on a *lend*. I'll be back. *I'll know!*"

Then he turned towards the door, opened it and walked out.

✖✖✖✖

CHAPTER 11

The Night-Mare

Ride a Cock Horse
To Banberry Cross
To see a fine lady
On a white horse.
Rings on her fingers
And bells on her toes,
And she will have music
Wherever she goes.

For several days after the confrontation, Rian did not want to be alone in the store. She also asked Kevin to drive her home early each night. He worried about her more than he cared to admit. Everyday she seemed to grow more nervous. Rian had always been sensitive, but, basically, she was pretty level-headed, and Kevin simply couldn't figure out why this guy had frightened her so much.

On the other hand, there was the call from Marty. That was uncanny. He was beginning to consider calling her to see if she could shed some light on the situation. He even thought of questioning Viviene. He knew she had read Rian's cards the day the stranger showed up, and wondered if she would tell him what she thought was going on. He'd need Rian's permission though. Viviene believed revealing a private reading to a third person was a terrible breach of trust.

"Listen, get some rest!" Kevin said to Rian one night as she got out of his car. "There's absolutely no need to stay all worked up about this guy! I want you to take a few days off. Go to the ocean or something. I'll watch the store... or close for a week if I have to. Things are really slow anyhow."

"Kevin, I couldn't do that."

"Rian, I mean it. You need a vacation. After the Fourth of July, why don't you go to the ocean? It won't be too crowded, and you can relax. Call a friend, and go have some fun."

"Maybe ... I'll think about it."

As Kevin drove away, he headed towards Viviene's house.

Rian went up the stairway and into her apartment. The first thing she did was to go into the bathroom and open the medicine cabinet. The doctor had given her mild tranquilizers for her nerves and panic attacks, in case she felt really bad.

This is *really bad*, , Rian rationalized. She turned on the tap and drew a glass of water. She swallowed the tablet, took off her clothes, and got into a warm shower.

It is all too much, Rian thought. *Too much.* Her mind wandered to the events of the last few days, the tarot reading, the stranger, the book, and finally the strange call from Morgana. None of it made sense, and yet, there were a few things that tied together. The reading, the book and the names seemed connected. But where do I fit in?

As she stepped out of the shower, her hair dripping wet, she told herself she must get a firm grip on herself. She dried herself off, slipped into an oversized white tee shirt and lay down.

Then, she rolled over on her bed, picked up the telephone and dialed a number she knew by heart. The phone rang several times, but all she got was an answering machine. *Damn. Why does she have to call me with all this stuff and then not be there?* Rian thought. She left a message and hung up.

Kevin's right I do need a vacation. I'm going bonkers.

Rian dialed another number. "Hi, Jamie, it's Rian!"

"Hi! What are you up to?"

"I need a vacation. Want to drive down to the ocean for a few days?"

"Wish I could, but I can't get off work right now."

"Sure?"

"Positive. Believe me, if I could I'd go in a minute. Try Nancy, I think she lost her job."

"Really? Bummer."

Jamie laughed. "She hated the job. She'll probably go if she has any cash."

Rian hung up the phone and laid back on her pillow. She was feeling much better. The tranquilizer was having its effect. She closed her eyes, and then almost immediately she was sleeping.

❈

Rian dreamed she was riding a beautiful white mare. So fast did they go, and snug did she sit on the horse's back, that it seemed they were one. She felt euphoric. Oddly, she also was aware that she was dreaming!

Rian had read about lucid dreaming. It was the ability to control one's dreams, to be aware that you were dreaming. *This must be it then*, Rian thought happily. *This is so amazing! I wonder if I tried...I could just travel anywhere I wanted?* She continued to gallop, and the countryside whizzed by her. *I know*, she thought, *I'll fly!*

And it seemed so easy. She simply willed herself to climb up into the sky higher and higher until she could see the earth far below. But then she became frightened, and for a moment she lost control of her dream and began to fall. *Wait*, thought Rian, *I can control this*. She pulled herself up, and now she was one with the horse.

I'm going to land now, she decided, and she did. Then she slowed down. She was trotting along a trail and smelled water. She walked down to a lake which was so clear you could see the surrounding trees mirrored in it. She walked up to the lake and took a drink, and felt a breeze blow her hair, her mane. Which was she, the horse or the girl? As she drank the water, she suddenly noticed two people standing by the lake. One was Morgana, and the other a man that she had never met.

"Hello, Rian," said the man, "My name is Dru. I'm honored to meet you." He pronounced her name Ree-ahn.

Dru took Rian's hand. He seemed familiar somehow, but he made her feel uneasy. Then Rian hugged Morgana.

"We are here to help you," Morgana said. "It's best to meet like this for now."

"Am I a horse or a woman?"

"Don't you know?" said Dru. "Can you remember?"

Now Rian, Morgana, and Dru seemed to melt into more wooded surroundings. "Does this place feel familiar to you?" asked Dru.

"Well, yes, I think so."

"Listen carefully." Morgana's words seemed to be coming to her telepathically.

"You may not understand what I'm about to tell you, but you must be told. You must be prepared."

"O.K." Rian felt uneasy.

"Remember the information you discovered about the name, Morgan?"

"I remember ... some of it." Rian wondered how Marty (should this be Morgana?) knew about that?

As if Morgana could read her thoughts, she answered, "I can't explain everything, but this you must hear and accept. Rian, you are connected to a great Welsh Queen of Annwn, the Otherworld. She ruled the dream world, and her totems were horses and birds. Her ancient name was Rigatona and, like Morgan, her name means Great Queen, but she's usually called Rhiannon."

"What do you mean? What is happening to me? I'm dreaming, aren't I?"

"Yes, but it's a true dream. It's really happening, Rian."

"Are you dreaming, too?"

"Not exactly, we are meeting you in an astral pathwork."

"You mean like a meditation?"

"Yes... sort of. A carefully protected one. Rian listen, you are being sought out by a man who is attempting to use you."

"What?"

"He is unworthy. He is pretending to do an errand for the Ancient One. The great Awakener. It is your blood, Rian, your lineage. But he is not the true one. He has destroyed the true messenger and is trying to take his place … trying to deceive you through your dreams."

"What are you talking about?" Rian wanted all this to end.

Rian sensed Morgana pleading, "Don't fight us on this, please!"

"Who is he? What does he want from me?"

"He is an impostor," Dru answered. "He believes he can redeem himself if he can send you back."

"It's good that you kept the book," said Morgana. "There are clues in there to your identity. And, he accepted the money. That means he must give up his claim to it."

Rian decided it was time to wake up. As if Dru could read her mind he spoke. "Ree-ahn, not yet! Wait! Watch!"

Rian felt herself getting angry, growing strong, changing. No longer was she the wonderful white horse. Her color seemed to be darkening, darkening.

Dru stood near her, his white hair waving in the wind, his open hand pointing at her.

Her coat turned black as night. Crows and ravens flew around her. She took off, galloping faster and faster as if mad. She ran, but never tired, her body covered with sweat. Then, she stopped, reared up and gave out an unearthly sound.

❈❈

At the same time, her body covered with sweat, Rian sat up in bed screaming.

❈❈❈❈

CHAPTER 12

The Pathwork

"We lost her."

"Dru, can't we get her back?"

He shook his head. "No, she's awake."

Dru rubbed his hand through his hair. "The thing is, she woke up so suddenly, I'm not sure she'll remember anything."

"Why did you do that?"

"Do what?"

"Show her that dark side. It woke her up!"

"I didn't!"

"Then, how did it happen?"

"Don't know. I just wanted to empower her. To give her more confidence. I wanted that ride to be on Rhiannon, not the Mora."

"Dru, you mean she transformed herself?"

"Possibly...but I wouldn't worry too much. It's better for her to be angry than frightened."

Earlier, Morgana and Dru had gone up to Ivy's small sitting room. There they cast a circle, calling on their totems and their powers.

Dru took his name from Druid, which was a tradition

that he had worked in for many years. The Druids in the old Celtic religion were bards and teachers, and families from Rome would send their children to the British Isles to study with them. The Druids were also connected to the tree spirits, especially the oak. Dru invoked the dryads, the tree elementals, and he called on the great wizard, Gwydion. Morgana invoked the crows for information, and the Lady of the Lake, Morgan herself.

First, they did a divination to see what was going on.

Dru suggested Ivy read the cards, since his daughter didn't know anything specific about the problem.

"I think," Dru commented, "she can be more objective, and anyway, she's a remarkable reader."

"Yes," Morgana answered, "That might be better."

Ivy agreed, and without telling her anything specific, they asked her to just do a reading on the situation at hand.

Ivy threw the cards. "What I see puzzles me," she began.

"What is it?" asked Morgana."

"Well, your niece Rian has something....which belongs to my father."

"What are you talking about?" Morgana asked.

"I associate my dad with the King of Staffs, as he connects to the tree. And crossing him is the seven of swords, which means to me that someone has stolen something of his. But the odd thing is that this happened a long time ago. Perhaps years!"

"Ivy, why do you believe Rian has this object?"

"Because up here, I see her as the eight of cups, an emotionally confused young woman trying to hide from her destiny ... and with good reason; she is being pursued by the Magician."

Dru and Morgan saw that the Magician was inverted.

"This object that was stolen, what is it?"

Ivy drew two more cards and turned them over, an eight of pentacles, and the Hierophant.

"Something you worked hard for, something philosophical. Ivy paused deep in thought, trying to see the message clearly.

"Of course! Your books or your teachings. Dru, I think the thief might have been one of your apprentices!"

Suddenly, Morgana remembered her dream.

"A few nights ago I had a dream that Rian was lying dead in the woods with a book in her hand."

"Can you describe the book?" Dru asked.

"It was small ... blue ... with ... something like a ... carousel etched on the cover ... and now ... this is funny, but as I talk about it I have the strangest feeling that I've seen it before ... somewhere."

Dru was silent for a moment. Then he said. "At my initiation a woman gave me a book like that. She was from New York I believe...an elder of our tradition, but a complete stranger to me. She came with a man whom I knew as Myrddin. The name of that book is *The Merrywells*.

Morgana frowned. She had forgotten to ask Rian the name of the book. "Dru, what happened to all those books you once had?"

"Everything's packed away, but if it's the one I'm thinking of, it's very unique, a hand-copied autobiography of the Lady Mere-Ama."

"The Norse Goddess of the waters. I suppose she would closely correspond to one of the Welsh Ladies of the Lake."

"Yes, but as I recall, this book was more of a narrative to record the events and myths which surrounded migration of a Celtic family to Britain. We know a myth is not an ordinary legend. It's a sacred story told on many levels."

"But, often it grows out of the lives of real people," said Morgana.

"Exactly. In the back of the book," Dru went on, "there were runes, herbal mixtures, and incantations. A sort of ancient Book of Shadows."

Ivy looked puzzled. She had been studying the cards while her father and Morgana talked. When they were done, she returned to the reading. This time she just stared at the cards without saying anything for several long minutes. Then her face changed. "Something's about to explode! Major changes imminent!"

Ivy's voice began to change. Her eyes closed halfway, and she appeared to be in a trance. Morgana had seen readers like this before, when the cards triggered something inside of their minds, and they became psychic readers not just intuitive counselors.

"Morgana, your niece Rian is connected to the Lady Rhiannon, and she is in grave danger. The man chasing her wants the book! It is Dru's book. He hunts. Hunts his prey to redeem himself. Not what he appears. Oh! No! Great Goddess! We must all be careful! He is a demon, a trickster! Be careful He is responsible for Dru's fate. He is an imposter and has taken over Dru's quest!"

Dru sat up straight. He turned pale.

"Morgana, he will destroy Rian. You must help her! He is a liar; a fraud. And he's very dangerous. Be careful!"

Ivy's head swung back and her eyes rolled back in her head as though she were going to have a seizure. Morgana and Dru restrained themselves. They knew better than to wake her suddenly.

After a moment, she took control and pulled herself back. Morgana wasn't sure if she would remember all she had said.

"That's enough, Ivy," her father told her. "Relax, honey. You did good."

After a while, Ivy calmed down, and Dru brought her some tea. They sat around and discussed the divination and the resolution, if any, for several hours.

They decided to undertake a pathwork in order to help Rian, and would attempt to contact her during her dream-time. They knew this channel had already been opened by the impostor, yet even so, they sensed they could communicate with her safely in this manner.

First, Morgana phoned Rian to see if they were on the right track and to warn her if they were, but after speaking to her, Morgana was sure that no ordinary phone call was going to help.

Next, they carefully reinforced their circle with candles and lit resin incenses. Then they anointed each other with a protective oil. Finally, they burned incense of wormwood to heighten their divination and psychic techniques.

Morgana had a photograph of Rian. She placed her picture on the altar and anointed her photograph with several more protective oils. Then, they placed her photograph underneath a crystal pyramid which had a light box underneath. When the light was turned on, Rian's picture was illuminated within the crystal, where she would be safe from any malevolent forces. They sur-rounded the little light box with burning incense cones to further protect their magick.

They carefully called the four Watchers of the East, South, West, and North to protect and guard them in their Sacred Space, especially Rian.

Then, they went into a guided meditation, or path-work, and concentrated on Rian, willing her to go home, get comfortable, relax, and fall asleep. This took nearly an hour. Finally, they planted their seeds, to re-link her with her ancient totem...the horse, and thus help her make the connection which would empower her.

In the beginning, everything seemed to go well. They helped Rian shift herself into a lucid dream. Then, they invoked her white horse, which she immediately connected to. This was not a surprise, as it was one of the central themes of her legend. In the dream-time all this would seem quite natural to Rian.

Then they let her go to relax and enjoy her freedom … her magickal power. Finally, when she seemed to be losing hold, they brought her back and met her. So far, so good.

The pathwork was two-fold: first, to help her con-nect to Rhiannon, her namesake, traveling between the worlds on her magickal horse; second to warn her of the baneful mission of the stranger.

But then something went wrong. Rian became con-fused. She wanted to wake up. Dru tried to keep her a lit-tle longer with enchantment, by opening her up to Annwn, but she became impatient and frustrated. They had forgotten that no one could ever catch Rhiannon's magickal horse! Without even trying, she instinctively shape-shifted into Mora, the strong and angry version of the dreaded Night-Mare, the night-riding spirit who entered bedrooms as a ghostly shadow and tormented her victims.

"It seems that on some level she connected to her more primitive form and just went with it."

"So," said Morgana, "What do we do now?"

"Well, for starters, we might look through your records and books," Ivy said to her father. "Didn't you once tell me they were all catalogued?"

"Yes, they were." Dru nodded.

"More importantly, we must find out which student betrayed you." Morgana added.

Dru shrugged. "There were many students over the years."

"Yes, but according to Ivy, he was only pretending. Isn't it possible that he was just hanging around? You know ... you had your share of groupies."

"I remember a few students back then who were experimenting with mushrooms. Not all were serious apprentices. It had to be someone who was there, when I first got into it."

Dru paused for a minute, thinking back. "On the other hand, it could very well have been a serious student ... who turned bad."

While Dru and Morgana talked, Ivy had been shuffling the cards quietly. Suddenly she stopped, laid them down on the floor and spread them out. Then she drew one. It was the King of Cups, inverted. "Or maybe," Ivy said very softly, "He was only a very good actor."

All three stared in silence at the inverted card.

Dru seemed visibly disturbed. "In that case," he said slowly, "it was all plotted out from the beginning." He paused again. "But I never saw it, never suspected...that. What you're saying is that somehow, he tricked me into my addiction in order to take my place, carry out my quest. It's diabolical! And why me, for what purpose?"

"To get the credit, of course," Ivy said simply.

Dru and Morgana looked at Ivy, a puzzled expression on their faces. Ivy had pulled one last card: *Judgment*. Nothing was said for a moment. The card of spiritual rebirth told them everything.

"To awaken Rian!" Morgana finally said softly.

"Yes," Dru replied, "To awaken Rian."

✳✳✳✳

CHAPTER 13

Ivy

Soft classical music was playing from the tape-player as Ivy sat in a meditative state in front of the little altar she had put together in her room. The altar was low, less than eight inches from the floor. Along with a burning candle and smoking incense cone, Ivy had placed a small goblet of water, a colorfully fluted Tunisian dish filled with salt, several shells she had collected, and a little blue Indian corn. Her tarot cards sat next to the candle.

It was a cool evening. Five nights had elapsed since she had done the tarot reading for her father and Morgana. She sat silently, her hands resting open in her lap, breathing slowly and regularly as she often did. She wore only a loose fitting blue caftan. Her long, beautiful red hair hung freely down her back. Her eyes were closed; her face was peaceful.

She sat that way for about twenty minutes. When she was finished with her meditations, she snuffed out the candle and dowsed the incense in the bowl of sand. Then she drank the rest of the water.

She immediately removed her caftan and hung it up, turned off the music and slipped into jeans and a

81

blouse. She went downstairs, picked up the phone and dialed her father's number.

"Hello."

"Hello, this is Ivy Parkington. I'd like to speak to my father, please."

"One moment."

A few minutes later Dru was on the phone.

"Ivy?"

"Hello, Dad, I just wanted to let you know...I'm ready."

"O.K., I'll be waiting."

Ivy went back upstairs to her room, grabbed her canvas pocketbook, then locked the door from the outside. She would not wear anything made from an animal. The exception was feathers ... if she found them herself.

She got into her car, and drove over to the bookstore where her father worked. When she pulled up in front of the store, Dru was waiting outside.

"Hi!" Ivy greeted him cheerfully.

"Hey, kiddo." Dru climbed into the seat next to his daughter.

"Is everything set?"

"Yep. Let's go."

Dru gave Ivy directions. They drove through the many hilly suburbs of San Francisco, over the Golden Gate bridge, and then headed north on Route. 101 towards Sonoma. After about two hours they turned off the highway, and drove another half-hour on some desolate side roads, until they pulled up in front of an unpaved gravel driveway. Dru told Ivy to pull the car into the driveway. They wound around until a small white cottage came into view.

Dru said, "This is it."

"Dad, how did you get all your stuff way out here?"

"With a truck."

Ivy and her father parked the car, and went up the walkway to the front door. Dru rang the bell. A short man with greying brown hair answered the door.

"Dru Parkington?"

"Yes. And this is my daughter, Ivy."

"Well, come on in. My name is Bill. Chris just went up to the store. He'll be back any minute, but I can take you both up to the attic."

Then Dru's expression changed. "Nancy!"

A middle-aged woman appeared at the door. She looked tired, but had a warm smile. If Nancy noticed how much Dru had changed, she didn't let on.

"Chris is Nancy's husband." Dru explained to Ivy.

She nodded. "And this must be your daughter, Ivy."

"Yes."

"Well, I'm so glad to finally meet you."

"Thank you," Ivy said politely.

"This is Bill," Nancy said. "He's been staying here a while. Kind of helping out. But listen, you don't have to wait for Chris. Bill and I can take you upstairs. Everything is just as you left it."

"Fine." Dru was anxious to get started.

They went up two flights of stairs to the attic, and Bill turned on the light. Ivy was surprised to see how big the attic was. The ceiling was low in places, but you could stand up in most parts of the room. It was filled with odds and ends. A few trunks and some loose clothing were lying here and there, but over on one side, pushed against the wall, Ivy saw a huge pile of carefully taped boxes and several bookcases.

"There they are!" said Nancy proudly, as if she had been waiting for this day for a long time. "Just as you left it."

Dru slowly walked over to the boxes, and ran his hands over them slowly.

"Dad, there must be more than twenty boxes here."

"More like thirty!"

"It will take a lot of searching to find one book." For the first time, Ivy felt a little discouraged.

Bill smiled reassuringly at Ivy. "Maybe not. All the boxes are labeled carefully. The book your father told us he'd be looking for would most likely be in a box labeled mythology, so that narrows it down a whole lot."

They began by looking for markings on the boxes. Dru was right when he said that everything was labeled.

There were boxes marked philosophy, history, psychology, science, fiction, and science-fiction. Others were labeled art, art-history, anthropology, archeology, alchemy, mystery schools, and hermetics. It went on and on. Ivy had never seen so many books outside of a public library!

Bill and Dru began moving the boxes around, searching for the ones on mythology. Nancy and Ivy crouched down and looked underneath, as the men pulled them out. The boxes were very heavy and it took a long time. Then they heard a voice behind them.

"How's it going?"

Everyone turned around. Ivy saw a well-built, sandy-haired man standing at the top of the stairs with a big grin on his face.

"Chris!" Dru stopped pushing the cartons around and went over to see his old friend. They talked and laughed for a few minutes, and then Chris joined the others.

Dru introduced Chris to his daughter.

"Whoa!" He stared long and hard at Ivy. "You certainly don't favor your dad," He chuckled.

Ivy tried to smile, but she felt uneasy. She didn't like this man.

The search resumed. Dru finally found some boxes on mythology. Chris and Bill helped him open the boxes, one at a time. There were four of them. Dru described the book to everyone so that no one would miss it, but after about an hour, they finally accepted the fact that it wasn't there.

Then, Ivy said they needed to find another box. "Dad, didn't you say that it would be labeled 'archives?'"

Chris looked startled.

"Yeah...sorry I forgot to tell you. Remember I kept a lot of notes and names of my students?"

Ivy shot a quick glance at her father, but then she smiled.

"Dad, can we take a short break before we look again?"

"That's just what I've been hoping." Nancy said. "Why don't you and I go downstairs and find some food?"

"Well, I will, if the rest of you come too." She was looking at her father.

"Sounds good to me." Dru took the cue.

Everyone went downstairs, leaving the boxes of books disheveled and scattered.

Nancy took them all into the kitchen, and put out

some doughnuts and strong coffee. Ivy ate no refined sugar, and drank no caffeine.

"I'm in training," she laughed.

"How about a sandwich?" Nancy looked helpless.

"No. Please don't worry about it. I'm fine!"

Suddenly Chris offered. "How would you like some mint tea?"

"That would be great!"

Nancy looked confused. "I'm afraid we don't have any."

Chris told Nancy there was a box in the shopping bag he had just brought back from the grocery store. "So, you're a real true vegetarian and health-food addict like your dad used to be?" Chris commented.

"Yes, I guess so."

"I admire you. I really do." His eyes alluded to more than that.

Ivy needed to speak to her father alone. After they had snacks, she asked for directions to the bathroom.

Nancy pointed the way upstairs.

The first thing she noticed was that the bathroom smelled of a strong incense unfamiliar to her. She pulled her thoughts together.

There was something wrong here. Something didn't fit. Aside from the way Chris looked at her — she was accustomed to men looking at her that way — she didn't trust him.

In fact, there was something wrong about the whole picture. Ivy looked around the bathroom. It was sparse. After all, a woman did live here, but she noticed none of the usual feminine bathroom articles, no bath-salts or scented soap. The towels were old and rough; the soap had never been used. Ivy opened the medicine chest. Empty. No comb or brush here either.

Dru had picked up Ivy's feelings.

When he heard Ivy coming down the stairs, he said, "Think I'll go next."

Dru casually got up and walked up the staircase. On his way up he passed Ivy coming down. She stopped on the steps and whispered quickly to her father. "Listen, Dad, be careful. I don't feel these folks are the people you think they are. As soon as you find the box of archives, let's go." She walked past him and returned to the kitchen.

Chris was watching her. He sensed that something was wrong.

He thought, *She couldn't know.*

After the treats, they all went up to the attic again. Dru found the box marked 'archives.' He put it aside, and Ivy sat on it. The men replaced the other boxes, and they all walked downstairs.

"It's getting late, Dad," Ivy said. "I have a class in the morning."

Dru was grateful for an excuse to leave. He seemed troubled by what Ivy had said. Before they drove up to the cottage he had told her that Chris was a long and trusted friend. "He's always there whenever anybody needs help. Everybody in the community likes him!"

Later, driving home, Ivy said. "Dad, I'm sorry, but every instinct I have tells me these people are not your friends."

Dru was visibly disturbed by her statement. "You said that before! And I don't understand. Why?"

"Don't you think it's odd that these so-called Craft

people didn't have any herbal tea in the house, or that they thought it odd I was a vegetarian?

"No, not really."

"What about the bathroom? I opened the cabinet and it was empty. And have you ever been in a bathroom where a woman lived, and seen no fresh towels or scented soaps, not even a comb or brush?"

They drove silently for a long time.

Finally, Dru said wearily, "I'm tired. Can you drop me off at my place? We'll go through all this stuff tomorrow."

"Dad, you can stay over at my house."

"Thanks, but I think I'll sleep better in my own bed."

Ivy could see that the trip had upset her father. Perhaps she shouldn't have acted so suspicious of his friends. But she couldn't help it. She hoped the notes in the box of archives would hold the key to whomever betrayed her father, and who was threatening his friends.

When they pulled up in front of the place he lived, she helped him carry the box to his room.

Dru suggested that they go through it in the morning, but Ivy felt strongly that they shouldn't wait. She was also very afraid Dru would try looking through the box alone and find something compromising about his friends. She didn't want him to be alone if that were to happen.

"Let's do it together," Ivy suggested. "If we concentrate our efforts on finding notes only connected to the time-frame when you first began experimenting with drugs, it shouldn't take too long."

Dru sighed, but agreed. With his pocket knife, he cut the twine and tape which held the box closed.

Finally he opened the top, and he and Ivy looked

anxiously inside, but their anxiety quickly changed to despair. The whole box was filled with newspapers.

❦ ❦ ❦ ❦

CHAPTER 14

The Equinox

Rian lay on the beach down near the water. She had taken her brother's advice, feeling the need to get away. Kevin made arrangements with his part-time clerk to help take care of the shop during her absence. Failing to get a friend to go with her, she went alone. The sun and surf were doing her a world of good, and she no longer felt troubled. The nightmares had stopped.

Even better, she had met a man who was staying at the same motel. They had lunch together a few times, and later today he was supposed to meet her at the beach. He told her he was from Annapolis, which was about an hour or so from Rian's house. He loved to surf and that was why he was here, at least that's what he told Rian.

Rian let the ocean waves roll over her feet. She built a sand castle and then knocked it down. She watched the children playing nearby. It was beginning to get late, and her friend hadn't come. She wondered if he really would. Finally, thinking she was stood-up and beginning to feel sunburned, she got up, picked up her little beach chair, and headed back to her motel room.

When she opened the door the telephone was ringing. It was him. "Hi, Frank," she said.

"Where were you? I looked all over."

Rian made a face to herself. *Sure.*

"Well, the sun got too hot, so I decided that unless I wanted a third-degree burn, I'd better go in for a while."

"Wanna meet at the beach at sunset?"

"Umm … O.K. I'll see you later then."

Rian hung up the phone, and took a shower. Afterwards, she felt drowsy, laid down and fell into a short, dreamless sleep. When she woke up, she changed and walked over to the boardwalk, where she grabbed some dinner.

Later, she almost reconsidered meeting Frank on the beach.

Well, why not? she thought. *It is a public beach.*

Rian went back to the motel, put on some shorts and a tank top, picked up her beach chair and blanket and headed back down to the beach. It was dusk.

Only a few people were still hanging around. Some guys were playing volleyball about thirty yards away, and two women were sitting on a blanket nearby watching a child. Gulls were flying over still hoping to get a treat from the beachcombers.

Rian stared out at the ocean as the sun set. The sky took on a red hue, and everything felt so peaceful. She honestly didn't care if Frank showed up or not. In fact, she felt grateful she was able to relax.

She watched the sea for a long time. The moon was coming up. In the background, she could hear music playing at her motel and an occasional squeal from a gull, but other than that, all was quiet. The air was still warm.

Rian closed her eyes for a few moments, then

opened them. The moon was just coming up over the horizon, and she began to feel a little odd, as though this scene had all happened before ... *deja-vu*. A fragment, a moonrise. *Where was this familiar feeling coming from?*

Then suddenly she thought of Marty and another night long ago. Another moonrise ... but it wasn't summer ... it was autumn ..., no, the eve of autumn ... the last night of summer ... and Marty finally agreed to take her ...

A long-lost memory, only bits and pieces at first, slowly began to creep into Rian's thoughts ... she struggled to capture it, and then finally, like a floating feather, it settled into her mind.

❈❈

Rian had nagged her, begged her to go! Marty finally gave in and helped her put a costume together, a gold-threaded Indian cotton skirt and blouse, a wreath made from grape-vine, and gold chrysanthemums for her hair.

They drove out to a farmhouse which belonged to one of Marty's friends. It was an old, faded, two-story frame house surrounded by hills and trees. There, about thirty people gathered in a small living room. Many brought drums or Native American rattles, and wore symbolic jewelry. Most dressed in some kind of garb and wore leather pouches either around their neck or around their waist. Like her, most of the women were wearing wreaths of autumn flowers in their hair. There was an abundance of food.

Rian noticed Robin was there, too. After everyone settled down, it was he who talked about the ritual they were going to do.

"The Autumn Equinox is the time when the day and night are equal." He held up an old-fashioned balance scale. "We have scales, and each of you may use any element you wish to balance yourselves. Remember, air represents new ideas, thoughts, and creativity; fire, energy and willpower; earth, courage and stability; and water, emotions. We will use incense for air, candles for fire, stones for earth, and a cup of water for ... water!"

Everybody clapped and laughed with anticipation.

After Robin explained the ritual, the group went outside and formed a circle around a blazing fire. A large flat stone sat in back of the fire pit. On it were two more large balance scales and some other artifacts, including a ceramic goblet, two golden twisted candles and a cauldron of burning incense. A basket of fruits and vegetables lay next to the stone altar. Far off in the dusk, Rian could make out endless fields of ripe corn.

As it grew dark, Rian watched a full moon rising over the horizon. At first, the scene reminded her of some of her childhood days in summer-camp, but there was something decidedly different about this. It seemed almost enchanted, and she felt very excited.

The ceremony began with each person being smudged with sage smoke as they formed a large circle. Then, a woman wearing a thin crown with a silver crescent on it lit a torch at four points and invoked guardians of the North, South, East, and West.

The group began chanting and drumming. Many of the chants had Native American overtones. One chant grew into another, out of which developed myriads of harmonies and counterpoints, most of which were about the sacredness of the earth. After a while, Rian's head began to buzz. She felt other-worldly, as though the farm had disappeared and she was in another time and place, growing less and less aware of her surroundings. Time passed, Rian did not know how long, and then she heard a low, deep chime. The chanting stopped.

A man's voice began to speak.

"Relax," he said hypnotically, "Relax and breathe deeply." He began some deep breathing exercises which lasted several minutes. Then he started a trance induction. "You're walking down a path. On one side it is day. On the other side it is night. On one side is the moon, the other is the sun." He paused for a while. Rian followed the pathwork. She could imagine everything as he described it. He continued the guided meditation until Rian was barely aware of the crickets singing in the night anymore. She was floating ... moving out of herself.

He continued. "Where the moon is, you will see the Goddess of the Harvest; where the sun is, you will see the Green Man; the God of Vegetation." He paused again. After a time, Rian heard the low deep chime once more. "In this grove you may each balance yourselves. Come to the sacred altar, and gather the elements you need."

One by one, Rian saw each person go up to the altar while the rest of the group chanted and drummed. After a while Marty got up to go, too. She felt her hand being taken as Marty got up from the ground and walked towards the altar. Rian followed closely.

She watched Marty take a votive candle from the altar and place it on one side of the scale. On the other side she poured just enough water in a paper cup to balance it. Then she added some stones to the other side, which tilted it again, and finally a smoking smudge stick to balance the stones. When the scale was completely balanced, Marty closed her eyes, put her hands out over the scales and chanted over and over:

> *"Balance me. Balance me*
> *As I desire me.*
> *Balance me. Balance me*
> *As I desire me.*
> *Air, fire, water, earth*
> *As I desire me.*
> *Balance me, balance me*
> *As I desire me."*

After a few moments, Marty took the elements from the scale and placed them back on the altar.

She whispered to Rian, "Wanna try?"

Rian hesitated. She was embarrassed. "No, I don't think so!"

"O.K." Marty took Rian's hand and led her back to their blanket. As they sat there, Rian slowly came back to herself.

Rian noticed a few other people who didn't go up to the altar. She thought, *they must be new too.*

As the last person finished the balancing ritual, the atmosphere lightened up markedly. Participants began talking quietly and laughing. Then the woman wearing the silver crescent held up a goblet of wine offering a libation to the Goddess of the Fruits, and poured a little into the fire. Marty explained quietly that she was the Priestess for this circle.

The man who had led the meditation held up a dish of corn cakes and offered it to the God of Vegetation. He repeated the same little ritual, throwing a little piece of cake into the fire.

"Why do they throw food into the fire?" Rian asked quietly.

"It's a libation, an offering, a gift," Morgana explained.

The remaining cakes and wine were passed around. Now all of the intensity was swept away. Everything seemed normal again and in place. People were laughing and talking. One girl played a guitar and sang some songs, while another played the flute. Drummers accompanied the musicians. Several people got up and danced. It was all very merry, and Rian was enjoying herself completely .

Someone said, "I'm getting hungry. Let's open the circle!" There was vocal agreement to that suggestion.

The same woman who lit the torches, went to each quarter and bid them farewell. Then everybody started hugging each other. Marty explained to Rian that the East, South, West, and North were connected to Air, Fire, Water, and Earth; and that these were the four elements necessary for life.

Driving home later, Marty asked Rian, "Did you have a good time?"

"It was awesome! Will you take me again?"

"Look, Rian, I loved having you, but you know how your mother would feel if she found out. Let's just play it by ear, O.K.?"

"O.K., I won't say anything. Don't worry."

Rian closed her eyes as they drove back home. She thought she'd never forget how she felt during that ceremony, but Rian was only fourteen, and the immediate events that followed would dim Rian's memories of that night for years to come.

That event happened as soon as they walked in the house. Resting in her beach-chair, Rian suddenly remembered it all now ... why Marty really went away.

It was the middle of September, and her parents

were out of town. When they got home, it was after two in the morning. Rian's mother had returned unexpectedly, and noticing costumes and grape-vines lying all around the house, was waiting. All hell broke loose.

❊❊

Rian felt terribly guilty. *If only I hadn't insisted on going, Marty might never have left. It was all my fault!*

Rian suddenly felt cold and began to tremble. Now she understood why Marty had left so suddenly. It was because Marty had taken Rian along. Though she didn't understand the process, she could only assume that she felt so guilty and traumatized by the argument, and especially Marty's subsequent departure, that she blocked the earlier part of that night out of her mind for years.

A voice interrupted her memories. "Penny for your thoughts. Sorry I'm late."

Startled, Rian turned around, looked up, and saw Frank standing behind her.

❊❊❊❊

CHAPTER 15

Enchantment

Frank surprised Rian. She was so immersed in her memories, she barely remembered him for a few seconds.

"Hey there ... remember me? Sorry if I woke you." He paused and knelt down close to her. "Were you sleeping?"

"No, daydreaming," Rian answered sitting up quickly.

"I met a few old friends at dinner and had a little trouble getting away. You know how it is down here. Time just gets away from you. When I come to the ocean, I leave my watch at home."

"Really? Why?"

"Because I have a high-pressure job and when I take a vacation, I prefer to lose all track of time."

Rian thought for a moment. *We can certainly lose track of that.*

"Wanna go inside? There's a great band tonight."

"I hate to tell you this, but would you mind if we went another time? I'm really tired."

"I can see that. Hey, you look upset! Anything wrong?"

"Sort of. I was just remembering something I had forgotten for years. Sitting out here brought it all back, I guess. I'm just trying to sort it out."

"Good memories or bad?"

"Well, both."

"An old boyfriend, right?"

"Guys. You think everything is about you."

"Isn't it?" He smiled, flirting.

"No, it's not."

"You know, I think all you need is something to cheer you up. Why don't you go inside, put on something smashing, and we'll go out on the town."

Rian thought for a moment. *Maybe that would be the best thing to do. After all, I did come here for a vacation. Why think about all this old stuff now?*

"Maybe you're right. O.K., pick me up in about half an hour."

"Wise decision!" He winked.

Frank helped her up and they walked back to her motel together. Rian suspected that he'd like to come in, but she did nothing to encourage him.

At the door she said, "See you in a little while!"

He left, and Rian went inside to change. She showered and dressed and waited for Frank to return. He didn't. Finally, she came to the conclusion that he wouldn't, when the phone started ringing. She answered it.

"Coming soon?" It was Frank.

"Where are you?"

"At your motel bar. Come on over."

Rian frowned. "Oh, O.K. I thought you were coming by here."

Rian wondered why Frank kept changing his plans. *Oh well*, she thought, *he's probably just wasting an evening.*

Rian went to the bar. Frank was sitting there. A

blonde on one side, and a redhead on the other.

"Hi!" said Rian trying to be cheerful.

Frank turned around and blinked at what he saw. This woman looked smashing! Rian had put on a sexy dress; a very short skirt with an off the shoulder top that showed off her beautiful tan. She was wearing makeup, which she rarely did, and her long dark hair, which she usually wore pulled back or braided, was pulled high up on one side with a pearl comb, the rest tumbling loose down her back. Frank was visibly impressed.

"Whoa! You look great!"

"Thanks, you look pretty good yourself."

"Care for a drink?" he said guiding her to a table.

"Ummm, O.K. I'll have a piña-colada."

Frank went up to the bar and ordered the drinks. Rian looked around to see if she could spot anybody she knew. Lots of her friends came down to the Ocean in the summer. Finally, she rested her eyes on the band. Frank was right, they were really good. There was a guitar, bass, drums, keyboard, and a couple of horns. The drummer and guitar player took turns lead singing. The place was jammed, and Frank had to wait a while for the drinks. In the meantime, Rian watched the band. The guitar player was very good, and in fact, Rian thought there was something familiar about him, but she couldn't figure out what. She didn't think she had heard this band before.

Frank put the drinks on the table.

"Great band, huh?"

"Yeah, great!

"So, you must be feeling better."

She smiled at him. "Yeah, I am."

"What do you do back in Baltimore?"

"My brother and I own and operate a couple of New Age book stores."

"What's New Age?"

Rian hesitated. This question was never easy to answer when talking to someone who was totally unaware of such things. Finally, she just gave the usual answer as casually as she could. "Well you know.. new thought, alternative healing, different sorts of spiritual paths, that kind of thing."

Frank looked blank. "Wanna dance?"

"Sure."

They both got up and started dancing. Rian was having fun for a change. She put the thoughts about dreams, Marty, and the shop out of her mind.

Rian started watching the guitar player again. *Where have I seen him before?* He caught her eye and stared back, as though in recognition.

After a while, the band went on break. Frank went back up to the bar to get more drinks. Rian sat back and watched the band as they put their instruments down. They all headed over to the bar except for the guitarist. He headed straight for her table.

"I think I know you."

"Yeah. You look familiar to me too," she smiled.

"Where do you live?"

"Outside of Baltimore."

"Me too. Go to school?"

"Well, I did. I'm out now. I own a little shop in Millcott City."

"Millcott! I hang around there a lot! Which is your shop?"

"The Apothecary. Heard of it?"

He looked at her more closely. "Oh, I know who you are ... you're ... Rian!"

"Yes ... How do you know?"

"Because, I've been in your shop. It's a great store!"

Rian looked at him carefully, then she recognized where she had seen him. "Of course, you are one of our customers! I'm sorry, it's just ... you know, down here everything seems ... different."

"Yeah, that's true, So, uh ... are you here with that guy?"

"Not really. I just met him a few days ago, and we decided to get together tonight. He's staying at this motel."

"Yeah, he's here every night."

"Wouldn't surprise me, he likes the band."

"Yeah, the band."

Rian laughed. "He does seem kind of flighty."

"Look, I have to go back to the bandstand in a minute. What are you doing after?"

"I don't really have any plans."

"You know, I'd really like to spend some time with you. How about getting together with me when I finish up?"

Rian liked him, and she certainly preferred his company to Frank's, whom she noticed now had his arm around the redhead.

"O.K. I'd like that. I'm sorry, but I don't remember your name."

"Scott Erecson. Some people call me Scotty."

"O.K., Scotty, I'll see you a little later."

Frank returned about the same time the band started up again. They danced and drank, but Rian couldn't wait for the band to be done, so she could spend more time with Scott.

They played their last set, and began packing up. Frank was getting a little drunk, and Rian would be glad to get away from him.

"Look, Frank, I know one of the guys in the band. He comes into my store a lot. I think I'd like to talk to him for a while, so I'm gonna say goodnight now."

Frank looked stunned. "What do you mean? I thought you were my date!"

"I suppose you did, but I really want to talk to him, so let's just let it go at that."

Frank got up from the table. "Sure, no prob." He walked back to the bar, where the redhead was still smiling at him.

Scott joined her. She felt attracted to him immediately. Rian couldn't understand why she had never noticed him in the shop before. He sat down. Rian thought he had the longest eyelashes she had ever seen. He was tall and his deep-set eyes were greenish, but at first she thought they were dark like his hair. And there was something mischievous about his smile, the way he laughed and … something seductive, too.

"You play great," Rian said warmly.

"You … look great!" He stared at her for a moment. "I wouldn't have recognized you. In the store you always look so casual. Quite a change!"

Rian tried to remember the types of items he bought, but there were so many customers, she couldn't.

"What are you interested in at The Apothecary?"

"Oh, this and that. I like the martial arts. Now and then, I delve into a little metaphysics. I've got a friend who lives in one of the apartments up there, so when I visit him I always stop in the store. I've seen you lots of times."

They both felt it. This chemistry between them. They both wanted to get out of the lounge.

"What do you say we get out of here?" Scott said.

"O.K." Rian gathered up her purse, and Scott picked up his guitar.

"Wanna take a walk on the beach?"

"O.K."

He took her hand, and she felt her knees go weak. It had been a long time since she felt this way and a part of her told her to use caution, but she wasn't listening very carefully. Everything was too electric.

Walking down the beach was almost too much. They stopped, talked, and laughed. They kissed and nuzzled, and they walked again. They talked about the things they liked, about his music, her store, his budding curiosity in metaphysics, her studies in holistic healing, his interest in martial arts.

The band, she found out, was his. He had formed it about three years ago, and they were doing very well. He told her all about himself and his background, and she told him all about herself. It was the first time she could talk to anyone like this since Richard. The difference was that she and Scott shared so many of the same interests.

Later they walked back to the motel. Rian changed, picked up a blanket and a deck of cards, and then spread the blanket down on the sand. They both sat on the blanket, talked, played cards and watched the sea. In fact they spent the whole night on the beach getting acquainted. Rian hoped this wasn't a regular pastime with Scott, but she also wasn't naive enough to think it hadn't happened before, perhaps many times. After all, she wasn't the only woman who admired his talent and good looks, but she didn't want to think about that now. She wanted to believe he really liked her.

Scott fell asleep while Rian stared out at the sea. A fog was coming in. Suddenly an image slipped into her mind, the fragment of a dream. She was lying on the beach or on a boat with Richard, and there was some kind of image emerging from the sea—a woman shrouded in blue.

As dawn approached, Rian sat on her blanket, arms clasped around her knees, and watched the fog settle in on top of the waves. It was getting so thick she could no longer see the horizon. The air had grown cool; the sky pale gray. Rian felt like lying down for awhile. But then, something she saw stopped her.

Shadowy and illusory at first, the mirage gradually became denser and took on a shape. Rian's squinted her eyes and watched, unsure of what she was observing.

The shrouded blue woman of her dream was moving through the waters towards her and Scott. Rian couldn't move. She watched the apparition transfixed, as it came closer and closer. She wanted to awaken Scotty, but was too caught up watching the mirage to say anything.

She didn't have to. Scott had awakened and also had seen it.

※※※※

CHAPTER 16

Elizabeth

Elizabeth worried much more than she should, at least that's what her husband always told her. He was out of town on a business trip for a few days, and Rian was at the ocean. It was not unusual for her to feel nervous when she was home alone in the remarkable three-story Victorian house. She always felt isolated, surrounded by more than ten acres of rolling land.

The lower outlying areas of the property were dense with trees and brush, giving the estate privacy, but as you got closer to the house, all of the brush, and some of the older trees, had been thinned out so that there was enough space to walk easily between them. Most of the remaining trees were very old, their trunks thick and gnarled. Many of the lower branches had been cut back, leaving the upper ones to serve as a large umbrella. The results were that parts of the property gave the impression of a little story-book forest.

To fill in the open spaces, where disease had slowly done away with all the grand old elms in the area, Elizabeth had planted some fast growing pin-oaks and a few pink and white dogwoods and cherry to add color to her little forest. Since sunlight did not get through this umbrella easily, grass was sparse, but enough of it grew to maintain the impression of green. In the area just surrounding the house were lilac, wisteria, yews, juniper, boxwood, and several varieties of holly, all bordered with more flowering trees and a well-kept lawn. A split-rail fence surrounded the entire property, and a gardener, who had been with the family for years, maintained everything.

Elizabeth prized her rose garden the most. Planted years ago by her grandmother, she personally cared for the many older varieties rarely seen today with their hardy stems, large flowers, and lush scents. She looked over the array of magnificent late-June blossoms, cut several, and brought them into the house. She filled a vase with water and carefully arranged the roses. Accompanying her, as always, was her beloved black poodle, Starlight.

She noticed that darkness was approaching, and as was her habit when David was away, she walked over towards the wall to turn on the outdoor lamps. She was interrupted by the ringing of the telephone. It was her husband, Dave. They spoke for a few minutes. He promised to be home by Friday. This was Wednesday. Her thoughts drifted back.

This weekend would be their thirty-fourth wedding anniversary. She remembered when she had first met him. It was near the end of the Korean War at one of those patriotic dances.

Back then, the USO sponsored carefully chaperoned social evenings for the Bainbridge Naval Boot Camp, which was about twenty miles outside of Baltimore.

Elizabeth was only seventeen, and she thought Dave looked just like James Dean. Most of the sailors were very young, just out of high school.

Since Dave was from Baltimore, they remained friends, and about two years after he was discharged from the Navy, they decided to become engaged.

Though Dave McGuire seemed a clever and personable fellow, he grew up in a blue-collar neighborhood, and didn't seem quite sophisticated enough to fit into the Chambers family. After the Navy, he went to college for a year, didn't like it, and dropped out. Jobs were scarce, and he could find no secure employment, but Elizabeth was determined to marry him anyway.

At first, her father, Justin Tracy Chambers, J.T, was opposed to the marriage, but when he saw the two were dead-serious about each other, he gave in. David had no money saved, but he and Elizabeth were so much in love, they would have lived in a tent just to be together. In the end, of course, the couple decided that renting a small trailer would be more practical, but J.T. balked at that. So after they married, they moved into the big Victorian house with J.T., Marianne, and Marty.

"Plenty of room for everybody." J.T. decided.

After a few menial jobs and Marianne's prodding, Elizabeth's father offered his new son-in-law a position in his booming post-war construction business. David learned quickly. He did so well, in fact, that when J.T. was suddenly killed in a boating accident, David took over and ran the business smoothly and profitably, to everyone's relief.

Elizabeth felt restless. She put down a novel she had started and turned on the television. The news was always bad. Tonight, two generals and two news commentators were arguing about whether or not to invade some third-world country. Elizabeth thought miserably, *God just what we need, another Vietnam.*

She switched channels to something lighter, but reruns of sitcoms had just about worn out their welcome with her. Finally she settled on a quiz show. At least she could participate. She reached into a basket, took out her needle-point, and relaxed.

Outside, the sun was setting, casting long shadows across the lawn. As the sky darkened, an owl glided slowly by, his sharp eyes hunting for an unguarded nest. Below, a hungry squirrel searched for food. She found some sweet cherries on the ground, and happily stuffed its face, then scrambled up a tall tree to busily finish eating her morsels. Silently, the owl watched from another tree observing a dark hole near the squirrel's dinner table, and waited to see if she was still hungry enough to leave the tree for more.

As this ordinary evening event unfolded, another hunter crouched against an old tree trunk, irritated because the trees were too far apart to adequately conceal him. Little by little, he inched his way closer to his objective, darting quickly but quietly from one tree to another, waiting, then moving, then waiting again. As he moved further up the hill towards the house he could not yet see, he reached a wall of large, thick rhododendron bushes. Beneath their long, pointed, rubbery leaves and deep purple blooms, the hunter stopped and crouched down again. Secure within the protective shrubbery, he looked beyond, and mentally gathered information.

From the front, the house looked typically Victorian. It had several gables, porches, and a weather vane on top. His rune-casting revealed that the book he sought was in this house, but did not reveal its exact location. He knew once he got closer his instincts would tell him where to search.

From his vantage point amidst the rhododendrons, he observed many bushes next to the house where he could hide. Slowly, he moved away from the wall of shrubs, and crept silently forward, until he came to a driveway where a dark green Saab was parked. He knew who drove it. Having watched the property for days unobserved, he became aware that the girl and her father were away. But this garage was large he thought, and there could be others living here. Quietly, he crept towards the old-fashioned garage with its multiple doors, and peeped through the window panes. Except for a few old bicycles and garden tools, it was empty. *So far, so good.* He felt the knife in his pocket. "Just the woman," he muttered to himself. "Easy."

He approached the steps to one of the porches. The dog barked. *Damn! Too bad ... for the dog.* He kept moving around the porch. It went nearly half-way around the house. The dog was barking more and more furiously. The stranger knew the dog had picked up his scent.

Elizabeth was startled by Starlight's barking. "Star baby, it's only a rabbit! Come on, go in your basket." But the poodle wouldn't be calmed. She kept running furiously around the house from room to room, barking and whining at the windows and doors.

Elizabeth thought she had company for a moment. She walked towards the door, but something made her stop. From a side bay-window which she had to pass on her way to the door, she could see the driveway. Her Saab sat alone.

Star continued running around barking and growling.

Elizabeth became suspicious. Star didn't usually get this wound up over a rabbit. Maybe a neighbor's dog? No, she doubted that. The split-rail fence around the property was screened, and it was unusual for other dogs to get in. She looked out the window carefully, but could see nothing. It was dark now, and she had forgotten about the outside lamps. Moving quickly over to the lightswitch, she turned them on and looked outside.

The hunter saw the lights come on and quickly crouched down, blending into the bushes next to the house.

Starlight had run upstairs, and continued to bark. Elizabeth walked back through the dining room and into the kitchen. A screened window over the sink was half open. She quietly walked over to it and peeped out. For a second she thought she saw something move, and at the same time heard a crackling sound. Frowning, she backed off quickly. She looked again, but all was quiet.

Ordinarily, Elizabeth would have thought it just a wild animal, but Star's angry growling and barking had alarmed her. Wild animals frequently came near the house at night, and if Star was awake, she always got excited. Her tail would wag playfully, and her eyes would sparkle. When she was a puppy David had built her a doggie door in a kitchen wall. Once she ran through it and proudly chased three terrified deer out of the yard.

But now her bark was not playful. It sounded hostile, and her tail was stiff, her body rigid.

Quietly, Elizabeth closed the kitchen window and pulled the latch tight. Then, she went upstairs into her bedroom and locked the door. She knew all the doors on the first floor had dead-bolts, and she knew the house was rigged with an alarm system, but she still felt uneasy.

From her upstairs window, she looked out again. In the moonlight, she suddenly saw a moving shadow. Elizabeth froze.

When she regained some kind of composure, she picked up the phone next to her bed and dialed 911.

A woman's voice answered. "This is 911, may I help you?"

"Still watching the window," Elizabeth answered tensely. "Please! Send the police. Someone's trying to break into my house!"

"What is your address?"

"540 Willow Drive. Will you send somebody right away?"

"Yes, I am doing that now."

"What should I do?"

"Do not try to confront the intruder. Stay calm, and hide if you can."

"My dog is carrying on so!"

"Good, that will most likely scare him away."

"No, he's still there, or the dog would stop barking!"

"Is the intruder in the house?"

"No, he's out by the porch."

"Can you see him?"

"I just saw his shadow. I'm upstairs … Yes, there he is! I can see him from my window."

"Is there more than one person?"

Elizabeth's heart began to throb harder in her chest at the suggestion. She could only whisper, "I don't know."

"All right, listen carefully. The police are on their

way. Everything will be all right. Try not to panic! The police will be there momenta ... "

"Hello! *Hello!*" Elizabeth screamed into the phone.

The line was dead. Elizabeth was terrified. She knew Dave kept a gun in the closet, but she hadn't the foggiest idea how to load it, much less shoot it. At the same time she suddenly realized that Starlight had stopped barking. The next thing she thought horrified her. *Oh no! Did I leave the kitchen door open?*

She had. Starlight had gone into the kitchen, and outside through her little doggie door.

Elizabeth heard something again. She dimmed her lamp, and crouched next to the window. "Oh God, please don't let him hurt her," she prayed in a whisper. "Please!"

Outside, the stranger had slowly moved around the house, checking out the alarm system. He found the telephone wires first. Then he detected that the alarm system only covered the first floor of the house. *What luck!* he thought.

He discovered the outside steps to Rian's apartment. Instinctively, something told him that here was the entrance he was seeking.

His glee was cut short for a moment when he saw the dog. She growled protectively near the bottom of the steps. The stranger pulled out his knife and swung. Starlight darted away and he missed. Then she approached again, snarling.

Elizabeth heard one loud, painful yelp and she went numb. She started weeping helplessly, her hands sliding down the wall as she collapsed. For a while she stayed there, her head buried in her hands as she grieved for her beloved pet. When she had enough strength to get up, she slowly lifted herself to the window and fearfully peeped out, but saw nothing.

Where are the police? Did I give them the address before the phone went dead? Elizabeth couldn't remember.

The stranger had gone up the outside steps to Rian's apartment. Her door was locked, but he could see her little outside porch around the corner. He climbed across the roof and let himself down quietly.

Elizabeth heard the footsteps on the roof. Trembling with fright, she moved away from the window, and sought protection inside her closet.

The stranger stalked through Rian's room. He sniffed around like an animal, and touched the door feeling for Rian's impression. Hissing through his breath, he slowly turned the knob of the French doors to her apartment. They were unlocked. He laughed to himself as he congratulated his good luck. Then he stepped into Rian's dark apartment, moving his hands along the wall until he found the light switch. He took a quick look around, but fearing discovery, turned it off and lit a match.

Silently, he moved around the apartment. He opened the door to her bedroom and walked in. As his eyes became more accustomed to the dimness, he observed a bookcase across from her bed, a stuffed chair, and a desk. He walked over to the bookcase, and searched. It wasn't there. He opened the drawers quickly, but had no luck. He became impatient and noisier, and began throwing Rian's things all over the apartment.

He walked into the kitchen, but had no instinct of finding it there. Then he walked back into Rian's bedroom. Here is where he felt it. But he found nothing.

He moved back into the room off the porch again. This time he looked more closely, observing a few chairs, television, and a corner cabinet. At first he had taken the cabinet as one of those frivolous things women keep ornaments in. He lit another match, looked closer and discovered it contained a shelf of old books. His fingers and eyes searched each book slowly.

Interesting, he thought, as he observed how rare they were. His match burned his fingers, "Damn!" He dropped it and lit another.

And then, finally he saw it. "Bingo!" he heard himself say out loud. He reached into the bookcase and carefully pulled it out. He held the book in his hands fondling it sensuously, as though it were a woman. And then, as if to check its virginity, he opened it and turned the pages. Satisfied, he put it inside of his jacket and turned to go.

Elizabeth could hear something upstairs. She was pretty sure he was in Rian's apartment. Feeling even more panicky, she tried to think of getting away. She believed that she might get down the stairs and out the door, but then what? What if he saw her?

She tried to think where her purse was. She knew her car keys were in there. If only she could make it to her car, she'd be safe! Escape was possible. Quietly, she crawled out of her closet and moved towards the bedroom door.

The stranger let himself out, as he had come in. Then he froze. He heard a car engine. For a moment he felt confused, so he slipped back in and listened. Deciding that he might be safer inside than out for the time being, he stayed put. He couldn't see the driveway from the living room, so he walked into Rian's bedroom. Only one window faced the driveway, but he couldn't see up near the garage. He decided to get out of Rian's apartment. It was too confining. But if he could get into the main house, he'd be harder to find. And there was the woman ... if he had to ... he grasped the small sharp knife in his pocket.

There was no way into the house from the apartment. It was completely closed off. He went out on the porch again. Slowly and carefully he climbed up on the roof, and hid himself between the gables.

Then he saw a small upstairs window, in one of the lower gables on the other side of the driveway. The window was open, but screened. He tried the screen but it was locked. With his sharp knife, he cut through it easily. He ducked in and let himself into the main house.

Rian's mother had heard the noises on the roof again. At the same time, she thought she heard a car coming down the driveway. *It must be the police,* she thought. Feeling safer now that he was outside again, she carefully moved over to her bedroom door, opened it and waited there. *What if he has a gun?* She shivered. *He could shoot me as I go out to the car! What if the car I heard isn't the police?*

Elizabeth stepped back into her room, and paused. It has to be the police, she thought. Who else would be coming this time of night? Inside her mind she was getting all mixed up. One thought she didn't want to deal with was that the sound of the car she heard might have come from a loud engine out on the main road. She felt trapped.

An irrational idea had grabbed hold of Elizabeth: if nobody answered the door for the police, they might assume no one was home and just leave. The idea became so overwhelming, that in her confused state she actually felt compelled to go downstairs and open the front door.

She cracked her bedroom door and peeped out. They said hide, she remembered. *But who will let the police in?* The more she panicked, the more confused she became. She looked out again. The hall was dark, but she was afraid to turn on the light. She glanced back into her room, and tried to find something to protect herself with. She noticed a letter-opener on her secretary and picked it up. Then she started towards the door again. Her only thought was to let the police in. She carefully moved out into the hall and paused, her heart pounding. Slowly and quietly, she began to walk along the wall towards the stairs.

Not twenty feet away ... coming from the opposite direction, the stranger slid along the same wall ...

A few moments later, the intruder heard something outside. Quickly, he leaped over the staircase to the first floor; ran to the window and saw the police walking around on the driveway. He moved to the back of the house, and saw a porch off of the kitchen. Then he looked outside. *No one.* Opening the door quietly, he carefully found his way down into the yard and into the shrubbery. He could hear the police with their radios around front. Suddenly, he heard someone walking around the back towards him. He ducked down, and melted into another bush. Crouching low, he slipped around to the other side of the house and managed to move unseen in the darkness, out towards the trees.

He stopped behind the trunk of a tree, cautiously

looking around the other side to check things out. Without a sound, he darted among the trees and into the thick brush. Now, if he could only make it to the road, he'd be home free before they even got into the house.

There were three squad cars. Several officers approached the house, as two others started looking around outside. One of them found Starlight under some large boxwoods where she had managed to drag herself. She was whimpering softly, her leg badly broken. The officer ran back to the squad car and found a blanket; then informed the other officers about the injured poodle. He radioed to an emergency vet they used for their own dogs. Then he covered Star and stayed with her a few minutes stroking her head, and speaking softly to reassure her.

Meanwhile after no one responded to their knock, the officers skillfully got inside. Expecting anything, their guns were poised to shoot. Quietly they began moving through the house.

Suddenly the silence was broken. One of the officers yelled from the top of the stairs. "Oh my God! Somebody call an ambulance!"

Another officer ran up the stairs and knelt down slowly above the woman who lay in a pool of blood. "My God." He shook his head slowly, revolted by what he saw.

By now, the stranger had moved swiftly towards the road and started running. He ran until he reached the highway, crossed it, and found an old abandoned lean-to on the edge of a corn field. There he stopped and rested. He reached into his jacket, pulled out his prize and grinned through missing teeth.

❄❄❄❄

CHAPTER 17

The Premonition

About the same time, a young, dark-haired woman was looking out over the ocean. Slowly, she raised herself to her knees. The blue image continued to come forward. She wanted to run, but she couldn't even speak.

The mirage came all the way to the shore. It was a woman, and she looked familiar to Rian. Her face … who was this? Rian squinted her eyes again. Then she blinked. This woman reminded Rian of her mother!

By now Scott was sitting up. He too had seen something, but not as clearly as Rian. What he saw appeared to be a little water-spout. But it was more than that. It was hard to perceive. He thought for a moment it had a shape, but then he couldn't be sure.

Rian watched mesmerized as the woman came towards the shore. And then just as she appeared, she began to disappear. After a few moments, she was completely gone. And where she had been near the shoreline, Rian saw something in the sand.

"Did you see that?" Rian asked when she could finally speak.

"I saw something. It looked like a waterspout." He spoke thoughtfully. "I don't know, it had some kind of weird blue color around it."

"Look," Rian pointed. "Do you see anything down there by the water?"

"Where?"

"By the shoreline. Like a conch, or a shell, or something."

Rian slowly got up. The sun was up now, and she didn't feel quite so intimidated. She heard barking up on the beach, and looked around. Someone was jogging with their dog.

Scott took Rian's hand, and they both walked cautiously down the beach. Rian could see something sparkle where the surf just washed over the sand.

"See, over there, something bright in the sand." Rian pointed.

"Oh, yeah, I see it!"

They both walked towards the spot where the shiny object lay. Scotty knelt down and looked.

"Whoa. . . .This is some kind of dagger!"

Rian crouched down next to him. Neither touched it.

"Look at that hilt," she said. "It has gems on it. You think they're real?"

"Has symbols on it too," Scott observed.

Rian had a curious feeling. She felt that this dagger belonged to her, that she had seen it before. She slowly reached for the hilt, and pulled the blade out of the sand. It was small and very sharp. She laid the blade across her hand.

"God, Scotty, this knife is beautiful. Have you ever seen anything like it before?"

She took a closer look at the hilt. There were little symbols carved on it. But the one carving that caught her eye and made her jump, was that of a little horse with a jeweled eye standing on its hind legs. Underneath the horse was an inscription with symbols on it that Rian recognized.

"They're runes. I've seen them in a few books, but I don't know what they mean."

"I think each one stands for a letter, or symbol," said Scott. "Mind if I take a closer look?"

"Here." Rian offered him the knife, but then for some reason she didn't understand, something seem to pull her arm back.

"That's funny ... I felt like I couldn't do that."

The knife had a life of its own. And it had communicated to her that no one but she could touch it.

Scott disregarded the gesture. "Someone must have lost it. I wonder who would just leave a valuable knife in the sand?"

Rian looked at him. "She left it."

"Who?"

"The lady in the blue shroud."

What are you talking about? What lady?"

"Remember when you said you saw something like a blue waterspout?"

"Yeah."

"Well, what I saw was a woman in blue moving along the water. She came up to the shore, and dropped something into the sand."

Scotty looked at her curiously. Rian saw major doubt in his eyes.

She spoke defensively. "This was not a fantasy. I know what I saw. I watched it for a long time."

"O.K., I'll take your word for it. Finders ... keepers!" He smiled.

"No, it's not that at all. Don't you believe what I told you?"

"I believe you believe it."

"Thanks a lot."

Scott tousled her hair playfully and laughed. Then he turned, swung his arm over her shoulder and walked her back to the blanket. He pulled out his watch from his shirt pocket and looked at the time. It was nearly seven A.M.

"I really need a shower." He hesitated. "Would you mind if I used yours?"

She hesitated, too. "No ... I don't mind."

They walked back arm-in-arm to Rian's motel room. When they got inside, Scott took off his shirt. Rian watched him. He was beautiful.

He smiled at her. "Wanna join me?"

Yes.

She laid her knife down on the bed and undressed.

The shower was warm and refreshing after laying in the sand all night. It was also erotic. After she got out Rian put on a terry robe and tied a towel around her hair. Then she flopped down backwards on the bed. *Ahhh!*

Scott watched her, then walked over to where she lay and tugged at her towel playfully.

Rian held on, and started laughing. Scott stopped. Then Rian stopped. Both waited ... not yet sure of what the other really expected from all of this. Scott slowly undid the towel from around Rian's head. With the other hand he touched her long dark wet hair and gently pushed it back from her face. They knelt on the bed and looked at each other.

Slowly, Scott opened Rian's bathrobe and removed it from her shoulders, not taking his eyes from hers. When it fell to the bed, he took her in his arms and kissed her, ever so lightly, on the lips. Trembling, they began to touch and caress each other, a little reserved at first. Their caresses soon became more passionate and frenzied. Finally what they both had really wanted, and really needed that night, but wouldn't speak about, happened ... and then it happened again ... and finally more slowly, and more tenderly ... again.

Rian rolled over contentedly and fell asleep. She kept dreaming of a pulsating light which continued to arouse her. When she finally opened her eyes, she realized the blinking light was coming from her telephone. She looked over at it drowsily. A beach towel was partially covering the phone, which was why she hadn't noticed it earlier. "Scotty," she said softly. "There's a message for me."

Scott looked over.

Rian picked up the phone, and slowly dialed the front desk.

A young female voice answered cheerily. "Office! How may I help you?"

"Hello, this is Rian McGuire. There's a message blinking on my phone: Room 108?"

There was a pause ... then, "Miss McGuire?"

"Yes."

"There is a message from your brother, Kevin McGuire."

"Yes."

"It just says 'call home immediately.'"

"That's all?"

"Yes, that's it."

"What time did he leave it."

"The message came ... uh ...eleven twenty-five last night."

"Last night? O.K., thanks."

Scott rolled over in bed sleepily. "Anything wrong?"

"I don't know. The message was from my brother. He left it late last night. Wonder why he'd call that late?"

Rian felt uneasy. Something was wrong. She picked up the phone and dialed her brother's house.

"Hello?"

"Yes, this is Rian. Is my brother there?"

A sleepy voice answered. "No, he's not. I guess he's still at the hospital."

"The hospital? Why?"

"Don't you know?"

"Know what ... ?" Rian's heart started pounding.

"About your mother?"

"What happened to my mother?"

"Wait a minute ..." There was a long pause. "Here's a number he left for you to call him."

Rian wrote the number down on a pad by the phone.

"Thanks."

She hung up the phone.

"It's my mother; something's happened to my mother! She's in the hospital."

"I'm sorry. What can I do?" Scott started getting dressed.

"Could you hang around a little while longer?"

"Sure. Did you think I would leave?"

Rian dialed the number and someone answered. "Shock-Trauma."

"My God ... shock-trauma?"

"Yes, can I help you?"

"Well, somebody, my brother ... left a message for me to call this number. I'm out of town, and I just got the message. My name is Rian McGuire."

"Yes ... oh yes, of course. We've been expecting your call. Wait and I'll get your brother."

Rian started shaking. Scotty held her.

"Hello, Rian?"

"Kevin, what happened?"

Kevin told her the story.

"Oh my God! I'm driving right home!"

Rian hung up the receiver. She forgot about Scott, and the vision, and everything else. She unzipped one of her travel bags, rummaged around for a pair of shorts, tee-shirt, underwear and sneakers and got dressed. Then she opened the closet and started throwing all the rest of her belongings inside her luggage.

While she packed she attempted to explain. "My mother's in shock-trauma ... critical ... Her heart stopped once ... Somebody broke into our house last night ... attacked her with a knife! He tried to cut her throat."

"Oh my God ...Rian, I'm so sorry."

"I shouldn't have been out all night!"

"Rian, don't blame yourself."

Rian stood up for a minute and looked straight at Scotty. "I should have been there! My mother is dying, and I'm out on the beach screwing around!"

Scotty felt helpless. He wondered if she could ever think of him in the same way again. She was the first woman he had really felt close to in a long time.

"How about if I go with you? I could drive you home."

"But you work tonight!"

"I'll get you back by one, and then I'll come back here."

"What about my car?"

"We'll take yours. I'll get a ride back. Don't worry."

Rian suddenly wanted to be away from him. He reminded her of her guilt. "No, I'll be all right. I want to be alone now."

Scott tried to understand. "Rian, take it easy. O.K.?"

Rian put her suitcase in the car and ran around front and paid her bill. She took one last look inside, and noticed something shimmering on the floor, nearly hidden under the bed. She bent over and looked more closely. It was the knife. She picked it up, and then remembered the vision, the woman in blue who looked like her mother. For some reason it made her feel better. She paused for a moment staring down at the knife.

Maybe you were trying to reach me, she thought. "Bye, Scott, I've got to go."

"Can I call you?"

"Sure. See ya."

Rian picked up the little knife and held onto it tightly and drove away.

❀ ❀ ❀ ❀

CHAPTER 18

The Lake

Elizabeth hovered over her hospital bed. Beneath, she could see doctors working over her body, but she felt strangely detached from it all. She noticed the equipment, the monitors, blinking and beeping. Then, she noticed that one of the beepers had stopped, and one long beep came out of the monitor. A straight bright line lit up the screen.

Someone yelled, "We've lost her!"

"Paddles. *Stat*!"

Elizabeth stared curiously as the doctors applied paddles to her chest. Then someone yelled, *"Now!"*

She saw part of her body jump up off the table.

No beep.

"Again!"

Elizabeth had no wish to continue watching this drama. She slipped out of the room and down into the hall. The hall turned into a long dark tunnel. She began walking towards what appeared to be a bright light. The closer she got, the better she felt. No pain. No fear. In fact, she felt euphoric. As the light got brighter, she felt happier and more peaceful than she ever had before.

"This is so wonderful. I hope I never have to go back."

She looked out and saw a beautiful crystal clear lake. The light was the lake. Then she saw her mother Marianne coming towards her. She looked young and healthy.

"Welcome, Elizabeth. You've come home."

"Mother, where am I?"

"Don't you know?"

"It all feels familiar, but I guess I forgot. Am I dreaming?"

"No, Elizabeth. This is no dream. This is more real than reality. This is your home."

Then Elizabeth remembered. "Annwn, yes."

"I am sorry you had to leave the children—especially Rian."

"Rian?"

"Your daughter."

"Oh, my. Yes. She's still there! I must see her, tell her good-bye."

Another woman approached. "Why, here is the Lady Mere-Ama," said Marianne. The Lady, who was young and beautiful, was dressed exactly like her mother, except she wore silver cords around her blue robes. Her mother's cords were purple.

"Greetings, sister Elizabeth. We welcome you."

"I'm glad to be here, but I feel so confused."

"They are still trying to get you back there," she said.

"They don't want to let you go. Modern medicine." Marianne said, "Would you like to say farewell to anyone?"

"I..I.. don't know."

"Come, look into the lake with me."

As they walked towards the lake, Elizabeth noticed

several other women standing nearby.

As if Marianne could read her daughter's thoughts, she said, "There are always supposed to be nine of us living here. When someone leaves, another returns."

"Leaves?"

"Yes, returns to the physical plane."

In some unconscious way, Elizabeth understood.

As they walked towards the lake, Elizabeth noticed that Mere-Ama's face had changed, or shifted. It had grown more mature, and her cords were now scarlet. Elizabeth and Marianne arrived at the sparkling lake and looked in. The Lady Mere-Ama left them alone.

"Here, dear, look in."

Elizabeth looked into the lake. It was like looking into a mirror. She gazed down into the lake and scryed.

"Can you see anything?" said Marianne.

"No, only me."

"Look deeper."

Elizabeth looked into the depths of the lake and saw a picture taking shape. Two figures slowly came into focus. One was lying down, the other sitting up. She blinked her eyes. The figure sitting up was her daughter Rian. For a moment, Elizabeth felt connected to that scene; then she felt detached, and then connected again. She lost the picture, and all she could see was her own reflection dressed in a blue robe. Around her waist were white cords holding a little jeweled knife. On her forehead, she noticed a small blue crescent moon.

"Why am I wearing this, mother?"

"We usually dress this way here."

"Yes, of course."

Elizabeth looked down into the lake again. She saw

Rian staring back. "She can see me!"

"Yes, she has the gift of sight, if only she could remember how to use it. Would you like to speak to her?"

Elizabeth kneeled down closer to the lake, and tried to will herself nearer to her daughter, but a moment later she heard a little splash as her knife fell out of its leather sheath and down into the lake. She moved back.

"I've lost my knife!"

"It is too late. The lake has no bottom. You cannot retrieve it."

Marianne looked down into the lake, and saw the knife floating down and away. But the next vision she had, startled her. She saw Rian holding the knife!

"Look, Elizabeth. Look at your daughter."

Elizabeth looked down into the lake again. Once again, she saw a picture. Rian and a young man were standing on a beach. Rian was holding her knife. "She has it! But how ... "

"There are many mysteries in the lake, Elizabeth."

Elizabeth turned around. It appeared to be the Lady Mere-Ama again. But, though she still appeared beautiful, she also looked very old, as old as the sea itself.

"It is our choice to remember who we are, and where we come from, before we enter each lifetime You chose not to remember. Perhaps in your next incarnation it will be different. Your young daughter has lost the memories as well, not because she chose to, but because of trickery. Therefore it is important that she be awakened, so that her karma may be fulfilled."

"At first we tried through Morgana, or Marty, as you call her, and when that didn't work, we tried other ways," said Marianne. "Unfortunately, our plan to awaken her got into the wrong hands, that is why you are here now."

"What do you mean ... the wrong hands?"

Suddenly, Elizabeth felt a stabbing pain in her throat. She could not speak. She saw her mother and the Lady moving away. Terrified she tried to hold on to something, but she was being pulled, pulled away-and then darkness.

❈❈

On the expressway Rian drove in a daze. When she got into town, she parked her car in the hospital garage, found out where the shock-trauma unit was and got on the elevator.

As she stepped out into the waiting room, she saw Kevin and her father talking to a doctor. She quickly joined them.

They turned and saw her. Her father gave her a strong hug, and Rian started sobbing. "What happened to mom? Is she going to be all right?"

"Rian, this is Dr. Howell."

"Hello, Rian. We think your mother is out of the woods. We lost her for a few minutes very early this morning, but she seems to be responding to treatment at the moment. The next few hours should tell."

Kevin helped his sister over to a chair. She nearly collapsed in it.

"Kevin, what happened?"

"We're not sure. Apparently somebody broke into the house, and ran into mom. The police found her at the top of the stairs."

"Oh, my God."

"Mom knew someone was there because she called 911, and they sent the police. The bastard even got

Starlight."

"Oh no ..." Rian began sobbing. "My God, Kevin ... how did he get inside?"

"Well, all we know right now is that one of the screens was cut, so we think he got into the main part of the house through an upstairs window. The police think he climbed your steps and got up on the roof."

"But I thought we had an alarm system!"

"We do, but not for the upper floors." Kevin hesitated for a moment. Then he said as gently as he could. "By the way Rian, your apartment ... was ransacked."

Rian looked at Kevin strangely. "My apartment? I don't have anything valuable. Why would he do that?"

Kevin shrugged, and Rian just stood there shaking her head.

"Kevin ... how bad is it?"

"Well, mom had a rough night. She lost a lot of blood. But shortly before you got here, the doctor said her condition had stabilized."

"Stabilized?"

He shrugged. "He was very encouraging."

"I want to see her Kevin."

"Dr. Howell said we could go in for a few minutes fairly soon, just one at a time."

Rian nodded. "Has anyone told Marty?"

"I phoned her last night when I heard. She got a flight out early this morning."

Rian was overwhelmed with guilt. "I'm so sorry I wasn't here sooner. I ... I didn't notice the blinker on my phone."

"There's nothing you could have done anyway."

Their conversation was interrupted by a nurse.

"Dr. Howell said you can each visit for a minute or so. Is one of you Rian?"

"I am."

"Well she's been whispering your name. Why don't you go in first?"

Rian seemed surprised. She looked at her father and her brother, and they nodded.

Rian got up and followed the nurse into her mother's room. What she saw crushed her. Her mother was hooked up to several monitors, and there was intravenous tubing taped to the back of her hand. She was pale; her neck was bandaged up and her whole face was swollen and distorted. Rian barely recognized her. She felt herself trembling.

"Hi, Mom," she said softly.

Elizabeth opened her eyes. "Rian?"

"Don't try to talk now. The doctor said you're going to be all right. You're gonna be fine."

"Rian," her mother tried to speak again.

Rian leaned over the bed close to her mother. "Yes."

"Is … Morgana … here?"

Rian was startled. "Morgana?" She had never heard her mother refer to Marty as Morgana before. "You mean Marty?"

"Marty?" Elizabeth felt confused.

"Your sister, Mom. She'll be here soon."

"Yes … that … is … good." Elizabeth whispered very slowly.

"Does it hurt much to talk?"

Elizabeth closed her eyes and slept.

Rian left her mother's room quietly. Two police officers were talking to her father and brother.

David saw Rian. "How's Mom?"

Rian shook her head. "Oh, Dad, it ... she looks awful. She's so beaten up. She fell asleep while we were talking."

Rian's father went over to a chair and sat down. He put his face in his hands and wept silently. Rian went over to her father and rubbed his shoulder. "It's O.K., Dad. I believe Mom's going to be all right. She spoke to me."

"What did she say?"

"Well, she recognized me. I guess that's a good sign. And she asked if Marty were here. I mean she seemed coherent, except she said one funny thing."

"What?"

"She called Marty ... Morgana!"

"Really, that's odd."

"Is somebody talking about me?"

Rian turned around and saw her aunt.

"Oh, Marty, I'm so glad to see you!"

They hugged each other for a long time.

"How's Elizabeth?"

"The doctor thinks she's out of the woods," said David.

"What happened?"

As the family related the story, Morgana felt a chill. She listened carefully, but even before the whole story was out she started to get impressions.

She wanted to ask if anything was missing, but was afraid the remark would be misinterpreted. Instead, she asked, "Do they have any idea who did it?"

"No. They haven't had time to check everything out. The police have been fingerprinting all night long."

"Why don't we all go down and have a cup of coffee together?"

Rian guided Morgana away from the others.

"Marty, I saw her, and she asked about you, but she called you Morgana!"

"She did?"

"Well, you know how she felt about the whole thing. And now she calls you Morgana! I think that's so strange."

"Yes … it is." Then Morgana asked Rian about the book.

Rian seemed puzzled. "The Merrywells?"

"Yes, where is it?"

"In my apartment."

"Is it still there?"

"I guess so, why?"

"I've had this ominous feeling ever since I heard. Can we go back to your apartment for a little while?"

"I don't think we should leave right now."

"No, I suppose not." They finished their coffee, and returned to the waiting room.

David walked over to them. "The doctor was just here. He gave Elizabeth another pain injection, and said she'd probably sleep for several hours."

"Kevin, I'd like to go back to the house for a little while. Do you think anyone could give me a ride? I won't be long."

Rian looked over at Morgana. She knew her aunt wanted to get back to the house as soon as possible, and she wondered why.

"I will," said Kevin.

"No," said Rian, "I'll go."

Rian and Morgana talked briefly to the doctor. He told them that he expected no major changes for quite a while, so Rian and Morgana left the hospital.

As they drove up to Rian's house, they saw a police car parked in the driveway. Two officers approached Rian's Camaro, and she introduced herself and Morgan. After a brief conversation, the two women got out of the car, quickly gathered up their travel bags and hurried up the steps. Rian anxiously fumbled for her key and unlocked the door. Though Rian recalled hearing that her apartment was broken into, she was completely unprepared for what she saw. Her entire apartment was trashed. Most of her belongings were lying all over the floor, drawers were open, chairs overturned. Even glassware and dishes had been smashed in the sink.

"My God! What has happened here?"

Morgana held her niece for a while, as Rian wept. "Honey, I'm so sorry. Either your place was ransacked, or you're an awful slob."

Rian stared at her aunt, aghast, for making such an insensitive remark. Morgana smiled, and then Rian began to laugh through her tears at her aunt's ridiculous attempt at humor. It broke the grip of terror she had felt for hours.

Then she started shaking her head. "How could something like this happen? What could anybody want … here?"

"Rian, where did you keep that book?"

"What book?"

"Rian, the book … the one that man left in your store. the one I called you about! Where did you keep it?"

Rian looked at her aunt curiously "I'm not really

sure. I think in the bookcase."

"Is it still there?"

Rian went through the disheveled bookcase. "I don't see it. Maybe I left it in my bedroom."

They faired no better there.

"Rian, there's no time to lose. Is it here?

Rian looked at her aunt impatiently. "I don't see it Morgana! Do you think that man tried to get it back? I mean would he actually try and kill Mom for some stupid book?"

"Yes. Let's keep looking."

Rian and Morgana searched every inch of the apartment. It wasn't there. While they were looking, there was a knock at the door. Rian opened it, and two police officers stood outside. "Miss McGuire?"

"Yes? Oh. I'm sorry, please … come in."

The officers entered Rian's apartment, and she offered them a seat.

"Anything missing?"

"No," said Morgana quickly. "Just messed up."

Rian looked at her aunt, but said nothing.

"It looks like the main part of the house was not disturbed. This is probably where he got in. We fingerprinted the whole house. It's odd, but this was the only place vandalized. Miss McGuire, do you know any reason why anyone would break into your apartment?"

"No, of course not. How did he get in here?"

"Well, your front door was locked, but your porch door wasn't. We think he climbed up on the roof, and got in through your porch. There was no sign of a forced entry. When he realized there was no way into the main house from here, he probably climbed up on the roof again, and got in through an upstairs window. One of the screens was cut."

"I know. Mom never uses the air-conditioner unless it's over ninety-five. She just keeps the windows open." She paused. "Is it all right if I clean this place up now?"

"Sure." Let us know if you find anything unusual though, anything missing or anything that doesn't belong to you."

"Of course."

After the police officers left, Rian and Morgana began cleaning up the apartment. Rian told Morgana everything that happened on the beach. Her aunt was stirred deeply when Rian told her about the vision that looked like her mother. Then she showed her the little jeweled knife she found on the beach.

"What do you think, Morgana?"

"I think you had some kind of precognitive vision. But I don't know how to explain the knife! Are you sure it wasn't just lying there in the sand?"

"No, I'm sure she put it there."

Rian took out the knife and laid it on the table. "It's beautiful, isn't it?"

"Why, it's an athame!"

"A what?"

"A ritual knife." Morgana made no attempt to handle it.

Morgana was quiet for a moment, than she spoke.

"Rian, would you mind if I made a long-distance phone call?"

"No, of course not."

Morgana opened her handbag and took out a little address book. She called Dru's number, but there wasn't any answer. She tried Ivy.

"I took him to the treatment center, Morgana. He's really down."

"What happened?"

Ivy explained to Morgana about the incident at the cottage.

"As we suspected, the little blue book was missing, and when we got home and opened his box of records, it was filled with newspaper."

Morgana was puzzled. "I don't understand!"

"We suspect all the boxes were probably tampered with. Their phone's been disconnected ... they were supposed to be Dad's friends, you know. He's devastated. I'm really worried ... that he might have a relapse."

Morgana frowned, trying to comprehend what Ivy was saying. Then she said, "Ivy, listen carefully. Someone tried to murder my sister last night. He got in through Rian's apartment, stole the book, then got into the main house and stabbed my sister."

"Oh, no!"

Morgana explained about Rian's vision and the knife. Please tell Dru to call me as soon as he can. If I'm not at this number, call me at the hospital. We'll be there every day." Morgana gave Ivy the number.

As soon as she hung up, the phone rang. It startled them both. Rian picked it up. It was Scott. He asked how things were going. She explained everything, and then hung up.

"That was some guy I met at the ocean," Rian explained. "He was really nice," she said, still feeling guilty. "He's a musician."

"Is he the one you were with last night?"

"Yes."

"Did he see anything?"

"He said he saw something, but it was different from what I saw. He thought it looked like some sort of waterspout."

When the two women finished cleaning, they tried to eat something, but neither one had an appetite, so they drove back to the hospital. Though Morgana probed a little, Rian still didn't feel comfortable talking about Scott. In fact she didn't think she ever wanted to see him again. After they arrived, Kevin persuaded his father to go home with him and rest for a while.

"Now call if there's any change, or if your mother wants to see me."

"We will; we promise," said Rian.

Father and son left. Morgana and Rian sat down in the waiting room.

"Morgana, why didn't you tell the police about the missing book?"

"Because this is not a man the police could catch, much less hold. He's like a demon, a trickster, and the only way we can get rid of him for good is through magick."

"Magick? What are you talking about?"

"I'm trying to explain that everything that happens to us is not on this plane; this physical plane. Certain kinds of beings can go back and forth at will. Sooner or later, even if the police caught him, which I doubt they could, he would escape."

Rian suddenly remembered what Viviene had told her about the Trickster. She related the card reading to Morgana.

"Listen carefully, Rian. Do you remember when you dreamed about the horse?"

"Yes ... well, kind of. My dreams fade so fast. But how did you know about that dream?"

"It was a lucid dream, wasn't it?"

"Yes, I suppose it was. I remember riding around on a horse. You were there, and this other guy with white hair. Oh, and listen, you know what I also remembered on the beach?"

"What?"

"That ritual you took me to a long time ago. The Equinox!"

"You had forgotten that?"

"Yes. Isn't that weird? I remembered when you and mom had that big argument and you moved to California. But I had completely forgotten that you had taken me to that ceremony. I guess I felt guilty and responsible for your having to leave."

"That's incredible! I can't believe you forgot the whole thing!" For a while Morgana didn't say anything. Then she said quietly, "Rian, listen to me. This family has a very unique lineage. I know this will all sound very bizarre to you, but it's true. My mother was aware of it, but you and your mother are not. Some people remember, and some don't. We live many times you see, and each time we return, we often connect to the same people."

"You're talking about reincarnation? Is that what you're talking about?"

"Yes, but listen, each culture has it's own beliefs about this. Some religions don't accept reincarnation, so when they die, they will go exactly where they expect to go. But after a while, they become aware that they can move on. That is when they can begin to work out their karma."

"I've heard this sort of talk before ... at the store,

and it all sounds pretty far out to me."

"No, not at all. When you are between incarnations, you go through a learning process. And when you come back here, it's to learn some kind of lesson. You choose your own karmic path. Each lifetime brings our souls closer to perfection. That is called God, Goddess, the Universal Life Source, Buddha, or whatever your religion thinks of as perfection."

"I see, and how many lifetimes does it take?"

Morgana could see that Rian didn't accept any of this.

"Rian, I know it all sounds a bit strange, but think about it for a minute. Is it any stranger than say, "streets paved with gold, or burning forever in a fiery pit?"

"Morgana, all that stuff sounds hokey to me."

Morgana was silent for a moment. Then she spoke.

"Whether or not you believe it isn't terribly important. Hundreds of millions of people on this earth do. I tell you our family, which is in danger right now, is descended from the Morgans of the Lake. The book you found, The Merrywell book, has been handed down, hand-copied, for generations. The Morgans needed your help, so they tried to awaken you to your lineage, but the person who was supposed to help you was betrayed by this man, this entity, who was trying to get his powers back."

Suddenly, what Morgana was saying sounded familiar. Where had she heard all this before? She couldn't remember.

Morgana continued. "His powers had been taken from him ... on another plane of course, because he abused them. He thought if he could repair his error, they'd give him back his powers and he could return at will."

Rian looked at her aunt strangely. For the first time

in her life, she felt that Morgana might possibly be mad.

Morgana picked up her feelings. "I know it all sounds loony to you, but what about what happened to you on the beach early this morning? What if you told that story to anybody but me? Do you think they would believe you?"

Rian had to admit that her aunt was right about that, but she still thought the rest of it sounded crazy.

Elizabeth's doctor appeared. He spoke to them quietly, "your mother's awake, and she's asking for you and someone named Morgana."

Rian was startled by the name again. She looked at her aunt. Morgana looked surprised too. They both got up and went into Elizabeth's room. Morgana was shocked by her appearance.

"Hi, Elizabeth," Morgana said softly. "How do you feel?"

"Morgana!" Elizabeth whispered.

"Hi, Mom."

"Rian ... you're ... here, too."

"I was here before, do you remember?"

"Everything ... is so ... mixed up. The most ... incred ... ible ... thing happened ... to me," she whispered.

"Mom, you shouldn't try to talk."

"I ... must."

"What happened, Elizabeth?" asked Morgana.

"I ... saw the ... doctors ... working on me, and ... then ... I was ... I was ... in this incredible ... place!" She stopped for a minute to rest.

Morgana gave her a sip of water.

Elizabeth spoke with great effort. "There was this clear ... clear lake ... Our mother ... was ... there! She

... had ... me look into ... the lake, and I ... could ... see you ... Rian, with..a ... young man."

Rian's heart skipped a beat.

"Then ... I leaned over to ... look ... deeper ... into the ... lake, and this ... knife..I was ... wear ... wearing, ... fell into .... the water."

Morgana looked at Rian. She had grown pale.

"But ... then mother showed me ... that you ... had found ... it! It was so real ... not a dream." Her hand went to her throat in pain, tears came to her eyes.

"Mom, do you need the nurse?"

Morgana offered her some water again.

Elizabeth looked at Rian. Her eyes asked, "Is this true?"

Rian nodded affirmatively.

Morgana went on. "It has a little jeweled handle."

"And," added Rian, "a little horse on it."

Morgana looked at Rian. "It does?"

"Yes, and inscriptions too."

Elizabeth's puffy eyes opened up. "You ... have ... it?"

"Yes, Mom, I do."

"How is that possib ..."

Just then the nurse entered the room with a hypodermic needle in her hand. "I'm sorry," she said gently, "but I'm afraid you'll have to leave now."

Morgana and Rian returned to the waiting room. Rian was very confused. A student nurse came over to them.

"Excuse me, Ms. McGuire?"

"Yes.

"There's a phone call for you."

Morgana thanked her and went over to the phone. It was Dru.

Morgana smiled when she heard his voice. She felt

relieved. "Dru, I'm so glad you called. I guess Ivy told you what happened."

Dru hesitated. "Ivy? Well ... no actually I haven't talked to her today. I called your house and Robin told me where I could reach you. What's going on?"

Morgana told Dru everything that happened. Then she told him how sorry she was to hear about what happened at the cottage.

"Dru," she said gently. "I've been thinking. This all has to be connected. Perhaps we can help ... each other."

"I don't know, Morgana, I'm ... not exactly myself right now." Dru sounded down. "What do you suggest?

"That you come here."

He heaved a weary sigh. "Whoa! ... I'd like to ... I just don't know if I can." Dru didn't mention the treatment center. Morgana felt he would prefer she didn't know.

"If you could only get away ... come here for a few days, maybe we could sort some of this out ... and you could bring Ivy with you!"

"You know if I really thought I could help, I would do anything for you."

"Then you'll come?"

He hesitated again. "I guess if you think I could do any good. As for Ivy, I'm not sure ... she has her classes, you know."

"Why not ask her?"

"All right. I know she would want to come. What happened to your sister is just horrible ... awful thing."

"I'll wait to hear from you then." They talked a little longer. Dru seemed more positive when they said good-bye, and Morgana felt better too. She hung up the phone and then turned around to tell Rian, but when she looked over at her seat, it was empty. Rian had disappeared.

❊❊❊❊

CHAPTER 19

The Divination

Over a thousand miles away, the stranger waited for another train. He had hopped several in the last twelve hours. Lurking silently, always unobserved, he jumped from one freight to another, muttering and cursing to himself about what a close call he had. But it didn't matter; he had the book.

Now in the dusk, he waited near a depot for the next train. He stretched out by the edge of a wheat field that was just tall enough to hide him. He felt hot and sticky, so he undid his back-pack, and took off his jacket. Then he placed his canvas tote-bag in front of him. Reaching inside, he found the sandwich he had stolen from an unsuspecting railroad worker at the depot. He always thought it amusing how trusting people were. "Easy marks, easy marks," he muttered to himself. Then he started laughing.

He opened his canvas bag, and took out the food. "Damn!" he said angrily. "Don't they ever eat anything besides this crap?" He started eating the ham and cheese sandwich. It had been his last two meals, and he was sick of it. But he was also hungry, and so he ate. He looked inside the bag for the rest of the goodies. Usually, railroad men had chips, pretzels, Twinkies, and plenty of cold beer. This one was no different, except for the beer. Cursing, he reached inside his tote-bag for something to drink. He found an old can of beer, and drank it warm.

The stranger knew by the train schedule he found that another train would be along in about half an hour. He took some stuff out of his tote-bag, and made a little make-shift altar on the ground. Then, he found his charcoal and herbs. He also found the book. "Try en steal somethin' from me, will ya? Bitch!" He put the book down next to the other things. Then he lit a match and started burning the herbs. What he didn't burn, he ate. Then he took out two small, heavy black stones he kept in another pouch. He held them in his hand for a moment, and concentrated. Then he tossed them on the ground.

What he saw infuriated him. The woman would recover. *Goddamn!* He looked further. What's worse, she had communicated with her contacts, and she would talk. He threw them again. This time he got angrier. The stones told him his accomplices were trying to run out on him.

Do they really think they can hide from me? He threw them one last time. The divining stones told him he'd be betrayed.

Another thousand miles away, behind a hidden driveway, two people finished packing up a van.

"Is that everything?" Chris looked at the empty attic.

Bill stood beside him surveying the room.

He nodded affirmatively.

"O.K., I'll clear the house now."

Chris took a smudge stick of sage and copal and lit it. He waited until it was smoking heavily. Carefully, he moved all through the house letting the incense fill the rooms. Finally, he put the smudge stick in a bowl on some burning charcoal and left it still smoking in the house.

"Let's go."

The two men got into the van, and Chris started up the engine and pulled away.

Around back, in an old rusty ash can, another smoldering fire burned up the last of the newspapers.

In the wheat field, the stranger threw the little stones again and again, but always they gave him the same information. Finally, he put them aside, and went fumbling around in his pack again. This time, he found a little leather pouch of rune stones. Twenty-five in all. Each stone had a Norse letter carved on it, called a rune, and each rune had a special meaning.

Once again he concentrated, holding the little leather pouch in his hands. Then he reached in and one by one, pulled out three stones carefully laying them face down on the ground. Then moving from right to left, he turned up the first stone, the present situation.

Teiwaz. It resembled an arrow. This symbolized the spiritual warrior, but the rune was inverted, which warned him of danger from his own impatience and misguided energies.

Angrily, he turned over the middle stone. *Ehwaz.* He froze. The movement of the horse. It looked like the letter M, but it, too, was inverted. The rune told him of the challenge he was up against. It suggested that any movement at this time could be blocked.

Finally he turned over the third stone, for the outcome. This stone had no symbol on it at all. It was *blank*. Now he began to feel frightened. Drawing this rune after the first two could only mean very bad luck, death, or abandonment. At the very least it would mean the unknown, his path of *karma*.

Only an extreme act of cunning might change the outcome. He sat and stared at the runes for a long time until the rumble of a freight train brought him back to the present.

❆ ❆ ❆ ❆

CHAPTER 20

Rian

Rian ran, her eyes filled with tears. She ran from the hospital, from her aunt, from visions and nightmares, from the stranger, and from the stolen book. She ran from fears and broken dreams, from the attempted murder of her mother, and the crazy rantings of her aunt. She ran.

At first, she didn't care where she went. She ran down city streets. Sometimes, she didn't even know which street she was on. A few times she crossed against the light and nearly got hit by a car. After that, she slowed the pace to her familiar jogging rhythm, but never stopped running. The image of a white horse ran through her mind, but she fought it, even though the visualization calmed her fears.

She scarcely noticed that after an hour or so she was jogging in a very familiar residential neighborhood, with charming, old, well kept brick apartment buildings around her. She kept running. She had a direction, a purpose, albeit unknown to her.

After a while, she began to ease up, suddenly realizing where she was. She crossed the street and jogged up to a familiar apartment building, then stopped in front of the door until she caught her breath. She opened the heavy glass door and stepped into the lobby. The man at the desk recognized her.

"Miss McGuire! Hello! Been a while. Out joggin' I see! How ya doin'?"

"I've been better," was the best Rian could offer. "Would you ring up Dr. Sherre's apartment?"

"Oh, you came at the right time. He just got home. Want me to tell him you're here?"

"Yes." Rian was still panting. "It's important."

The elderly desk clerk plugged into the old-fashioned switchboard.

"Hummm," he looked a little surprised. "No answer."

"Never mind. Did you happen to notice if he had company?"

The clerk smiled. "He went upstairs alone."

"Thanks." Rian walked over to the elevator, and pressed the button. The door opened with a creak, and Rian stepped in. She pushed number five, and waited for the old door to close. The elevator was an antique, Rian thought. She never noticed before how slowly it went, and how much it creaked and whined. Each second Rian was slowly losing her nerve. After what seemed an eternity, it finally stopped, and the door opened slowly. Rian stepped out into a long carpeted hallway. Taking a deep breath, she turned to the right and began walking down the familiar corridor.

When she reached the door she was looking for, she nearly changed her mind, but determined to go through with it, she rang the bell anyway. For years she had her own key to this apartment.

"Be right there." She heard the familiar voice.

A few seconds later the door opened. A very handsome young man with wet, sandy hair opened the door. He was wearing a royal blue terry-cloth robe. He stared out at Rian.

"Rian!"

"Hi, Rich. May I come in please?"

Richard looked at her curiously. He'd never seen her look so disturbed.

"Sure."

He moved aside and Rian slowly entered the foyer. She looked around at the apartment she had once helped decorate. Feeling awkward at first, she could say nothing sensible, and when she finally spoke it had nothing to do with anything that was driving her to such desperation.

"I see you're still wearing that terry robe I gave you last Christmas." Rian tried to smile pleasantly.

"Yes." He looked down at the robe.

Rian walked over to the piano, and started playing around with the keys. Now that she was here, she didn't have the foggiest idea of how or where to begin.

"Still play?"

"Still play." Richard was alarmed at Rian's behavior. "Why do you ask?"

"It's just small talk. The truth is I've had a very bad fright, and I'm just not handling things very well."

Richard noticed Rian had started trembling.

"What happened?" He went to her and nudged her shoulders down gently, so that she sat on the sofa. Then he sat next to her.

"I ran here, all the way from the hospital."

"St. Mark's?" It was the closest one he could think of.

"No, University."

"You ran all the way?"

"Yes. I ran all the way. And I didn't even know where I was going until I got here." She paused. "I hope I'm not disturbing you or anything."

"No, of course not. The hospital ... what's wrong?"

"Someone tried to kill my mother last night."

"Oh, no. Oh, my God." He reached for Rian's hand.

Suddenly, Rian broke down and started crying. At first, the sobs came uncontrollably, and they brought relief, so she didn't even try to stop. Instead, she allowed herself the luxury of crying for as long as she needed to. Here with Richard, she felt she could do that. And finally, through her sobs, she began recounting the last few remarkable weeks to Richard.

"Rich, I feel I'm losing my mind! I just don't know what to do!" she said after she told him everything.

Richard could see that Rian was strung out about as far as she could go. He put his arms around her and held her for a while, comforting her as much as he could. When she stopped crying he brought her some tissue from the bathroom and she wiped her eyes and blew her nose.

"I'm a basket case, Rich!"

"Rian, listen to me," he said very calmly after hearing her story. "Someone's been playing cruel mind-games with you. You must know that these dreams and all the other stuff are just coincidences!"

Rian began crying quietly again.

"Listen to me," he said softly. "Dreams are made by your own mind, Rian. No one can put them there. They're your own fears, your own wish-fulfillments! And don't forget, we dream in symbols. So none of the things you dreamed about can be translated into actual occurrences." Richard wiped her eyes.

"As to the man who broke into your house … you can't prove it was the same man who came into your store. That's just your aunt's theory."

"But the book is missing! And as far as we can tell, it's the only thing missing."

"O.K. O.K. But I'm sure there's another explanation." Richard paused for a while. Then he spoke slowly.

"You know, I was just thinking. The way you described the man and his anxiety over the missing book, makes me wonder if his book might really be valuable."

"Rich, it was an old beat-up book. Even if it was rare, it would be worthless. Some of the pages were torn out … No, I don't think so."

"O.K … something connected to the book then."

"Like what?"

Richard thought for a moment. "Maybe something was hidden in it … you know, like gemstones or … drugs. Could he have been smuggling drugs inside it?"

"Drugs?" Rian had never thought of that."

Richard went on. "Is it possible, they could have been concealed … say, inside the cover?"

"How? It was just a regular cloth cover."

"They're experts. Read the newspapers."

Rian looked at Richard. Even though the idea was frightening, this explanation comforted her simply because it was sensible.

As Rian felt calmer, she also became more rational, and little by little the whole story she had just related was beginning to sound absurd even to her. She looked up at Richard. For a moment she wondered why she had ever broken off their relationship. Suddenly, she wanted to change the subject. She asked cautiously.

"How have you been doing?"

"O.K."

"I heard you were engaged."

"Where did you hear that?"

"I can't remember. I think Mom told me."

Richard went into the kitchen, and took down some glasses. He opened the freezer and got some ice. Rian heard him pouring something into the glasses. Richard said, "I am seeing someone, but I'm definitely not engaged."

"What's she like?"

"Why do you ask?"

"Just wondered."

He came back with two glasses of iced tea, and put them on the table. "She's very nice. A nurse ... here, have some of this."

"Thanks." Rian picked up the glass and sipped some of the tea. Then she switched gears again.

"How do you explain the knife, Rich?"

It didn't escape Richard how quickly Rian changed the subject when she realized he wasn't serious about anyone else.

He took a gulp of tea. "Somebody probably left it on the beach, Rian."

"Then how did it get into my mother's dream? Did I mention she had an N.D.E.?"

"A near death experience? Rian ..." Rich shook his head. "And even if she did, how could the two possibly be connected?" He paused, and put down his glass. "Would you like to hear what I really think?"

Rian nodded.

"O.K. I'm very sorry to have to say this, but in my opinion you hang around with some very eccentric people. It seems your aunt is a little nutty too. Now, for some reason you've been having a series of bad dreams. Everybody does from time to time. Most people put up with them till they go away, or they go to a therapist if it becomes serious enough. But you are surrounded with fortune tellers, psychics, and a so-called witchy aunt, and they put all these strange ideas in your head and try to make you believe them."

Richard hesitated for a minute. Then he added, "I'm really very, very sorry about your mother, Rian. If I were you, I wouldn't even worry about all the other stuff. It's just nonsense."

Rian thought about what Richard said. It did make sense. If Viviene had never read her cards and suggested that this man was going to manipulate her dreams, she probably never would have connected it in the way she did. And if Marty hadn't called her with that story ... but how did Marty know about this man?

"Richard, how did Marty know about that guy? How did she know about my dream? I never told her."

"Well, I'm sure there's some explanation. It had to be a coincidence. Listen, Marty believed she had some kind of vision about you, so she called to warn you. When she did, this man who frightened you just happened to be in your shop. You immediately put it together and believed her. Some people wouldn't have given it a second thought."

"But how did Marty know about my dream? The one with the horse in it. How could she have known that?"

"Are you sure, you didn't tell her?"

"Yes. I'm sure."

"Let's start over. When did Marty mention the dream to you?"

"I think at the hospital … after we got back from my apartment. She only spoke about part of the dream. But she knew it was lucid, and she knew about the horse. How could she have known all that?"

"I suspect you probably mentioned it when you were talking in your apartment. You were pretty upset. You could have told her then."

"No, I don't remember telling her about the dream. I only remember telling her about the … vision."

The more she talked about it, the more ridiculous the whole story was beginning to sound to Rian.

"The vision. You said you were with someone, and he said he saw some kind of waterspout, right?"

"Yes."

"Isn't it possible you were kind of dozing? You think you saw something, but you were actually having a little dream. You know how it is. Sometimes I fall asleep in front of the television, and part of what I dream is really coming from the TV. It gets mixed together. So, here you are dozing off and on at the beach, and a strange cloud formation comes up, or a waterspout. You open your eyes and think its something else. You think you see a woman in blue coming towards you, and she reminds you of your mother. I don't think that so unusual."

"I could have sworn I was awake."

"You probably were a little of both."

"Can you have a dream if you're awake?"

"Sure. You can dream you're awake when you're really sleeping."

"Is that a lucid dream?"

"No, I think a lucid dream is the opposite. You know you are dreaming, while you're asleep."

Rian nodded.

"Listen, I'm no dream expert, but I know a therapist who is. Would you like me to ask?"

"No, don't even bother, Rich." For the first time in a while, Rian was beginning to feel normal again. "Your theory makes sense."

Richard smiled at this sensitive girl he had loved for three years. Having her here with him made him realize that he still had very protective feelings towards her, and it startled him a little.

"Look, Rich, I don't want to make any trouble for you, you know, with your girlfriend."

He smiled and looked at her. "Don't worry about it."

"Well, I do, a little."

"There's no reason we can't be friends."

"Sure?"

Richard reached out and placed his hand on her shoulder. "I'm sure." But he realized he would have liked more than friendship.

Rian was exhausted. She felt like she had never lived such a night and day in her life. Before she could say anything more, her eyes closed and her breathing became slow and regular. Then her head fell limply on Richard's shoulder.

Richard picked up her legs gently and laid them on the couch where they had been sitting. Then he covered her with a light blanket.

For the first time in nearly thirty-six hours, Rian slept.

✳ ✳ ✳ ✳

Chapter 21

The Crystal House

When Morgana realized that Rian was missing, she nearly panicked, especially when she found her pocketbook still lying under her chair. She checked all the possible places, and when she couldn't find her, she called the store and then the house. Finally, she reached Kevin.

"Rian's gone."

"Gone?"

"Yes. I've been looking for her over an hour."

"Well, she was pretty strung out. Could be she's on her way home, or maybe she just went for a walk."

"I'm worried, Kevin. She just split … didn't say a word. Her pocketbook is still here."

"That's weird. She was so upset, she must have forgotten it. I'll call you if I hear anything."

"Thanks."

Kevin went upstairs into Rian's apartment, and began looking through her little address book she kept next to the phone.

Suddenly the phone rang. Kevin was startled.

"Hello?"

"Kevin?"

"Yeah?"

"Hi, this is Richard."

"Hi, Rich. How ya doin?"

"Fine. Listen … Kevin, I didn't want you to worry. Your sister is here. She's completely sacked out. I'm very sorry to hear about your mother. Rian told me all about it."

"Thanks for calling. Rian didn't tell anyone she was leaving the hospital."

"Well, she was really upset when she got here. I figured she might not have told anybody where she went. I called downstairs, but there was no answer."

"Well, Dad's asleep right now. He's been up all night."

"How's your mother doing?"

"Better. The doctor said her condition is stable. She's improving."

"That's good to hear." He paused. "Uh, listen … do you have a minute?"

"Sure."

He hesitated again. "Well, Rian told me a very unusual story. It had her pretty scared."

"What kind of story?"

"Were you aware your mother might have had a 'near death experience'?"

"No."

"Well, Rian thinks she did, and so does your aunt."

"Really?"

"The whole thing has Rian very confused."

"Why?"

"Because Rian had an unusual experience at the beach early this morning, and she has connected it to her mother's N.D.E.. It appears your aunt suggested the idea."

"I see."

"Listen, Kevin, I don't think this metaphysical stuff

is good for Rian. It frightens her."

"What do you mean? What's wrong?"

"Rian's an utter basket case. She's terrified of this guy she believes stole a book from her apartment. She was convinced he was some other-worldly character determined to do her in."

"She thinks the man who left who book in the store is the guy that broke in here?"

"She's sure of it."

"Why?"

"Because her aunt told her."

"Aunt Marty?"

"Yeah."

"Well, this is news."

"Do you believe it?"

"It seems pretty far-fetched to me. I just don't know. He was a pretty weird character."

"You've met him?"

"Briefly. I paid for the damn book. He was hysterical about it. What makes Rian think that man broke into her apartment?"

"She claims her apartment was the only place vandalized, and the book was the only thing missing."

"I better call the police then."

"If he broke in, and tried to kill your mother just to get his hands on some book, it must have been valuable."

"No, I don't think so. The book was in really poor condition. It couldn't have been worth much. But the guy did seem obsessed with it."

"Kevin, if that guy broke in and did what he did for a book, there must be more to it than that."

"What do you mean?"

"The only thing that comes to my mind is drugs."

"Drugs … ?"

"Is it possible drugs could have been concealed inside the book?"

"God, I don't know."

"Got any better ideas?"

"Frankly, no. You might have something. If it was him."

"Anyway, I'll have Rian call you as soon as she wakes up."

"I really appreciate your helping out, Rich."

"No problem. Talk to you later."

Kevin hung up the phone, and called the hospital. He told Morgana where Rian was, and that she was O.K. Morgana felt relieved. More than anything she wanted her niece to be safe, and for now it seemed as though she might be.

She was interrupted from her brief thoughts. A nurse told her she had another phone call.

Morgana went to the phone. It was Ivy.

"We can't get there until Monday night. Is that soon enough?

"More than I could have hoped for!"

"Great! I'll meet you at the airport."

"O.K. Wait, I'll give you the time and the flight number."

Morgana wrote it all down and hung up the phone. Then, she immediately began to think about where she could put them up. It wouldn't do to have them at the house. There was too much going on. There wouldn't be enough privacy. She went to a phone booth and began calling around trying to find a suitable place for them to stay.

Kevin returned to the hospital. He found Morgana in the waiting room and asked about his mother's condition.

"She's still under a lot of sedation, but the doctor said she was coming along much better than they expected. They might be able to move her out of I.C.U. tomorrow."

"That's great! She must be improving!"

"I just spoke to a resident, and he's surprised at how fast she seems to be healing," said Morgana.

"Look, do you know what's going on with Rian? Richard told me she was very upset about a near death experience that Mom had."

Morgana looked concerned. "It's true, Kevin." Then she told him what her opinion was of the intruder, the book, and Rian's connection to the whole thing. She also told Kevin about Rian's strange experience on the beach and how it connected to Elizabeth's report of her N.D.E.

"That's quite an amazing story," Kevin remarked.

Then Marty told him everything that had happened with Dru and Ivy. Kevin listened patiently. He tried to approach metaphysical happenings more objectively than most people, but he found this story much too bizarre even for him. The two talked for several hours trying to reason the whole thing out. Kevin decided he wanted to speak to Viviene about it.

"Kevin, remember I told you that Dru and Ivy were flying out here?" Morgana asked over a late snack.

"Yeah."

"Do you know any place I could put them up? Some place private?"

Kevin thought a minute. "As a matter of fact, I think

I do. I have a friend in Millcott who has a house there. She's visiting her family in Ireland, and I'm kind of house-sitting.

"Sounds perfect."

"Well, I'd have to check with her first, of course. When are they coming?"

"Monday night."

"I'll give it a try."

"Thanks a lot, Kevin."

Morgana decided to go home and get some rest. Kevin dropped her off at the house. Over the weekend, things began to look up as Elizabeth's condition improved dramatically.

Monday evening, Morgana took off for the airport in Elizabeth's car to pick up Dru and Ivy. They all drove back to Millcott, and Kevin met them out front with the key.

The only way to enter was through a narrow, low stone passage-way built between two shops. Then they had to walk up a flight of stone steps to get to the level of the back of the house. There was no front entrance.

When they entered the house Kevin turned on a light, and all three were instantly awestruck! Crystals of every size, color, and class were all around—on the floor, in the corners, on little tables. Morgana and her friends had never seen anything like it.

Kevin walked them through. There were only two-and-a-half-rooms on each of the three floors. A wrought iron spiral staircase connected each level. Each floor displayed colorful, hand-woven Indian throw rugs, and a small altar. And, as on the first floor, everywhere you looked were crystals. Some of the larger geo's looked very valuable. The house radiated energy. On the walls hung medicine shields and other Native American artifacts.

"Kevin, this place is incredible!" Morgana remarked.

"I thought you'd like it," he said.

On the top floor was a sleeping place for one. There was a mat neatly rolled out on the floor with a pillow and a colorful Indian blanket.

Morgana asked, "Who lives here?"

"Caitlin. She owns a little rock and gem shop downstairs in the front, and she also belongs to a metaphysical study-group. Sometimes I think they have their meetings here."

Morgana rolled her head around. "I can see why."

"You've been most kind to us." It was Ivy speaking.

"Glad I could help." Kevin thought he had never seen anyone quite like her.

Ivy and Dru put their belongings away in the closet. Then Kevin left to pick up some Chinese carry-out. Morgana, Dru, and Ivy sat down for a while and talked about everything that had happened. Morgana told them about Rian's sudden disappearance.

"I think it's probably a good thing that Rian is with her friend right now," Dru said.

Marty nodded. "Yes, I suppose. But Dru, I'm worried about her. She's so hostile to anything that ... could possibly be a solution to all of this."

Dru looked serious. "Can't blame her. She doesn't see it the way we do."

"I know, but if she would just be more open-minded, she could handle this whole thing much more effectively. Somewhere, inside herself, she has the power."

"Not all who are called can answer," Ivy said.

Morgana nodded. "I know, but I believe it's imperative we convince Rian that the Morgans are trying to connect with her."

"Perhaps if we knew why, it would be helpful," Ivy remarked.

All agreed, but felt it was more important to know where the impostor was right now, and what he was up to.

"I may be able to find out," said Ivy. She took out her cards. Directing her question to Morgana she asked. "Do you think it would be O.K. if I burned a little incense in here?"

Morgana shook her head. "I don't see why not."

Ivy took out an incense cone and a tiny brass stand from her purse. She lit the incense and then laid out the cards.

"Look," she said immediately as she laid them down, "the eight of wands."

"Flight," Morgana spoke.

"Yes, very fast too," added Ivy.

She continued the spread. "Five of pentacles crossing." Ivy laid down several more cards and then stopped. "This seems clear. He's run away, yet he's also been left out in the cold. This makes me feel he had accomplices." She looked up at her father.

"Chris and Bill?"

"And Nancy, too," Ivy went on. "They're all in this together."

"The devil card." It was Morgana speaking.

"He's in a bit of trouble at the moment, but he'll come 'round. He's a survivor. But now that he has the book, I don't think he'll be bothering Rian for a while.

He knows he has failed that part. He knows he's been discovered."

"Why," asked Morgana, "do the Morgans want to connect with Rian?"

Ivy shuffled the cards, and laid them out again.

She looked at the cards for a few minutes, and then spoke. "This tells me nothing. For those answers I think I would need to scry."

"Well, there are plenty of crystals here to work with," said Morgana.

"Oh, no. I couldn't. These tools belong to somebody else. I wouldn't use them."

"Of course … you're right."

Just then Kevin walked in with dinner.

They all sat on the floor and ate. Everybody was hungry, and the food hit the spot. It was getting very late. Dru looked at his watch, and noticed it was nearly midnight. They all decided to turn in. Kevin said he was going back to his parents' house, because his father would be needing him. Ivy and Dru thanked Kevin for finding them a place to stay.

"Thanks for everything, Kev," said Morgana. She kissed him, and he left.

After they straightened up, Ivy walked out the back door. "Look," she said. "There's a little courtyard out here!"

The three went outside. A small stony patio was built in the back. Not twenty feet behind was a sheer wall of rough granite. A waxing moon lit up the courtyard.

"An herb garden," commented Ivy. "Isn't that wonderful!"

"Umm," said Morgana. "Look at them—wormwood, mint, lavender, rue."

"Lots of sage," said Dru.

Each of the herbs was separated by pretty little smooth rocks. But the mint was trying very hard to get into the lavender.

"Dragon's blood!" Ivy pointed to the tiny smooth rubbery leaves. All three commented at how well cared for the little garden was. Then they went back into the house.

Morgana went home. Dru told Ivy to sleep upstairs on the mat. He was glad he had his sleeping bag. Ivy went upstairs, undressed and laid down on the mat.

The moon shined in through the window near her mat and illuminated all the crystals and artifacts in a magickal sort of way. *How could anyone really rest in a room such as this?* she wondered.

One large quartz crystal ball at least eight inches in diameter sat on the altar less than three feet from her mat. She stared innocently at it for a while, admiring the size, crevices and fractures within the sphere, and then without even trying, images began to take shape.

At first she saw a lake, clear as a crystal and felt she recognized it. It was the magickal lake, one of the lakes in Avalon. Ivy kept staring. Next she saw human shapes, eight women robed, standing by the lake. *Why only eight? There should be nine.* She looked deeper and began to sense a message. *Someone else should be there. Someone was missing. How odd.* The message continued. One of the ladies had disappeared. She had not left willingly as all did, but had been abducted. Her name, they said, was Rhiannon.

❈ ❈ ❈ ❈

CHAPTER 22

Viviene

Kevin rose early the next morning and called the hospital to check on his mother. She was stable. Then, he placed a long-distance call to Caitlin.

A friendly, sing-song voice with an Irish brogue answered, "Hello?"

"May I speak to Caitlin, please?"

"Of course."

A minute later his friend was on the phone.

"Hi, Caitlin, it's Kevin from home. I've been trying to reach you for days."

"Oh, really? Is everything all right?" Caitlin spoke in her soft, quick tones.

"Unfortunately, it's not. My mother was attacked in her house last Wednesday night. She was nearly killed."

"Oh, Kevin … that's terrible. Will she be all right?"

"I think so. The doctors are optimistic. Anyway, the reason I called is, do you remember my telling you about my Aunt Marty?"

"Yes. The lady in the Craft."

Kevin explained the whole situation to Caitlin as best he could, and asked for her help. Ordinarily, Caitlin was warm and generous, but now she hesitated.

"Kevin, I don't know. I'm really terribly sorry about your mother ... but ... I feel a bit uneasy about having strangers living in my house, you know. It's so special."

"It's up to you, Caitlin. I understand."

Caitlin hesitated again. "Well, I would like to think about it."

"Cat, I don't want to sound like I'm trying to influence you, I mean it's your house, but I know they're completely trustworthy. And I will take full responsibility. In fact, if you prefer, I will stay there with them. I know they will respect all of your things."

"Let me think about it, Kevin. Can I call you back later?"

"No problem. How's the trip going?"

"Very well. Listen, Kevin, I really hope your mother gets better. I'll send her some healing energy."

"Thanks, Caitlin. Look, I have to go to the hospital now. If you come to a decision, leave a message on my answering machine, O.K.?"

"I will."

Kevin hung up the phone, but stopped at Viviene's before she went to work. Called a *techno-pagan* by her friends in the Craft, she designed computer software when she wasn't reading cards.

"How's your mother?" Viviene said, pouring him some coffee.

"Better. I need to talk to you." Kevin told her everything. She listened carefully, but said nothing when he was finished.

"What do you think?"

"I think your aunt is on the right track."

"You believe all this?"

"Why not?"

"It sounds … hokey!"

"Well, that's certainly a reasonable explanation." Viviene took a sip of coffee.

"Viv, this business about the knife. That's totally absurd!"

"Outrageous."

"I really don't appreciate your sarcasm right now."

"Kevin, you can believe it or not. The fact is Rian believes it."

"I don't think so. Morgana doesn't think so."

"Of course she believes it. Why else would she run away?"

"Because she's scared. She's angry."

"Yes, but if she thought it was all nonsense, she wouldn't need to run. She'd ignore the whole thing. No matter what she may say, on some level she does believe!"

"You really think all this makes any sense?"

"Do you have a better explanation?"

This was Viviene's teaching mode. Always answering a question with a question … Sometimes it drove him up a wall. Now was one of those times.

Kevin answered, "I don't know. But this much I do know. My mother was brutally attacked. We're sure the man meant to kill her, and my sister is one step from a nervous breakdown."

"Yes, and it all started when the Rag Bone Man came into the store and left his book."

"The Rag Bone Man?"

"Yes. That's what I call them."

"Call who?"

"Umm … nasty elementals."

"Elementals?"

"The folk who live between the worlds. The faerie folk."

"I've heard of elementals before, but only in some sort of nature context."

"Yes, air, earth, fire, and water."

"What is a Rag Bone Man?"

"Kevin, faerie folk are different from us. They live by a different set of ethics. When they come into our world they can do good or evil. Some elementals start out O.K., but might get corrupted along the way. Some are inherently nasty. Those kind are usually called demons. Others tend to be helpful, good natured. We usually refer to them as angels or faeries. But faerie is a generic term. It includes all of them, boogies, sprites, undines, sylphs, devas, gnomes, leprechauns, banshees— all of them. Some good; some bad. Some … just benign."

"And this, uh, guy is a spirit? An elemental?"

"Well, he's not a spirit. Elementals are elementals!"

"Meaning?"

"They exist between two worlds, ours and the astral. Esoteric students would call it the 'Plane of Corridors.' or the 'Elemental Plane.' These creatures can travel through the corridors between both worlds, you see. They can communicate with us and beings on other planes."

"And you believe this guy is an elemental?"

"I think it's possible."

"What do we do about him?"

"Well, your aunt has told you why he's here. He's trying to get into the good graces of more evolved beings, because he's probably done some forbidden thing. But he can't, because he inherently has no ethics. He doesn't know how. And, of course, that makes him very dangerous."

"So what do we do?"

"I don't know. It appears that your aunt's friends are on the right track."

"Why Rian?"

"I read her cards a few weeks ago. Someone is trying to get through to her, but she resists."

"Who?"

"I don't know, Kevin. I think, from all you've told me, it's related to your family tree."

"Why do you say that?"

"Because of your mother's near death experience, because she spoke to her own mother there, and because of the athame passing between the worlds."

"The athame?"

"Yes, the special ritual knife. In magickal family traditions, tools are often passed down from one generation to the next. Rian said her mother gave her the athame in a vision. Therefore, it must have traveled between the worlds, probably carried by a friendly water-sprite or something."

"Another elemental?"

"Yes, exactly."

"This is so crazy."

"Yes. I know it sounds that way, but it happens. I've often wondered if that's where people get the idea of space creatures, U.F.O. travelers, and such."

Kevin put his head in his hands. He felt powerless.

"I've got to go to the hospital now."

"See you later?"

"Viv, I'd like you to meet Dru, Ivy, and Morgana."

"When?"

"Tonight."

Viviene hesitated for a moment. Then she said, "O.K. I think I can do that."

Kevin got up, put his coffee cup in the sink and left for the hospital. He had never felt so confused

A few minutes after he left, Viviene's phone jangled on the kitchen wall.

"Hello."

"Hi, Viv, it's Caitlin!"

"I expected to hear from you."

"What is going on there?"

Leaving out most of the details, she focused on the crisis at hand.

"Do you personally know the people staying in my house?"

"No, but Kevin wants me to meet with them tonight. I told him I would. He thinks the whole story is ridiculous."

"Do you?"

"No."

"Viv, would you mind checking them out? I don't mind that they stayed last night, it being an emergency and everything, but Kevin asked me if they could stay several days, and I didn't give him a definite answer. I'll go by whatever you think."

"I'll let you know, then. Suppose I drop by there this morning?"

"Thanks. I'd feel a lot better about it if you did."

"Talk to you later."

Viviene hung up the phone. She took a shower, dressed, and then drove over to Millcott. When she walked passed Rian's store, she noticed the "Sorry We're Closed" sign on the door. Further up the street, she came to the little stone passage at the front of Caitlin's house, walked through, and went up the steps to the back door.

At her knock, a man answered.

Viviene introduced herself. "I'm a friend of Kevin and Caitlin. May I come in?"

Dru stood aside, and Viviene walked in. Ivy was cooking breakfast. Viviene could smell a strong herb tea brewing, and noticed some hot rolls on the little kitchen table.

"Hello," said Ivy.

Dru introduced Ivy to Viviene. Her smile and her eyes immediately won Viviene over. She could sense a golden aura around her and trusted her completely. Next she looked closer at Dru. He was more puzzling. She thought he seemed unsettled. Viviene assumed he'd been through a lot.

Viviene was, as always, very direct. "I'm here because Caitlin, who is a close friend of mine, asked me to come and meet you."

"She is not comfortable with our staying here?" asked Ivy.

"No ... she just wants to be sure."

Dru explained their situation. He told Viviene that they had already discussed the option of taking a motel room while they were here.

Viviene was surprised at the remark. "You have?"

"Yes. This house is so personal." Ivy went on to explain that although she would never dream of using another person's magickal tools, a vision had come to her last night through Caitlin's crystal ball. "It just happened!" she said. "I didn't expect it."

Viviene asked her what she saw, and Ivy told her.

Viviene sensed that Ivy was one of those rare psychics whose ethics were above reproach. She also sensed that these two people might possibly be the keys to the answers they sought. As to Caitlin's magickal tools, Viviene saw no harm in using the crystal. It could be cleared after they left. If the vision came without asking, then the forces were trying to come through.

For years, Viviene had suspected that this house was built directly over a ley line. Many times magickal occurrences had happened here.

Caitlin did not think of herself as a psychic. She collected crystals and magickal tools, but rarely used them. Some of the crystals stored in her house were later sold in her shop. Viviene knew that she kept her personal tools locked in a box whenever she went away, because she gave Viviene the box for safe-keeping. Caitlin's magickal gifts were more of a practical nature. She could raise and brew nearly any herb one desired. In the winter, pots of herbs crowded the whole house. She created marvelous poultices, bath-salts, incenses and fragrant massage oils, frequently wholesaling them to Rian and Kevin's Apothecary.

Viviene, Ivy, and Dru shared tea, hot rolls, and jam. They also shared information. Before Viviene left, they decided to hold a circle there that night if Morgana and Kevin had no objections. The moon was nearly full, and it would be a good time.

❀❀❀❀

CHAPTER 23

The Encounter

It wasn't until the next morning that Rian finally awoke from her dreamless sleep. She was startled at first to see where she was. Then, her memories all returned.

Richard had gone to work, and she was alone. She smelled her favorite hazelnut coffee brewing in the electric percolator, and poured herself a cup. How nice, she thought, that he still remembered how much she liked that coffee.

After a few sips, she went to the phone and called the hospital. The nurse told her that her mother was still in I.C.U., but might be moved before noon. Rian felt much better. She took off her rumpled clothes washed them out, and threw them in Rich's dryer. Then, she took a long shower. The water felt soothing and healing as it ran over her. *It feels so familiar to be here,* she thought, *almost like a second home.* When her clothes were dry, she dressed and called Kevin. Her father told her he had left for the hospital, and that he, too, would be leaving in a few minutes.

Rian straightened up the couch, combed her hair and pulled it back with her barrette. She found a note from Rich and some money.

I had to go Rian. You didn't bring a purse, so I thought you might need some money for cab fare. I'll see you later at the hospital. Love, Rich.

Rian smiled. He thought of everything.

Rian called downstairs and ordered a cab. Less than a half-hour later she stepped out of the taxi and rode the elevator up to the hospital's waiting room.

After seeing her mother, Rian drove home. She went up to her apartment and picked up some additional clothes. For the next few days she stayed at Richard's, leaving only to visit her mother. She avoided the family because she didn't want to run into Marty and her rantings. The clerk Kevin had hired was still running the store.

One day she arrived at the hospital and ran into Kevin. He was alone.

"How is Mom?"

"Well, she's improving."

"I know that. But how do you think she is ... really?"

"They say she's doing O.K. She looks much better."

"Yes, I've noticed. Talks better too."

Kevin was quiet for a minute. Then he walked over to the fountain and got a drink of water. When he came back, he asked Rian. "Why'd you run off like that?"

"I don't know. I just had to get away from ... from everything."

"Did Aunt Marty tell you a lot of weird things the other day?"

"I don't want to think about any of that now. Rich and I had a long talk, and I think Aunt Marty is more than just a little fixated on the occult."

"I thought you really liked her."

"I do. I like her. But she's weird, that's all."

"Then, I presume you've decided to dismiss everything she told you?"

"What do you know about all this?"

"Aunt Marty told me too."

Rian looked irritated. "And what did she tell you?"

"The whole story, Rian. Everything."

She nodded. "I see. And do you believe it?"

"I don't know what I believe. But it does sound pretty bizarre. I talked to Viviene about it."

"You told Viviene?"

"Yeah."

"You told her how upset I was?"

"She knows how you feel, Rian. She already knew something about it anyhow. Remember when she read your cards?"

Rian frowned. "I remember. That's what started it all."

"Come on, Rian. You were bent out of shape before that. It was that guy that started it."

"Well, maybe it was. Maybe he just scared me; I admit to that. But the rest of it was suggestion. First Viviene, then Aunt Marty. They made every unusual occurrence seem like a para-normal experience."

"Look, I don't want to upset you, but Marty sent for a few of her friends to come here and help figure all this out. They flew in last night."

Rian looked horrified. "Oh, no! I don't believe it!"

"They're very nice, Rian. I've put them up at Caitlin's."

Rian was still horrified "And does she know, too?"

"Yes, a little. We're all going over there tonight to meet and talk."

"Oh, great! Everybody knows. Why didn't you just put an ad in the newspaper?"

"Come on, Rian."

Rian started to walk away from Kevin. Then, she turned her head and said coldly. "Please, Kevin, leave me out of the whole thing."

Just then a nurse came up to them and asked if they would like to visit with their mother.

Kevin and Rian stopped arguing immediately and went into Elizabeth's room. Her neck was bandaged, but she looked much better. There was color in her face. She tried to smile.

They visited until the nurse told them they would have to go. Nothing unusual was said until Rian and Kevin turned to leave. Then Elizabeth said casually, "Is Morgana coming?"

Upon hearing the name, Rian blanched.

"You mean Marty?" Kevin asked.

Elizabeth looked confused for a moment. Then, she seemed to laugh at herself. "I don't know."

"Mom, you never called Aunt Marty that before," said Rian.

"Yes, but that was before … I remembered."

"Remembered what, Mom?" said Kevin.

The nurse smiled at them. "You'll have to take up this conversation a little later. Your mother needs her rest."

"Rian, will you be back later?" asked Elizabeth.

"Of course I'll be back. Now just rest." She kissed her mother, smiled at her, and then left the room. Kevin was already waiting in the hall. When they came out they saw Morgana and their father.

Rian and Kevin decided to go for a walk. Rian barely

spoke to her aunt before she walked over to the elevator. Morgana followed her.

"Rian, please don't be angry with me."

Rian wheeled around angrily and confronted her aunt. "I can't believe you've brought strangers here to get involved in my life! I think you're really overstepping your bounds here, Aunt Marty, I really do. I'm very upset that you would do a thing like that."

Morgana tried to talk to her, but the elevator door opened. Rian turned away and got in with Kevin.

"You were pretty hard on her," said Kevin in the elevator.

Rian was silent. When they got to the parking lot they said their goodbyes, and Rian decided that she wanted to return to work. She drove over to The Apothecary and relieved Kelly, who went back downtown to the Harbor store.

Ivy and Dru left the little house and decided to spend some time looking around Millcott City. Both were enchanted by all the unusual shops. Ivy loved one of the stores which featured fantasy items.

It was called The Pinochio Factory, and it was stocked with magic wands, puppets, and flower garlands. Everything seemed magical, from the jewelry to the exceptional dolls, faeries and elves. Standing up on the eaves of the first floor was a life-size mechanical bear blowing bubbles out across the street.

Ivy bought a dried flower garland for her hair. She was having a wonderful time. They visited the myriad of antique shops up and down the street, and then as they came down to the end of the block, they walked into The Apothecary.

A young woman with dark hair was at the counter. They wandered around the back of the store looking at all the herbs and incenses and Dru pointed out a small clay cauldron which he found quite interesting. It had fetishes attached to it, and there were runes carved around the middle.

"Like that, don't you, Dad?"

"You bet. Wonder how much?"

"Doesn't matter, it's probably a lot more than we have."

"Yep ... you're right. Sixty-five dollars."

Ivy winced. Suddenly the sales-clerk came up to them.

"May I help you?"

Dru turned around and stared at the young woman. Rian looked at him curiously. He looked familiar. She assumed he had been in the shop before.

"Nice shop you have here. Been here long?" asked Dru.

"A few years. Is this your first trip to Millcott?"

"Yes, and I'm very impressed."

"You look so familiar to me. Are you sure you haven't been here before?" Rian studied his face. The silver-white hair, the sound of his voice.

"No, this is the first time I've been east in years, but I am enjoying it. This smudge pot is quite unique. Too bad it's out of my price range."

"Yes, it is unique ... made by a local artist."

Ivy was checking out the many incenses. Rian walked over to her. Ivy was looking at the loose resins. "This is very good quality myrrh," she remarked.

"Would you like some?"

"No, I guess not." She knew she had very little money. "Actually, I would like to have some dried wormwood. Do you have any?"

"Why, yes." Rian showed her the jar.

"Thank you."

Rian walked back to the front. Something kept nagging at her. She was absolutely sure she had met that man before. But how could it be if he hadn't been in the area for such a long time? Another customer distracted her and she forgot about the encounter for a few minutes.

A little later they both returned to the front room. Rian had just rung up a customer, and packed her bag when she turned around and saw Dru standing there.

Suddenly she felt light-headed, and her mind shifted into that place people often refer to as *deja vu*. She saw a man with silver white hair, his hand pointing at her saying, "Wait! Watch!" Then she felt herself galloping as fast as she could, no longer human. The flashback all happened in a split second, but it was strong enough for her to remember, and long enough for all the perfectly rational arguments made by Richard to fall away.

❊ ❊ ❊

CHAPTER 24

The Circle

Kevin and Morgana picked up Viviene and they drove to Caitlin's house together. Viviene had called Ivy earlier, and told her to go ahead and prepare a circle using the first floor altar. It was the one they always used for open circles and when they had guests. By the time they arrived, Ivy had already been meditating for quite some time upstairs. With Viviene's permission, she had also scryed into the crystal that showed her the vision the night before, but nothing came of it. So, Ivy had gone downstairs and prepared the circle.

On the altar she placed a dish of salt, some burning wormwood incense, and her little athame. Dru had bought some candles in Millcott, which he placed in two candle holders sitting on the altar. Viviene told Ivy to bring the large crystal ball downstairs for use during the ritual. When Ivy hesitated, Viviene reassured her that Caitlin did not use that crystal exclusively for personal use.

Now, they all sat together in the circle. "The purpose of this ritual," said Dru, "is to try to understand why Rian is being pursued, and who is doing it."

Everything they already knew was reiterated— Rian's encounters with the Rag Bone Man and her subsequent dreams and visions, Viviene and Ivy's' tarot readings, Morgana's warning dreams, the disappearance of Dru's notes, and, finally, the attack on Elizabeth and her N.D.E.. Then, Ivy told the group about her vision the night before.

Viviene dimmed the lights, and Ivy lit the candles. Her hair shimmered in the firelight, and Kevin, who was doing his best to concentrate, couldn't take his eyes off her. She seemed to glow all over. Morgana got up and sprinkled salt water around the circle, and Dru walked around with some incense. Then, Ivy drew an imaginary light around the circle with her little athame and said some words of power. The circle was bound.

Ivy began to concentrate on the crystal. The room was filled with magickal energy, from the heady scent of wormwood, to the crystals shimmering in the candle-light. The powerful group of psychics sat silently, meditating together on their quest.

Suddenly, the atmosphere was shattered by a noise outside the door. Startled, everyone looked up. The noise came again. Morgana grasped her athame, stood up, and waited. Everyone listened.

Finally, Viviene whispered, " I think there's some-one outside the door."

Morgana nodded. She walked over to the east quar-ter, hesitated for a moment, and then drew an arch in the air with her athame, mentally pulling the energy into her knife as she did. Then she walked through the arch, turned around, and drew the arch again in the opposite direction, releasing the energy back out again. This act created a gate to enter or leave the magick circle. Cau-tiously, she walked over to the door and slowly opened it.

A familiar voice asked softly "May I join you, Morgana?"

Morgana was startled. But when she heard her *Craft* name and saw Rian's face, she relaxed, and reached out to her. "I'm really glad you came," she said. "Come in and sit down."

Morgana once again opened and closed the gate as she ushered Rian into the circle. Ivy and Dru recognized her, but said nothing. Rian looked around awkwardly, then quietly sat down next to her aunt.

After everyone settled down, Ivy began again, but now the mood in the room had subtly changed. Before Rian came in, the circle was filled with anticipation. Now, it was intense.

Ivy silently called upon her inner contacts to give her the sight. Everyone sat quietly, deeply concentrating. After a while, the room seemed to grow cooler, and a glow began emanating from around the crystal sphere. Whether the aura came from the candlelight or not, did not seem important. Ivy looked deeply, and as gradually as before, images began to gradually appear.

Finally, she spoke. "I see the clear lake of Annwn, but I see eight women instead of nine." She continued to scry, and then after a little while, spoke again. "The images are changing ... a white mare is running up to a woman, who looks like Rian ... She is alone ... and she mounts the horse ... but wait ... this horse ... I sense is not really hers ..." There was a long silence.

Now Ivy started to go into a trance, that state Morgana had seen her in before. Her eyes became glassy, and she was far away.

"The mare, oh no, it is not hers! My God ... what is

this?" Silence. "Something is very wrong, I can sense the danger ... but Rhiannon cannot ... Oh! This is not right!" Ivy grew silent again.

"She rides so fast, like lightening! My God ... she has slipped right through the veil ... .and now it is too late. They are outside of Annwn ... the horse is changing ... shapeshifting! It's turning into a ... a ... bull with the head of a man!" Ivy paused. " Ah, the poor Lady Rhiannon. The beast has thrown her off! She's been tricked ... abducted, and she cannot find her way back ... what an evil creature!"

Ivy paused. "I see the ninefold sisters in Annwn now. But I fear one is an impostor who has trespassed into the forbidden land."

Morgana spoke. "Has he shapeshifted ... into a woman?"

Ivy paused again. "I don't know. Wait, it appears he has taken the guise of Rhiannon's mare again. Sometimes through the veil, it is hard to tell ... but they fool no one in Annwn. Now the sisters are calling the High Priestess."

Morgana spoke again. "What does she do?"

Ivy waited. "She is banishing him forever ... .he has done the unforgivable. He trespassed into their realm to steal magickal secrets."

"What has happened to Rhiannon?" asked Dru.

"Ah, the Lady Rhiannon cannot find her way back. Perhaps she does not wish to. She sees but one option now, and that is to withdraw her magick from Annwn and return to this world ... " Then Ivy chanted sadly.

"She left the web, she left the loom,
She made three paces through the room
She saw the water-lily bloom,
She saw the helmet and the plume:
She look'd down to Camelot ... "

There was a long silence. Ivy looked again into the crystal. "The intruder is being banished. He may never travel freely through the planes again, until what he has done, can be undone." Another pause. "The Queen is transforming him into an ugly man with missing teeth and horrible eyes! She says his outside appearance will now forever reflect what he is inside."

Rian spoke softly. "So, now the creature thinks he must restore me to Annwn if he is ever to return to his own realm?"

"Yes." Ivy answered. "But the sisters will never allow him to do it. It would be unethical to restore her to Annwn before her time. But the sisters do have a plan. They have chosen someone to help from this world, someone who is true and rightful ... but only to 'awaken' her; to help her connect with her true-identity! Only then will the creature's evil spell be broken."

Morgana touched Dru's shoulder gently saying, "And the person chosen to 'awaken' Rian was you, Dru."

"Ah, yes, and we know the rest. The impostor tried to take my place."

"Yes. And he will continue to pursue Rian. He must be sent back."

"But," said Morgana, "how is that possible? He has been banished! We must find another way to rid ourselves of him. He is dangerous to us all."

Ivy was beginning to wind down. She was perspiring

profusely. Her father dipped his hand into some cool water from the goblet on the altar and put it on her forehead and the back of her neck

Ivy began to breathe quietly. Her eyes closed, and she fell into a deep sleep. Morgana opened the circle and Dru carried her upstairs and put her to bed.

No one spoke for a while.

Finally, Viviene went to the kitchen, and, as was the custom after a ritual circle, she gave out food and drink. This helped the practitioner return to everyday consciousness.

Rian sat quietly. She had no memory of anything Ivy spoke of, but neither was she so sure about her own identity any longer.

"Guess I was born too soon, huh?"

Dru spoke. "My dear, the sisters have always watched over you. You are one of their own. But yes, you were tricked, and now there is an imbalance in their land. Such imbalance sometimes throws off the beneficial magicks that they weave for the world. Nine is the magickal number, you see."

"Does that mean I must die?"

"No, of course not," said Morgana, "not until your natural time. But by being awakened to your lineage, you can serve quite well right here, by simply acknowledging them, or even communing with them. Do you understand?"

"Yes, I think so, but how?"

"You need only believe, Rian, and accept your true nature."

Kevin spoke. "I hate to play the devil's advocate here, but what if all this is just Ivy's imagination? How do we know it really happened?" Yet even as he spoke, on some level he sensed Ivy saw the truth.

"Do you think she could just make this all up?" said Viviene.

"I didn't say that. I think she truly believes it, but it all sounds … it's just so hard to believe."

"So, what do we do now?" asked Rian.

Everyone looked a little grim. Then Morgana spoke.

"Since we cannot send him back," she said, thoughtfully. "We must think of a way to bind him."

There was a period of silence. Finally, Rian asked a question. "Don't you think it's strange that though his freedom has been restricted, he can still move easily in and out of people's dreams?"

Everyone agreed that Rian's observation was true.

"He must have found a way to circumvent some of the restrictions. He still gets around rather well," Morgana commented dryly.

"Elementals are very wily," said Viviene. "They have their ways. It is said that some have friends or even slaves on other planes that can help them. And, sometimes, if they're smart enough, they can even cultivate susceptible humans."

Dru's face changed, and he took a deep breath.

"I don't think we will figure all this out tonight," he said. "To be one step ahead of an elemental is no easy task."

Even so, they talked far into the night after they shared food. Everyone had a different idea, but no one could quite figure out how to get rid of the Rag Bone Man.

❈ ❈ ❈ ❈

CHAPTER 25

The Familiar

Summer passed into autumn, and autumn into the first days of cold and snow. As the Winter Solstice drew near, Rian's mental health had returned, and Elizabeth recovered. The memories of her N.D.E. never dimmed, but her understanding of the matter did. She no longer referred to her sister as Morgana, but she felt no hostility when Rian did.

Both stores grew very busy with the approach of the Christmas season. Viviene started coming in one extra afternoon, and Caitlin struggled to keep up with Rian's orders for her aromatherapy section. Ivy, and Dru returned to California soon after the circle, but Morgana stayed for a while longer and helped care for Elizabeth after she came home from the hospital. For the first time in their lives, Morgana and Elizabeth had grown close.

Rian resumed her friendship with Richard, but not as before. She never told him about the circle at Caitlin's house, nor did she tell him that now she was at least partially open to the possibility that she might be connected to an ancient magickal lineage which needed her input to stay in balance. Still, her so-called input was limited. Now and then, she would attempt to meditate about it, but that seemed about all she knew how to do. Further-more, since her dreams had returned to the ordinary run-of-the-mill sort, and the stranger had not returned, Rian came to believe that just her acknowledgment, her limited belief, was enough.

Kevin, however, had given the intruder's description to the police. He was far from convinced that his mother was attacked by some being from another plane. Viviene said he was wasting his time, but Kevin did it anyway, and his relationship with Viviene cooled. He frequently wrote to Ivy, and sometimes she wrote back. He invited her to visit, but she politely refused, citing taking care of her father and school as the reasons. One day just before the holiday season, he decided to try again.

"Hello," came her charming voice over the phone.

"Hi, Ivy," said Kevin. "How are you doing?"

"Fine, who is this?"

"Your pen-pal from Millcott. Remember me?"

"Kevin, of course!"

They chatted for a little while. Ivy seemed genuinely pleased to hear from him, and that gave Kevin courage. "I was wondering if you'd like to pay us a visit over the holidays. You could stay at my parents house if you want. There's plenty of room."

Ivy hesitated "Gee, I don't know. I'd have to discuss it with my father. I don't like leaving him alone."

Kevin was disappointed. "Why can't you leave him?"

"He's ... had a few minor relapses again, Kevin."

"Oh, I'm sorry. I didn't know that."

"Actually, he's much better than he was, but I'd still have to think about it."

Kevin felt let down after he hung up the phone. Ever since he had met Ivy, he couldn't get her out of his mind. He wanted to see more of her, but now it looked as though that might never happen. He rationalized that she probably thought he was too old for her anyway, and was trying to let him down gently.

He thought of talking to Rian about it, but when he got to the store she was busy checking in a large shipment of books. She gave him a bunch of invoices, and he took them upstairs to the office.

Rian heard a customer come in, and was grateful for the breather. She looked up and saw a familiar face. Not exactly the same; he had grown a beard, but she still recognized him.

"Scotty!"

"Hi, Rian, how's it going?"

"Gee, it's been a long time!"

"I tried to call you a few times last summer, but you were never home."

"My mother was in the hospital for over a month. Then, we all took turns taking her to physical therapy and check-ups." Rian was excited to see Scott again, but she tried to appear casual. "She had to go back in for some plastic surgery, too. Between that and work, it's been rather hectic."

"It must have been terrible. How is she doing now?"

"Oh, she's pretty much recovered … physically. Emotionally, I don't know if she'll ever be the same. You don't forget something like that. My dad never leaves her alone anymore. He stopped traveling."

"Yeah, I can understand that."

Neither said anything for a minute or so. Scott

started browsing around the store. They both felt awkward.

It was Rian who finally broke the silence. "Scott, I'm sorry things turned out the way they did ... I would have preferred otherwise."

He looked over at Rian, and said quietly. "I would have preferred that too. I've thought about you many times."

But whenever Rian thought of Scott, she also thought of the night her mother was attacked, for they seemed to be linked indelibly in her mind. "It's been difficult for me to forget what happened to my mother the night we were together. I was out enjoying myself, and my mother was nearly murdered!"

"Rian, what happened, happened. It was terrible, I agree, but don't you think it's time you put it behind you? Even if we hadn't been together that night, it wouldn't have changed anything."

Rian walked away for a moment, then she walked back. Her hands were clenched tightly. "I understand that Scott ... intellectually, I understand it. I don't know how to explain. Maybe I felt I was behaving irresponsibly ... staying out all night where no one could reach me. God, suppose my mom had died that night?" Her eyes began to fill with tears and she turned away. "You see what I mean?"

Scott hesitated for a moment. Then he reached around, touched her chin very lightly and turned her face towards him. "But Rian, she didn't die. She's O.K. now. And none of this ... was our fault." He spoke softly and looked at her in that special way. Rian gazed back, and in spite of herself, felt the old chemistry stirring inside of her.

She rubbed away the tears and tried to compose

herself. "Yes, I know. I know these feelings are irrational."

"Not irrational; understandable. I just don't like to see you being so hard on yourself, that's all."

She nodded. "I know you're right. Maybe it doesn't seem like it, but I really appreciate your coming here and talking things over with me." She looked up at him and smiled.

He smiled back, and looked at her the way she remembered from last summer. Her hand brushed his briefly. They were both definitely feeling the attraction again.

"So, are you playing somewhere nearby?"

"Yeah, at a new place, down by the harbor. It's called "The Ark.""

"I've heard of it. It's near my brother's store."

"Wanna come hear us play some night?"

She hesitated again, then smiled coquettishly. "Maybe I'll come. When?"

"Tomorrow night?"

Tomorrow was Friday. She worked late. "I work till ten, but if I'm not dead tired, I promise I'll be there."

"Then don't work too hard." He picked up a new Tai-Chi book Rian had just unpacked. "Can I buy this book?"

"Wait a minute. I have to check it in first, before I can check it out!" While Rian put the books away, the two chatted for a long time. Finally, Scott had to leave. Rian was happy that he had stopped by. Seeing him again did wonders for her morale.

Shortly after he left, Viviene arrived. When Rian looked up, she noticed that Viviene seemed pale. "Hi, Viv. . . .What's the matter? You don't look very well."

Viviene moved over to the window. "Nothing."

Rian knew better than to press her, so she continued unpacking the books. But Viviene kept going back and forth to the window as though she were looking for something.

Finally, Rian asked again, "Viv, why do you keep looking outside?"

Viviene stared silently at Rian for a moment. Then she turned away and said, "I don't know ... I thought it looked like snow."

Suddenly Rian had a funny feeling. Viviene looked frightened.

"Viv, what is it?"

Viviene turned towards her abruptly. "Rian, where'd you park your car?"

"In the lot, across the street."

"Rian, go home ... now."

"What?"

"I said, go home!"

"Why?"

"Rian ... I think I saw him."

Rian felt stunned. She didn't have to ask who. "My God."

"Listen to me, Rian. He cannot harm you. You must meet him on his own terms. Recognize him, and remember who you are. He has tricked you before, in another place, another time. Do not be fooled again."

"Where is he?"

"I think I saw him near the store, just before I came in."

"Out front?"

"No, he was walking down the street, near the bridge."

"Viv, maybe you're wrong. Maybe it just looked like him."

"I suppose it's possible." But then she shook her head.

"I'm not afraid anymore, anyhow."

"Really?"

"Really. I know what he is. He won't fool me again. Anyway, why would he? He has that book."

"Rian, the book was just a means to an end. It's you he wants."

"Why?"

"He would want to send you back to Annwn, that's why. Remember what we talked about in the circle at Caitlin's last summer? Remember, we said in his mind, your death would mean that your spirit would be free to return to Annwn?"

"You mean ... you think he still wants to kill me?"

"Yes! In spite of it all, that creature still believes your physical death would break the spell the Morgans put on him."

"But last summer you said such an act wouldn't do him any good!"

"Of course it won't. But he doesn't see it that way. He doesn't reason as we do. He just wants to undo what he did."

Rian continued putting the books on the shelves. She was beginning to feel nervous. "Even if I went home he'd find me."

"Not if you meet him as an equal. You must use your inherent magickal powers."

Rian laughed sarcastically. "What magickal powers?"

Viviene hesitated. Then she said seriously, "Rian,

would you like me to teach you?"

Rian continued putting the books on the shelf. For a few minutes, she said nothing, but she felt herself growing more and more uneasy. Then she stopped and looked straight at Viviene. "Yes. Teach me."

Viviene smiled. "Good. I'll call Caitlin. If it's all right with her, we can go to her place after work tonight. We may not have much time … and, I'd still feel much better if you went home to wait. I've helped out before. I can watch the store for a few hours."

Rian hesitated. "All right," she agreed. "Call me later when you know."

Later that night, Rian parked her car in the lot across from her store, and began walking up towards Caitlin's house. Viviene met her. "Thought I'd walk with you," she smiled.

Rian smiled gratefully. It seemed out of character for Viviene to behave protectively.

As they walked up the street, Viviene asked. "Would you mind if Caitlin sat in on this? She's … part of my group, and she might be able to help."

Rian thought about that for a moment, then said, "No. I guess not. It is her house, after all."

Caitlin greeted them at the door and took their coats. She was attractive, small, and delicate, with large dark eyes. Her soft brown hair was cut very short. There was already some incense burning, and the atmosphere seemed charged. Rian felt a little tense.

Caitlin smiled and asked. "Shall we sit around the altar?" Her voice was soft and gentle.

Viviene nodded. "Yes, I think that would work best."

The three women sat down cross-legged in front of the low square table. Rian recognized the same altar that was used last summer, except then it had a cloth on it. Now the bare inlaid wood was not covered. A few large crystals had been placed on the altar, and two unlit candles sat next to each other. Under the little brass cauldron was a hot-pad. Other than that, the altar was bare. Caitlin poured a little more incense on the coals, and a woody-spicy scent rose into the air.

Finally, Viviene began. She looked over at Rian and spoke very seriously. "I think I should begin, by explaining to you some of the laws of magick." She paused, as if she wanted to make sure the words came out just right. Then she said carefully, "Magick … is the art … of changing consciousness … at will." Viviene emphasized the words changing and will.

Rian looked puzzled.

Viviene continued. "What that means is, learning intuitively how to connect with the inner and the outer forces of the universe … that are available to us all. Part of working magick is learning how to focus and direct our will … from here." She placed her index finger in the center of her forehead just above her brow, held it there for a couple of seconds, and then put it down again. "Our minds are so powerful, Rian, that if properly trained and exercised, one can actually influence and manipulate the energy forces around us. And that produces change!"

Rian shook her head. "It sounds pretty complicated."

Caitlin spoke up in her quick soft voice. "It does, but it's not … really. Many people have the gift. They have the natural ability, but never learn how to use it. Others are not born with much ability, but learn how.

Some people probably use it everyday without even realizing it."

Viviene added, "Personally, I think magick is a technique ... you know, like playing the piano. The more you practice, the better you get. But you are born to it, Rian! You already have some natural talent ... so it shouldn't come too hard."

Rian sighed. She still felt dubious. "What would I have to do?"

"There are many different kinds of magick," continued Viviene. "Some are called sympathetic magicks. That's when you do something on this plane to cause a corresponding act to occur somewhere else. For instance, see this?" Viviene pointed to a dried-up article that looked like a shriveled orange, sitting just under the altar on a piece of paper towel.

Rian looked down and saw it. "What's that?" she asked.

Viviene explained. "It was a carved pumpkin several months ago. But someone wanted to get rid of a problem. So, the person took a piece of parchment-paper, wrote their problem on it, and put it inside the pumpkin. As the pumpkin dried up, so did the problem."

"That's it?" asked Rian.

"No, the most important part is that the practitioner had to concentrate very carefully on what it was he or she wanted to do, and also speak the words."

Rian thought about that for a moment. Then she smiled. "Is that what they called an incantation?"

Viviene paused and shrugged. "Yes, but we usually call it a *rune*. Now, listen carefully, because this is the important part." Once again Viviene spoke slowly and precisely. "While they wrote it down they concentrated, visualized, and above all, willed their desire." She paused again, watching Rian." The pumpkin is only a prop, you see ... something to focus on. It's the mind that really does the changing. Each time the person visualized, willed and spoke the rune, that is, the words of power, the magick was being charged ... like a battery."

Rian smiled a little weakly. "Did it work?"

Caitlin answered. "It definitely did, Rian. And now, the person will bury what's left of the dried pumpkin, to put it all to an end."

Rian nodded.

"I know of another good spell for protection," Caitlin went on.

Rian looked up, interested. "Really? What is it?"

"When I feel things working against me, I take a lemon and cut it into four quarters. Then I pour salt on each piece, charge them, and place each slice in the four directions of my house. As the sour lemon dries up, so does the negative energy which surrounds me. If the lemon doesn't dry, but gets moist or moldy, then I have to repeat the spell. Sometimes, three will dry, and one will not. That tells me that the strongest negative energy is coming from one particular direction. So, if the lemon in the west corner doesn't dry up, I know that corresponds to water, to my emotions."

"Just like the tarot cards?" said Rian

"Yes, it's the same," answered Viviene.

Caitlin continued, "Without realizing it, I may be emotionally drained. Often you can just sense it. Negative energy feels like black holes, you know? ... or gloomy shapeless colors."

"Yes, I've studied about that," said Rian. "A healthy person gives off a strong vivid glow, but a sick person's aura is usually weak or dark."

"I call those murky colors smudges," said Caitlin. "But smudges can also reveal danger as well as illness."

"Can you see auras whenever you want?" asked Rian.

Caitlin shook her head. "No, I can't, but I know a healer who can accurately diagnose illnesses by reading an aura. He diagnosed a food allergy I had once, and he was completely accurate. When I stopped eating that particular food, all my symptoms disappeared."

Rian nodded again. She was remembering something.

"There are other protective magicks," Viviene continued. "If you have a photo of someone who's been causing you grief, you might take their image; turn it to a mirror, and then tape it there with the conscious intention that anything harmful they wish upon you will reflect back on them."

"And if you don't have a physical link, you could try visualizing that very same image in your mind and get similar results," added Caitlin.

"Interesting," commented Rian.

Viviene thought about that for a minute. Then, she shook her head and said, "I don't think it will be that simple for you, Rian. You're just a beginner, and you haven't learned the art of imaging yet. Furthermore, you are working with an elemental, who can shapeshift, so that changes ordinary kitchen magick to something much more serious. You need to meet him on his own ground."

"How do I do that?"

"Possibly by creating a familiar for yourself."

"What's a familiar, a cat?"

Viviene shrugged and smiled. "It could be. But a familiar or fetch can also be a little spirit or creature you create in your own mind to help you. Such an image is called a thoughtform. But thoughtforms can be more complicated than simply creating a little creature. They can be moving images, or even whole scenes. Like an elemental, the thoughtform can exist in both worlds. The difference is that you are in control. You create, direct, and dismiss it. It belongs to you, therefore you hold the ultimate power."

Rian asked, "And what about an elemental?"

"It is sort of a nature spirit," Viviene answered. "One whose existence on the inner planes is independent of us. Except while dreaming, few of us have the talent to travel through those inner planes, but your thoughtform can. And because you are connected to Rhiannon, you could wield much power there. You need to make contact, that's all."

Rian thought for a moment. "O.K., so how do I do that?"

"You must create it," Viviene replied. "Remember the book I suggested you read?"

Rian nodded. "The one about creating sacred space?"

"Yes."

"Well now, it's time you learned to cast a circle yourself," said Viviene. "When you are in protected space, think about the thoughtform you wish to create. If you use a fetch be sure to give it a name. More importantly, when you no longer need its services, never forget to dismiss it." Viviene handed Rian a little notebook. "Here, I've written down all the instructions. Follow them carefully. A thoughtform isn't created overnight, you see. To strengthen it, you have to keep charging it up."

"Like a battery," added Caitlin smiling.

"Exactly. Above all, do not let anyone know what you are doing. Don't let the 'cat out of the bag' so to speak. If you do, and you're not in protected space, others on the inner planes might pick it up and then you could be discovered by unfriendly forces."

"You mean the elemental?" asked Rian.

"It's a definite possibility."

Rian looked puzzled.

Then Viviene explained, "When you begin to practice magick, your mind becomes like a telephone wire to the inner planes, Rian. If you make your contacts carelessly, you can be picked up."

Rian nodded. "I see what you mean. Sort of like a party line."

"Exactly. Now, watch me," said Viviene.

Viviene cupped her hands slightly, and turned them towards each other. Then she pulled them apart and pushed them almost, but not quite back together again. She did this several times. Then she said. "Now, you try."

Rian imitated Viviene for a moment, and then Viviene asked her. "Do you feel anything?"

"Yes … pressure building between my hands."

"Good, that's what you're supposed to feel. Now you are building energy. What you need to do is to think of what your thoughtform will be. Make it up, and when the image is very strong in your mind, throw it into this little ball of power you are building between your hands.

I always imagine it as one of those bubbles you blow from a pipe."

"Yes," added Caitlin. "Keep it clear and weightless, so you can put an image inside, and send it off easily."

"All the while keep concentrating and reciting its purpose," Viviene went on. It works much better if the charge rhymes, has a definitive meter ... a vibration. Want to give it a try?"

Rian nodded, and began to do the little ritual. She cupped her hands and tried to think of some kind of creature. It was easy. A white horse came immediately into her mind. And its legs kept moving in her head as though it wanted to run, but couldn't.

Rian told Viviene what she was seeing.

"Yes, that makes sense, of course. The horse is your totem. Rhiannon's alter-ego. Now, if you can, try to put yourself in the image with your familiar. Build a bond between the two of you ... ." She waited.

Rian continued the exercise. She closed her eyes and attempted the visualization.

Viviene waited a little while. Then she said. "O.K., Rian, now this is more difficult. Without losing the image, see yourself being threatened, and visualize your thoughtform overcoming the threat." Viviene waited again.

Then she asked, "Got it?"

Rian nodded.

"Perfect! Now begin again. This time for real. Here, sit in front of the altar. Caitlin and I will sit on the other side. You can try it here first, and then afterwards create the image at your own altar. If possible, do it everyday."

"And then?"

"You must decide. Keep it near and call on it when necessary, or send it out to confront the creature on it's own … or both. If the time ever comes, Rian, you'll know."

Suddenly, what Viviene was saying took a turn in Rian's mind. Why, she thought, is everybody so sure this creature is an elemental … and not a thoughtform? She wondered if thoughtforms ever drifted away, or what became of them if they were not dismissed.

Viviene dimmed the lights, and Caitlin lit the candles and the incense. Then she walked around and cast the circle with the salt water and incense. Rian remembered the Equinox.

Caitlin drew a protective light around the altar with her athame.

Suddenly, Viviene took Rian and Caitlin's hands and swept them all up together. She said:

"By the powers of the East
"By the fires of the light
"By the mysteries of the deep
"And the silence of the night
"In this circle of enchantment
"Where all space and time take seed
"Come forth ye powers of all magicks
"And assist us in our deeds!"

Slowly, she brought their hands down. "Now," she said to Rian, "it's time to begin."

❅ ❅ ❅ ❅

CHAPTER 26

The Link

Ivy hung up the telephone after talking to Kevin. She felt disappointed. It had been five months since she'd stayed in Millcott, and Kevin had just invited her to visit again during her winter break. Ivy wanted to go, but she was still afraid to leave Dru alone. She realized that even though her father was doing better, he still needed to go to the treatment center. Occasionally, one of the doctors would even suggest to him that he check in for a few days, and Ivy would worry and fret the whole time he was gone.

She picked up her handbag, swung it over her shoulder and went out to her car.

Later, driving her dad home to his new flat, she commented sweetly, "You know what I miss?"

"What?"

"A white Christmas."

"You do, huh?"

"I do. What would you say about going East for the holidays?"

"East ... where ... to New York?"

"Yes ... I would like to spend some time with Mom during the holidays, but I was also thinking about Millcott.

"Millcott? Oh, I get it. You want to visit Rian and

208

Viviene, huh?" Dru smiled at his daughter.

"Sure, why not?"

"And what about Kevin?"

She shrugged. "Yes, and Kevin."

"He still writes?"

"He called this morning and invited me to visit him during the holidays next week. He said I could stay at his parents' house this time."

"So, what'd you tell him?"

She shrugged again. "I didn't give him a definite answer."

"Why don't you go?"

"The truth?"

"Of course."

"I don't like leaving you here alone, Dad. Come with me."

He laughed for a minute. "Don't you think I can take care of myself?"

"Sure I do. It's other things that worry me."

"Our old friend?"

"He's still out there."

"Well, I guess the truth is I wouldn't mind going, but I doubt if I could get away this time of year."

"I know, but you could ask."

"Actually, I am thinking about cutting back my hours at the bookstore. I'd really like to start conducting workshops again ... I need to feel more independent."

"Dad, that's wonderful!"

"It would help if I could locate all my old books."

"I've been thinking about that. I know it's just a hunch, but I think we should go back to that house."

"I told you I've been up there twice, and I've been

trying to locate Chris for months; nobody's heard from him."

"Let's try again."

"Might be a wild goose chase, you know."

"Might be."

"You have a hunch, huh?"

"Yes."

Dru watched Ivy carefully. "O.K. when?"

"Since this is my first day of vacation, how about today?"

"Right now?"

"Yes."

"It's a long ride, we won't get back until dark."

"I don't have any plans tonight; do you?"

Dru leaned back in the car and looked at his watch. It was about one o'clock. If they drove up there now, they'd make it about four; only an hour before dark.

Ivy continued to drive quietly, while Dru turned the idea over in his mind.

Finally, she spoke. "So, what do you think?"

"I think we better get some gas first."

Ivy turned the car off of the road and headed out towards the highway. For a while they drove along thinking their own private thoughts. Then Dru spoke.

"So, what's your hunch?"

"I can't explain. You know, just one of those feelings."

"Maybe I should try and call first, just to see if anyone is living there now."

"If it'll make you feel better."

They stopped at a public phone. Dru pulled out his address book and dialed the number.

The operator told him that the phone was disconnected. Dru got back into the car and said, "Phone's still out."

Ivy stopped for gas, and then headed north. Dru refrained from questioning her about her hunch. Mostly, they talked about other things, and listened to the radio. About two and half hours later they pulled up to the gravel driveway. Dru pointed to a 'No Trespassing' sign. Ivy disregarded it and drove up to the house. It was definitely abandoned. Even the doors and windows were boarded up.

They got out of the car and walked up to the porch. "I'd like to look around the back," Ivy said.

Dru looked at his daughter. He could see that something was up, and he knew better than to question her remarkable intuition.

They walked around to the backyard. Ivy saw an old, rusted metal ash can. As though she had expected it to be there, she walked straight up to it and looked inside. Except for some trash which was pretty murky looking, she saw nothing unusual. Ivy stopped, and thought for a minute. Then she spoke.

"Dad, I had this dream the other night, and I can't get it out of my mind."

"What'd you dream?"

"We were up here, I saw a big, old rusty ash can, just like this one, but when I looked inside I found something important, and then I woke up!"

"What'd you find?"

"I don't know, I can't remember!"

"Are you sure it was this place?"

"Yes."

Ivy walked over to the back porch steps and sat

down. Dru followed and sat down next to her.

"Can you remember anything else in the dream, any fragment?"

"I know it was here," her voice trailed off. "There was a big old ash can ... you and I ... and ... " She stopped talking for a minute. "Wait, we dumped it, turned it over or something, and there was something important ... "

Ivy suddenly got up from the steps, and ran over to the ash can. Dru followed quickly. It was very heavy, but they managed to turn it over, and dump it. They started sifting through the trash.

"Wish I had a pair of gloves," said Ivy. "This is awful."

"There's a pair in the trunk of the car," said Dru. "I'll get 'em."

A minute later he came back with a pair of garden gloves, and Ivy put them on. They continued searching.

"Look, Dad," she said, pointing to some charred newspapers in the can.

"Newspapers. Probably the same ones left over from the stuffing in my boxes," he commented angrily.

"I'm not talking about the newspapers, look at this."

Dru looked. Ivy pulled out a half-burned dark-blue paper bag, with some printing on the front. It said *Ap t hec ry*, in faded letters.

"What's that?"

Ivy smoothed it out on the ground. Then she opened her handbag, pulled out a pen, and filled in the letters — Apothecary. "The Apothecary!" she said brightly. "Rian's shop." Ivy opened what was left of the charred bag, looked inside.and smelled of the contents. "Sandalwood."

Dru looked into the bag and sniffed.

"Dad, remember when Rian told us about that horrid man? She said the first time he came into her store, he bought some sandalwood chips. This bag is exactly like the ones in Rian's shop."

"So, he has been here. You were right. He is involved with Chris and Nancy in some way."

"Dad, does any of this ring a bell? I mean, do you remember Chris ever introducing you to anybody with a couple of missing teeth?"

"Well, I'm not sure I'd even remember something like that."

"You know what I think?"

"What?"

"I think he can change his appearance for short periods of time, but it doesn't last. I also think he's discovered a way to slip through the veil, but he just can't hold on to it."

"That would explain how he manipulates the dream plane."

"He's very clever, and apt at it, too. He probably has to be very selective with his guises, since after time, he always reverts back."

"He didn't disguise himself for Rian."

"I know, but that's because he didn't think she'd recognized him. She never saw his true appearance."

"That's true." Dru thought for a minute.

"Well, one thing we know for sure. They were all in this together. How do you suppose he corrupted them? Chris was such a ... I thought he was a good friend."

"Maybe he was, once. But elementals can be very seductive. And if he did it anonymously, they may have become involved with him very innocently at first. Then, when they realized what he was up to, perhaps it was too late."

"So, now what?"

Ivy started looking around again. "I want to get inside the house," she said.

"That's called breaking and entering in case you haven't heard."

"Only if you're caught."

Dru went out to the car, and found a some tools. He brought them back, and ripped a few boards off the back door. When he exposed the door knob, he turned it. It was locked. He broke the little window pane above it, and turned the knob from the inside. It opened.

Ivy and Dru walked cautiously through the empty house. There was no furniture, nothing. A few ashtrays were laying around. They went upstairs and walked through the rooms.

Ivy noticed a broken window. "Look, Dad."

Dru walked over to the window. "Well now, I guess we're not the only ones interested in this place."

Ivy looked in another room, and found nothing.

"Dad, let's go up in the attic."

"I thought of the same thing. But you stay down here."

"No way, I'm coming too."

"Look, now I've got a hunch, and it's that you shouldn't come up." Dru sounded very adamant.

She insisted. "Dad, I'm going with you."

He shook his head in frustration. They climbed the steps to the attic, Ivy behind her father. Dru opened the door, and Ivy scooted around him and looked in. What she saw both astonished and repulsed her; scattering cockroaches, paper bags, garbage, scraps of fur and feathers, bloodstains, and the bones of dead animals. The attic smelled like a garbage dump.

"My God!" said Ivy, putting her hand over her nose. "Something was living up here!" Both were too stunned to say anything more for a minute. Then, slowly they took a few steps inside. The next thing Ivy noticed was that all of Dru's boxes were gone.

Suddenly her sweater caught on something sharp. As she went to unhook herself, she noticed a small piece of black cloth caught in the same place with her sweater. Ivy pulled at the cloth as she unhooked herself. Suddenly, she drew her hand back as though she had encountered something evil.

While Ivy was unhooking herself, Dru had ventured further into the attic. Ivy called to him softly. "Dad, Dad, come here! Look at this … " Ivy was grimacing.

Dru turned around. "What is it?"

She pointed to the cloth. It was still on the hook. "Dad, it's him!" she said grimly. "I know this piece of cloth was from something of his."

Dru walked back to Ivy and looked at the black cloth closely. He nodded, also feeling the connection. He thought for a moment. "Ivy, do you have something neutral I can put this in?" he asked.

"No, but I'll look around." She went downstairs into the bathroom, remembering how unused everything looked the first time she was there. Sure enough, she found the roll of unwrapped tissue paper still sitting on the window sill. Ivy took it upstairs to her father.

Carefully, Dru wrapped the piece of cloth up in many layers of tissue before removing it from the hook.

Then he pulled on it slightly, and it came off.

Finally, he spoke. "This is what we've needed," he said with satisfaction in his voice. "We've finally found a *link*."

✖✖✖✖

CHAPTER 27

The Awakening

Rian set up her altar very carefully with the things she needed. At Viviene's suggestion, she had done a little research beforehand, and discovered from many old myths that the white ghostly mare who sometimes struck fear into the dreams of people was called Mora, or Mara. This seemed to fit Rian's purposes very well.

She had prepared everything according to Viviene's instructions, checking the little notebook along the way. The hardest part was creating the incantation or rune, and choosing a name for the familiar. Finally she came up with one. After doing the ritual and creating the energy ball within her hands, she began her recitation:

> *"Mora, Hear my words; Heed the spell!*
> *"If danger threatens, serve me well."*

It was very simplistic, Rian had to admit, almost silly, but Viviene had said, "That doesn't matter. Keep it short, specific, and give it a meter. The important part is making the mental connection between the words and the image." As Rian sat cross-legged in front of her altar, she closed her eyes and conjured an image of herself growing strong and powerful with Mora by her side. When the image grew strong in her mind, she threw it into the ball of energy she had created between her hands. Then she held onto it and kept repeating the rune.

Finally, when she felt played out, she took the energy ball, and in her mind's eye, carefully placed it on her shoulder where she would keep it stored until she charged it again.

Suddenly, her phone rang. *Damn!* she thought, *I forgot to take it off the hook.* Viviene had warned her about that. Disregarding the phone as best she could, she allowed the answering machine to pick up the message, and continued.

She ended the rite by taking her athame, the one she had found on the beach, and erasing in a counter-clock-wise manner, the protective light of fire she had drawn around her altar at the beginning. Then she touched her athame to the little copper cauldron which sat in the center of her table and said out loud. "This rite is ended." Finally, she used her candle snuffer to douse the smoking charcoal in the sand, and then snuffed out the candles.

The first night she did it, she felt lighthearted when it was over. *Why, I am really a little witch,* she thought, laughing to herself afterwards. She made herself a peanut butter and jelly sandwich, and drank a glass of milk. The book emphasized one must always partake of food after doing magick, to ground and center oneself.

As she ate, she listened to the message from her answering machine. She was surprised to hear Scotty's voice. "Hi, Rian, it's Scott. I'm sorry you couldn't make it tonight. I'll call you again soon. Bye ... ." The machine clicked off.

Oh Scotty, she thought. *I'm sorry. It's not that I don't want to see you.* Suddenly, Rian felt exhausted. This magick stuff took a lot out of her. She undressed, got into bed, and snuggled up under the covers. Just before she drifted off, she thought of Scotty again.

Rian began to dream she was at her shop, but the shop looked different. She had the impression that she was in an old attic. She was unpacking some books, but several were missing.

Someone was there with a notebook and pencil in his hand, making sure she checked the books in correctly. Then she said, "I found it! Look, here it is." She held up a faded blue book, but when she looked inside it was not the book she thought it was. Instead it seemed to be the little instruction book Viviene had given her. Then she said, "I'm sure I ordered it." At the same time she seemed to realize it was not part of her inventory.

Suddenly, her phone rang. Rian was sleeping so soundly she barely heard it at first. When she did become aware, she rolled over in bed and fumbled with the receiver. "Hello," she said sleepily. There was no answer. "Hello?" Still nothing. Rian replaced the phone in its hook and fell back to sleep.

❈❈

Once again she dreamed. The scene had changed. She was back at the lounge where she first met Scotty. The music was playing, but she was dancing with Frank. She felt Frank breathing down her neck and told him to "Back off!" He kept holding her. His grip was tight. Then, she wasn't sure it was Frank, his face was changing, but he still seemed familiar. She fought him. No one around seemed to notice her predicament. In fact, the harder she fought, the louder the band played.

Scott walked over. He struggled with whoever it

was, and finally succeeded in freeing her from his grasp.

"Why is the music so loud?," asked Rian.

"Frank likes it that way. It brings people in from the beach. He has a lot of power, you know."

"He does?"

"Yeah, you're in his domain. Didn't you know that?"

Rian was surprised. Frank's domain? She thought about that for a while. But he never wore a watch. He worked in Annapolis.

The music got louder. Then Scott said, "I've got a present for you. If you know how to use it, it will turn the music off." Rian was grateful for that. He pinned a silver disk on her dress. It was about three inches around, with Celtic knot-work embossed on it. Three horses were woven into the knot work.

"That's really nice, Scotty." But the music didn't stop, it only changed. The drummer was banging away on a cowbell. Rian wanted to run out. Instead, she began to wake up. The cowbell kept banging, and Rian slowly realized that it wasn't a cowbell, it was the telephone ringing again.

❈❈

Rian sat up in bed. *What's going on?* she thought angrily. *Who the hell keeps calling me at this hour?* She looked at her clock. It was after midnight.

Rian grabbed the phone. "Hello?" No answer. "Who is this?" Click. The phone went dead. "Damn!" Rian threw the receiver down on the bed. "Why do people do this? It's so sick!" Then she recalled her dream. *Scotty? Maybe he's pissed because I didn't meet him. But,* she thought, *that doesn't seem like him. He wouldn't do that.*

As she calmed down, she realized she had a nasty headache. She dragged herself into the bathroom, and took a couple of aspirin. Then, the phone rang again. Rian had an unlisted number. Whoever was calling, she thought, knew her. "Hello?" No answer. Rian listened. She thought she heard music in the background. "Scotty?" Click.

Rian dialed a familiar number.

An annoyed voice finally answered. "Hello?"

"Hi, Rich, it's me. I'm sorry to call you so late."

"Rian, what's the matter?"

"Have you been trying to call me tonight by any chance?"

"Just now?"

"Yes, I've had three calls in the last half-hour. Two while I was asleep. Whoever it is just keeps hanging up."

"Well, it's not me. Why would you think I would do a thing like that?"

"Oh, I didn't think you … I thought maybe it was just a bad connection or something."

"Listen, Rian. I don't mean to cut you off or anything, but I have an early flight in the morning, so I want to get some sleep."

"Oh?" His sharp tone startled her. "Well, I'm really sorry."

"That's O.K. Listen if you want to find out whose calling, next time it happens, dial back star-69."

"Why?"

"Because that will dial back the number."

"Really?" Rian picked up a pencil next to the phone and scratched the number down.

"Yeah, now I've really got to go. Talk to you later."

Rich hung up ... He wasn't alone, Rian thought. She felt hurt. Her feelings for him were so confused. Sometimes she thought she loved him, and other times she wasn't sure. But suspecting he had another woman in his bed disturbed her.

Rian couldn't sleep. She turned the TV on for a while, and watched a late movie. After a while, she grew drowsy and finally drifted off on the couch. But once again as soon as she fell asleep, the ringing phone woke her up. Still, no one was there.

Frustrated, but more prepared, Rian picked up the scratch pad. Then she dialed star 69. The phone rang a few times. Then a little whine came into the receiver. A recorded voice said, "I'm sorry, the number you have dialed is not in service. Please hang up and dial again."

Rian was fuming. "Not in service?" she said out loud. "What is going on?" She picked up the phone and dialed the operator. A voice answered. "Operator."

"This is 555-3787. Someone has been ringing my phone all night, and hanging up. I can't sleep. Is it true that if you dial star 69 it will ring the number back?"

"Yes, it will."

"Well, that's what I did this last time, and a recorder came on and told me the number wasn't in service!"

"Are you sure you dialed properly?"

"Very sure. Does that mean the phone is out of order, or busy, or what?"

"No. It means it's not a working number. It's not hooked up."

"I don't understand. Are you sure?"

"Would you like to speak to the supervisor?"

"No, I guess not. Thank you. Goodbye."

"I would suggest you call the business office tomorrow, and make a report. I'm sure they can help you."

"Thanks." Rian hung up the phone. After a moment she took it off the hook and stuffed it into her closet. She laid back on her pillow, but couldn't sleep. Finally, she got up and walked around the apartment, as if she were trying to find a friend. Her eye fell on the little jeweled athame still lying on the table she was using for an altar. She picked it up and it nearly jumped in her hand. She could feel the power emanating from it, into her, back to it. The energy kept exchanging. Whether from her imagination or sheer exhaustion, she couldn't be sure, but she accepted it, and gripping the athame firmly in her hand, she went back to bed.

Not a working number, she thought … *not in service … not … in … service …* and then she knew. She knew it was him.

❋❋❋❋

CHAPTER 28

The Visit

The snow fell softly as Ivy and Kevin walked up the driveway to Elizabeth's house. Dru preferred staying in a nearby motel. He felt self-conscious about the formalities of such a grand house.

Already three or four inches had fallen. The evergreen trees surrounding the old Victorian house were tinged with snow, and the whole scene resembled a Christmas card. Ivy was wearing a dark green coat and matching knit hat. Her bright red hair curled up around her face, and tumbled loosely down her back. Her face was pink from the cold. Kevin thought he had never seen anyone so beautiful.

Kevin opened the front door. Morgana was already there. She was spending the holidays with her family for the first time in years.

"Hi, Ivy!" She gave them both hugs. "Here, let me take your coat. Kevin, why don't you take Ivy's suitcases up to the guest room."

The room, which was once occupied by Kevin's grandmother, had never been changed. Marianne had a passion for collecting antique furniture. This bedroom was a reflection of her taste.

224

Ivy followed Kevin upstairs, carrying a few things she wanted to put away. A smile lit up her face as she stepped into the room. It was lovely, with a high double bed, a writing desk, and a soft chair covered with a rose floral chintz pattern that matched the curtains in the bay window seat, and the dust ruffle on the bed.

As she looked around the room, she noticed that above the desk, carefully placed in a wood and glass cabinet, was a collection of miniature carousels that Marianne had once treasured. She had collected them since she was a young woman. Her own mother, Tamara, had brought her the first one from Europe.

Elizabeth always thought it odd that her mother left them behind, after she moved to New York. A few times Marianne spoke of them, but never took them with her. Elizabeth and Marty eventually assumed that perhaps their mother felt the collection belonged here at the house.

As Ivy looked around the room, her eyes fell on the collection. She put down her camera and a small suitcase she was carrying, and walked over to the cabinet.

"How beautiful," she commented. "May I?" She placed her hand lightly on a single carousel sitting next to a tiny, iridescent glass vial atop the writing desk

"Sure," said Kevin. They had been in the cabinet so long, he never noticed them. He walked over and looked at the little carousel. "They really are unique," he observed.

As Ivy turned the carousel over in her hands, she noticed a little key.

"Look Kevin, I think it winds up."

"Give it a try."

She did, and suddenly it began to play a little tune. Ivy smiled. "Kevin, this one is a music box!" The two started listening and discovered it was playing a melody they both recognized. "Silent Night." said Ivy. "And look, it's also a tree ornament. See the little loop?"

"You're right," said Kevin wrapping the loop around his finger and swinging it. "That's pretty neat."

"Oh, Kevin, be careful."

Kevin replaced the ornament next to the vial.

Then Ivy noticed a photograph hanging on the wall. There was a very attractive dark-haired woman, a light haired man, a light haired younger woman, and a child about seven or eight.

"Kevin, who is that?"

"That's my grandparents, my mom, and Marty."

"Oh, I didn't recognize them."

"Well, it was a long time ago."

"Yes, I see the resemblance now. Your grandmother was lovely. She reminds me of Morgana, and Rian."

They both walked downstairs. Everybody was gathered in the dining room. Starlight, who still limped a little, ran over to greet everyone. "Hi, girl," said Kevin. He started playing with the dog. Elizabeth walked in with a tray of sandwiches, and put them down on a table. Rian followed carrying a large cut-glass bowl of eggnog, which she placed beside the tray.

"Everybody, come and get it!" said Rian's father. Kevin and Morgana walked over to the table.

"Where's Robin?" asked Rian.

"He'll be back soon," said Morgana. "He's visiting some old friends."

Everyone gathered round the table talking, laughing

and snacking. Morgana felt so happy to be home for the holidays. "Who is watching the shop?" she asked Rian.

"I've always got part-time help this time of year."

Elizabeth noticed the way Kevin looked at Ivy. She had to admit she could see why. The young woman was not only beautiful, but sweet and gentle. She liked her instantly.

The phone rang.

Rian answered it.

"Hi, Rian, How ya doin'?"

Rian was surprised to hear Scott's voice.

"Hi, Scotty!...Sorry I didn't get down last week. I've just been working so late. How did you know I was here?"

"Well, I tried the number you gave me, but I got the answering machine, so I called the store, and they gave me this one. The reason I'm calling is because I'm off tonight. I thought maybe we could get together."

"Well, I'm downstairs at my parents' house. We have out of town guests, and they just got here this afternoon ... so ... I don't know."

"I understand." He hesitated. "Well, I won't keep you."

"Scotty, you're not. It's just that this is a busy time for me. But I promise ... hey, I know. We're having a little open house here tonight. Why don't you stop by?"

"Are you sure?"

"Yeah ... really! Anyway, I'd like you to meet some of my friends."

Rian gave him the address. Scott said he would come.

Later, after lunch, Elizabeth who had taken an

immediate shine to Ivy gave her a tour of the house. When they got to the top of the stairs, she stopped for a moment.

"This is where it happened, you know."

Ivy looked surprised for a moment. Then she realized what Elizabeth was talking about.

"Oh, yes. I know about that. My father and I were here for a few days when you were in the hospital."

"Yes, they told me. Thank you for helping out."

"It was only a little moral support. My father and Morgana have been friends for years."

"You must be very close to your father."

"Well, my parents divorced when I was a child. I grew up in New York. So, last year my mom brought me to California to get re-acquainted with my dad. I've been with him ever since. Guess I'm making up for lost time."

Elizabeth took Ivy through the rest of the house. Ivy was very impressed. As they moved through each room, Elizabeth pointed out some of the antique furniture and told Ivy about their origins. Starlight followed Elizabeth everywhere.

"You have a beautiful home, Mrs. McGuire. It's a collector's dream."

"That's quite a complement coming from you. I understand you're very talented. "Marty told me you attend college in San Francisco on a Fine Arts scholarship."

Ivy shrugged. "Actually, it's only a partial scholarship."

"Still, quite an accomplishment. I understand you also design jewelry."

Ivy smiled and nodded. "It pays the rent."

"You're much too modest. Marty says your jewelry is sold in some of the finest boutiques in San Francisco."

"It is doing well. I guess I inherited the fashion flair from my mom. She's a designer too. But, actually, I'm much more interested in serious sculpture than fashion."

"I'm sure you'll do well with that too." Elizabeth smiled and the tour continued. Finally they reached the top of the stairs again. Ivy knelt down to pet Starlight, but the dog growled and quickly backed away.

"Sometimes Star's skittish with strangers, though up till just now it's only been with men. When that horrible man attacked me last summer, he must have kicked her or hit her with something. He broke her leg badly. If the police hadn't called their vet right away, she probably would have died." Elizabeth knelt down and picked up her little dog.

Ivy found that story interesting. *Animals were wonderful trackers. Even elementals had a scent to a dog.*

They both returned to the living room. Rian was telling everyone about a midnight holiday party in Millcott city next week.

"It's Friday night," she said. "I hope you can all come."

"Yeah," said Kevin. "It is fun. All the stores are open till midnight. A lot of them serve food and wine too."

"Hey, Morgana," said Rian. "A friend of mine is coming by later. I think you might like to meet him."

"Who?"

"His name is Scott Erecson. Remember, I told you I met him at the ocean last summer?"

"Yeah."

"Well, he called me a little while ago, so I invited him over."

"Oh? I thought you were dating Rich again."

"No. I haven't seen much of him lately."

"What happened?"

"I don't know. Things just kept changing between us."

Elizabeth looked over at Rian for a moment and said nothing. Then she just walked away.

"I think Mom heard us talking. She still would like me and Rich to get together."

Morgana nodded. "Well, I guess you can't really blame her."

"No, he's a great guy."

"But you prefer someone else these days?"

"Perhaps I just like variety."

"Don't be coy with me, Rian!"

"I think Rich is seeing someone else anyway."

"That would change things."

"It does, but I don't think Rich and I were really going anywhere. I mean I felt bad at first, but ..."

"Now that you have someone else?" Morgana smiled.

"Morgana! I don't have anybody else!"

"How did you find out that Rich was seeing someone?"

"Well, one night last week I called him kind of late, and could tell he wasn't alone. He wasn't very friendly, either."

"Uh-oh."

"I have very mixed feelings about Rich. I guess I'm not ready to talk about them yet."

Morgana nodded as they walked over to the others.

❈ ❈ ❈ ❈

CHAPTER 29

The Silver Disk

Elizabeth's party was a huge success. Robin returned, and several of Morgana's old friends dropped in to see her again.

Ivy mentioned to Morgana, "It sounds strange to hear people calling you by that name."

"Yeah, I guess it does. It sounds a little foreign to me too … now."

"Marty … It's unusual."

"It's a contraction of Marianne-Tamara. The first name was my mother's, the second, my grandmother's."

"I like that," said Ivy. "It's nice to have family names. It gives one a sense of belonging."

She shrugged. "I suppose it does. I used to hate it, but now I really don't mind."

Out in the kitchen, Rian was helping her mother put the finishing touches on the buffet. She shook her head, overwhelmed by the amount of food her mother had prepared.

"You've really outdone yourself, Mom. Plum pudding? You haven't made that in years!"

Elizabeth looked at her daughter thoughtfully. "This year is very special to me, Rian."

Rian understood. She gave her mother a big hug. "Yes, it is special. We're all together again. And most of all, you're here; we didn't lose you." She hated that creature, not so much for what he had done to her, but for what he had nearly done to her mother.

Rian heard the doorbell ring again. People had been coming and going all evening.

Maybe that's Scotty, she thought. *I'd better look.* She opened the kitchen door, and heard someone call her. "Rian! There's a friend here to see you."

"Mom, I think Scotty is here. I'd like you to meet him."

She walked out to the entrance hall to meet Scott. They chatted briefly and then she introduced him around. A few minutes later, Elizabeth, David, and Morgana set out the buffet.

"It's really nice of you to have me over," Scott said to Rian. "I didn't expect anything quite so ... fine."

"Well, I really felt bad about the other night. I got your message on the answering machine, but you didn't leave a number, and I didn't want to call you at work ... by the way, you didn't try to call me again that night, did you?"

"No, just the one time, why?"

She shrugged. "Nothing important."

"Nothing?"

"It's just that later that night someone kept trying to phone me, but ... the connection was bad."

Rian decided to keep most of that incident to herself. She had noticed that since she had been doing the ritual, she felt more empowered. She kept uncommon things to herself, and listened very carefully to her instincts. At the same time, on a different level, she felt she had a deeper understanding of what was going on inside of other people.

After dinner, Morgana began talking to Scott. "So you're the fellow who was with Rian that night."

"I guess you mean the night of the accident."

"Oh, that was no accident, I can assure you," Morgana remarked.

Scott didn't know how much Rian's family knew about the night they spent together. Suddenly, he felt awkward.

"I'm sorry. I know it wasn't an accident."

"Rian told me that you saw a little waterspout."

"She did? Hummm, I don't remember that."

Rian walked up to Scotty. "Don't remember what?"

"The waterspout that night," Morgana said.

Rian looked hard at Morgana. Her eyes told her aunt that she didn't like discussing this subject with Scott.

Then Scott said, "I do remember one thing, though."

Morgana looked at him.

He continued, "Remember that jeweled knife you found on the beach?"

"Yes, I remember that."

"You had a weird dream about someone giving it to you or something?"

"Yes … "

"What happened to that knife? It looked valuable."

"I still have it."

"Really?"

"Yes, it's upstairs."

"So, you kept it?"

234/ THE RAG BONE MAN

"Of course I did."

Suddenly Scott felt a little embarrassed. He shrugged. Then he laughed a little. "I don't know. Maybe I thought you put an ad in the 'lost and found' or something."

Rian realized where Scott was coming from. From the real world, from this place, what he said made perfect sense.

"Well," said Morgana. "It was really nice to meet you, Scott. Think I'll go see what Robin's up to. Talk to you a little later."

Morgana was aware that Rian, on some level, now accepted the existence of the Rag Bone Man, as Viviene called him. But she was not aware that Rian was actively preparing herself to magickally confront him. If she had, she would have been quite frightened. Rian after all, was a novice. For a novice to confront a seasoned and treacherous elemental was quite dangerous.

Later, Rian and Scott took a walk outside in the snow. She felt good being with him again. They talked about his band, and her store. He told her he had traveled a lot lately, but that it was getting tiresome and the band was going through some changes.

"The drummer is leaving. He's moving to L.A."

"So, what will you do?"

"I'm auditioning a few others. One of them seems pretty good."

"Yeah?"

"He's from ... come to think of it, I don't know where he's from. He plays pretty good though."

"So, where's your next job after this one?"

"Oh, I'll be here for three months. Then I'm booked

in Annapolis for another three."

"Pretty good! Will you be going back to the ocean this summer?"

"No, I'm going back to school. Think I've finally got enough money saved to finish. I'm just tired of traveling all the time. I want to get my degree."

"So, what will you do, teach music?"

"That, or arrange. I don't know. Hey, enough about me!" He reached into his jacket and pulled something out.

"I've got a little Christmas present for you."

"You do? Well, thanks!"

He gave her a little box. It was wrapped in red shiny paper and had a gold bow on top.

"Ummm, nice wrapping. Shall I open it now, or wait till Christmas?"

"Aw, live dangerously. Open it now."

Rian leaned up against a tree, and carefully removed the wrapping paper.

"Oh, Scott." The gift didn't completely surprise her. But it did. "It's beautiful ... thank you!" She turned it over in her hand feeling for the texture of it. "Will you help me put it on?"

Scott took the gift out of the box. Then he pinned the silver disk with the horses and knot work on Rian's coat. She didn't blink an eye. It was as if Rian sensed in some way what would be inside before she opened it, and it all seemed perfectly natural.

✠✠✠✠

CHAPTER 30

The Carousel

Ivy flopped into bed that night. She couldn't remember ever sleeping in anything so comfortable. The bed was piled high with ivory laced goose-down comforters. The pillow cases were matching ivory lace. She laid there for a while, feeling like a princess. *I wonder,* she thought, *what it must be like growing up in a house such as this.* Ivy had been raised in the city, although she had spent some of those years in a girl's boarding school. Her mother worked hard in the fashion industry to keep up their New York apartment, and Ivy had always slept on a pull-out sofa-bed in the living room. Suddenly she had a very strong desire to call her mother, but it was late.

I'll call her tomorrow, she thought. *At least I'll be able to spend Christmas and New Year's with her.* Last year, she had been nursing her father during the holidays.

Ivy couldn't sleep. She pulled back the comforter, and turned on the little lamp beside the bed. Then she got up and walked over to the desk. Her eye fell on the iridescent vial sitting on the desk. She picked it up, opened it and sniffed. It was rosemary oil, sacred to the sea, and used for healing and memory. *Rosemary for remembrance,* she thought.

She looked up at the cabinet with its beautiful carousel collection. Feeling a little guilty, she tried to open the door to the cabinet. It was locked, but an old fashioned brass key was lying in full view on top of the desk. Now she felt like Alice in Wonderland. The key said, *Turn me!*

Ivy couldn't resist. She tried the key. It worked. The cabinet door opened. She looked at the collection with wonder. Ivy recognized fine art, and these little carousels appeared to be very valuable. Some were porcelain, others crystal, or carved wood, many beautifully hand-painted.

She hesitated for a moment, then reached into the cabinet and picked one up. It had a little catch in the back. She turned it, and the carousel began to move around.

How delightful, she thought! How do they work? There must be springs or something inside. Then she laughed to herself. *Probably magick! They're too old to have batteries.* She continued to look through the collection. She picked each one up carefully and tried to connect them to the country of their origin. Finally, she decided that most of them were probably from Germany, Austria, and Eastern European countries. Perhaps, some were from Russia.

She tried to wind them up or look for secret catches. It was like a little game. Some played music and went around, others had little springs which made the horses move. Some did nothing at all. Then she picked one up which didn't seem to have any catch or key. She turned it around and upside down, but found nothing. Just as she was about to replace it, she felt a thin, round groove underneath. As she slid her fingers over the groove a panel in the bottom of the carousel sprung open. Startled, she turned it upside down again, and looked inside. It seemed hollow, but as she looked more closely, she saw something was in there. She felt deep within the carousel, and pulled out a small photograph. It was a picture of a woman, with a child on her lap who resembled Morgana, and a man she didn't recognize.

She stared at the photograph for a long time. Then she looked over at the picture on the wall. There was no mistake. This woman was Marianne, Morgana's mother. But the man was not Morgana's father...and the child...she wondered who the child was. Ivy turned the photograph over. There was an inscription on the back. It read: *To Marianne, a picture of us with our beautiful daughter... Central Pk... Sept., 1950. Love, Carl.*

Ivy read the note over and over. Then she ran her finger over the images, and closed her eyes. Ivy's intuitive mind made the connection. The child, she was sure was Morgana, but who was this man? Was he Morgana's father?

Without meaning to, Ivy sensed she may have stumbled onto some sort of family secret. She felt uneasy. She had no right to be fooling around with these carousels. In fact, it wasn't like her at all to do such a thing. Why had she felt so compelled to pry? Was she supposed to find out? Did Morgana know?

Ivy opened her bedroom door, and walked down the hall to the telephone. She called Dru's number at the motel.

"Hi, Ivy."

"Hi, Dad. I need to talk to you."

"Sure. What's on your mind?" Her father sat on the edge of his bed, while Ivy told him what she had discovered.

"Dad, you're so close to Morgana. Do you think she knows?"

"Well, if she does, she never said anything. She always talked very fondly of her mother."

"What kinds of things did she tell you?"

There was a pause on the line. Then he said. "Not very much. I remember her telling me that her mother had re-married after her husband died. A playwright from New York, I think."

"Really? What was his name?"

"I have no idea. If it's the same man who came to my initiation with her, I told you, I knew him only as Myrddin."

"Then Morgana and Elizabeth might have different fathers."

"Why do you say that?"

"I don't know. Elizabeth and Morgana are so different. They don't even look alike."

Dru was quiet for a minute. "The only thing I remember Morgana confiding to me about her mother's background, was that she went to college in New York, and nearly married another man; a student. I suppose it was before she married Morgana's father. Anyway her grandfather disapproved, and forced her mother to break off the relationship."

"And …"

"And nothing. Morgana said her mother had stayed close to her friends in New York. She told me how much she liked it when her mother took her up there to shop, or see a show."

"And that was all?"

"That was about it. At least, that's all I remember."

"That's so odd ..."

"Why?"

"It just is. I have this feeling..."

"Ivy, don't say anything. You don't really know." There was an edge in Dru's voice.

"I do know! I'm sure. It's Morgana who doesn't know. What if her father's still living? Why was the photograph kept hidden?"

"Don't you think he would have told her?"

Ivy hesitated. "Humm ... I suppose so ... especially since her parents are both dead."

"So you'll leave it alone?"

"Maybe they had an understanding about Morgana."

"Meaning?"

"I don't know. Maybe they thought it best she never know."

"Then, Ivy, for heaven's sake, why would you tell her?"

"Because something has changed. That's why I discovered the photograph. I think Marianne wants Morgana to know."

"Listen, wait on this. Think about it. There's no proof ... and you could cause a great deal of trouble! If you're wrong, you'd be making a fool of yourself."

"The photograph is all the proof we need. If Marianne took Morgana, not Elizabeth, to New York all the time, you can bet it was more than to shop or see a show. It was probably to spend time with her father. Dad, his name is Carl. If that was the name of the man she eventually married, it would all fit."

"Why must you push this, Ivy?" Her father sounded

very irritated.

"Because, I didn't really get to know you until I grew up, and I think Morgana should have that opportunity too...if its true."

"Ivy, I think it would be a terrible mistake to get involved here. As your father, I insist you stay out of this."

"Dad, it's not that I don't respect your opinion, I just need more time to think about this ... anyway, I have to go now before I wake somebody up."

Instinctively, her last remark told Dru that she wouldn't respect his wishes."

"Ivy, I meant what I said. Don't interfere!"

Ivy returned to her room. She straightened up the cabinet and then took another look at the photograph. There was no doubt about it. This man, Carl, and Marianne shared a child, and Ivy sensed it was Morgana. She wondered if there were more clues, and if any of this could be connected to the creature and Rian. But Ivy already felt uneasy about what she had discovered. She would not look any further.

Tired, she slid into the luxurious bed and turned off the lamp, but it was a long time before she fell asleep.

While Ivy and the others slept, Rian and Scott were getting reacquainted in her flat upstairs. At first Rian felt self-conscious about her little altar. She hadn't had time to put everything away. The little bowl of water, and the copper cauldron still sat there. The smell of incense lingered in the air, and her athame lay conspicuously next to the two unlit candles.

Scott noticed the low table immediately. He saw the

cushion still sitting in front of Rian's little altar. But he took a completely different point of view than she expected of the whole scene.

"Do you practice yoga," he said.

"Why do you ask?"

"The altar, the incense, candles." Scott smiled. "You meditate don't you?"

She hesitated. Then she shrugged. "Yes...I suppose you could say that I do."

"I don't know why I didn't assume it. After all you do own a metaphysical store. It's only natural."

"And you buy esoteric books in my store," she smiled. "So I suppose you meditate, too."

"I try to ... whenever I can ... " He gestured towards the altar. I see your little copper cauldron. Would you be into Agnihotra?"

Rian tried to think. She'd never even practiced yoga, and wasn't up on any special meditation techniques. "Oh, no, I just sit quietly you know, and listen to a tape or something."

He nodded. "Got any favorites?"

"Sure, a few." Rian was anxious to change the subject. "Hey, would you like a beer or something?"

"No. Thanks. I've really gotta go in a minute anyway." He started to pick up his coat from the back of the couch. Then he hesitated for a moment and looked at Rian. "You know, I've thought of you a lot. I really wanted to see you again, but I wasn't sure you'd want to get together anymore ... after the last time."

She nodded. "First, and last time. But I think I'm getting over all those guilty feelings now, Scott. I'm changing."

He picked up his coat and put it on. Rian smiled at him and said. "Thanks again for the present."

At the door, they finally did kiss goodnight, and both of them felt all of the old feelings resurface. "You know, I really like you a lot Rian," he said. "I'm glad we got together again." And then he was gone.

After he left, Rian leaned up against the door and took a deep breath. She understood why they both felt cautious, but she also knew this was only the beginning, and she felt they would be together for a long time to come.

❈❈❈❈

CHAPTER 31

Revelations

The sunshine streaming in Ivy's window woke her up. She had never slept in such comfort before, and it was nearly impossible to tear herself out of the bed.

All night, she kept dreaming she was sleeping on a cloud. She got up, showered, and dressed. When she walked outside of her room, she heard conversation coming from downstairs. She could hear voices. Kevin was there. She smelled the bacon and eggs, and wondered how she could gracefully refuse such a breakfast.

She need not have worried. Morgana had already told her sister that Ivy was a vegetarian.

Elizabeth, eager to please, baked fresh rolls for Ivy, and served them with her own preserves.

"I'm not a vegan," Ivy smiled. "I do eat eggs and diary products." Upon which Elizabeth immediately scrambled her a platter full.

A few minutes after Rian arrived at the store, her phone rang. It was Scotty. She smiled. "Hi!"

"Wanna have lunch with me today?"

"Sure, can you come over here?"

"About what time?"

"Ummm, between one and two?"

"Sounds good. See you then."

Later that evening, Rian went down to hear Scott's band play. They were as good as ever. She noticed the new drummer, and asked Scott about him. "So, what do you think?"

"He's good."

Scott nodded. "Nice guy, too. I like him."

"Where did you say he played before?"

"I didn't. He told me it was on some cruise ship. He's just sitting in tonight. Gary will be back tomorrow."

"Oh. When's he leaving permanently?"

"Not till the end of this gig."

"Well, that gives you plenty of time to audition lots of drummers."

"I already have. This one's the best so far."

Later, Rian and Scott went out with some of his friends from the band and had breakfast at a local diner.

"Do you always do this after you play?"

"Sometimes. Playing all night makes us hungry."

That's how it went the rest of the week. Scotty would stop by and have lunch with Rian. She would stop by the Ark at night, listen to the band and go out for breakfast afterwards.

One evening, she said, "I can't go tomorrow night."

"You can't?"

"No, It's Millcott's holiday party. All the stores are open till midnight. Sometimes the whole thing doesn't wrap up until after one. Wish you could come."

"I'd like to."

"I know, but you have to play."

He shrugged. "You never know. I might be able to slip away early. Sometimes I can get somebody to sit in for a few sets. Like the night of your Mom's party."

"Oh. How do you manage that? I mean wouldn't he have to know all the parts you play, and practice with your band first?"

"Not necessarily. We have charts for all the tunes we do. We don't use musicians who can't read charts."

"What's a chart?"

"It's like a piece of music, with the outline of the tune on it. All the chords are written in."

Later that night after playing, they went up to Scott's place and he cooked her breakfast there.

"Not bad," she said. "But I think the eggs are a little better at the diner."

"Is that right?" he said sarcastically.

"Yep, no question about it. Maybe if you just tried cooking them just a little longer, they wouldn't be so …. gooey." She made a face.

He shrugged. "O.K., so cooking's not my long suit. I have other talents."

"Really?" Rian looked at him coyly. "I haven't seen them lately."

Scotty stopped laughing, and looked back. Their eyes met for a long time. Slowly, he moved his chair nearer to hers.

"Well, let me show you some," he said softly as he started to kiss her. Then he stopped and backed his chair away. "Oh, wait, I forgot. You don't like gooey."

"Scot-ty."

He laughed. Then he stood up, and pulled her up with him. He put his hand under her chin, tilted her face up and kissed her. Then he pulled her head to his chest. She could feel his heart pounding, or maybe it was hers. They stayed that way for a moment, but then slowly he let her go, turned around and walked out of the room.

Rian watched him as he left.

When he returned a few minutes later, he was carrying an acoustic guitar. He slumped down on the couch and started finger-picking it.

Rian looked at him. "What are you doing?"

He started humming along with the music. Then he stopped. "I'm showing you my other talents," he said, his eyes on the guitar.

"You are so weird sometimes."

He continued playing, still not looking at her. His voice sounded serious. "Rian, did you know I once played in Nashville, with a country band? Bet you didn't know that, did you?"

Rian couldn't quite figure out what this whole scene was about. "Nope."

He was quiet for a minute. "Well I guess there's a lot more you need to know about me, and a lot more I need to learn about you."

Rian looked at him curiously. Now she understood. *He still doesn't trust my feelings,* she thought. *Not yet. He likes me a lot, but he's not sure where I'm coming from.* On some level, she was grateful that he was taking things slowly, at least sexually. But now that she was feeling more relaxed with their relationship, she was ready to move on.

She no longer experienced the awful guilt which had kept her from seeing him all those months. She was healing, and she wanted to convince him of that. But they'd only been seeing each other for such a short time. Even though she was enjoying the relationship, there were still some lingering doubts and fears to overcome, and she wondered if he was still troubled about that too?

It's always the same when you start sleeping together, she thought. *Either you get very serious, or the relationship fizzles out ... and I'm not ready for either ... not yet anyway.*

Ivy had spent a lot of time with Morgana and Dru. They had visited with Viviene, and she, in turn, had introduced them to Caitlin. Ivy and Caitlin really hit it off.

During one of their conversations, Ivy said. "Tell me, Caitlin, don't you find living in a house with all these crystals mind-boggling? The energy here is so intense!"

"No, I'm used to it. I've collected the crystals slowly, you see."

They all discussed the circle they did last summer when Caitlin was in Ireland.

"I've heard something about it," said Caitlin. "I've also heard that you are quite a psychic," she said to Ivy.

"It comes when it comes. I can't always depend on it."

"Oh, you're too modest," said Morgana. "I've seen you call, and I've seen it answer."

"Only sometimes. Sometimes, nothing happens at all."

One afternoon, Ivy and Morgana went shopping. At lunch, Ivy said cautiously. "What were you parents like? There's a picture of your family hanging in the room I'm staying in."

"Well, my mom was great. When she was young,

she wanted to become a doctor. Her father wouldn't hear of it. Then she fell in love with a drama major at college and her father broke that up, too. Took her right out of school."

Ivy nodded sympathetically. "What was your father like?"

"J.T.?" She shrugged. "He was very nice, sure of himself ... kind of traditional, I guess." Then she paused. "I really wasn't that close to him ... you know."

"Why was that?"

"I don't know. I guess I was more like my mother. Unconventional, different. Elizabeth was more like dad. Conservative.. quiet."

"In the photograph, I noticed Elizabeth looked a lot like your father. Dad once told me you and your mom went to New York frequently. I grew up there you know."

"Yes, Dru told me. My mother took me to New York many times. She had lots of friends there. We always got tickets to the new musicals. Mom loved them."

"And Elizabeth? Did she go too?"

"No. She never would ... Elizabeth didn't like big cities ... and she was older then. She was already dating my brother-in-law, Dave. She never wanted to go."

Ivy hesitated. "Your mother remarried a man from New York, didn't she?"

"Why, yes. How did you know?"

"I guess my dad told me." Ivy had since found out from Kevin that his grandmother had indeed married a man named *Carl. Carl Meriden. Meriden ... Myrddin. That fit too.*

"Did you know him very well before your mom and he got married?"

Morgana looked at Ivy curiously. "Yes, I did. He was a famous playwright. I always saw him when we went to New York."

Ivy leaned a little across the table. "Could he possibly have been the man that your mother loved as a young girl?"

Morgana cocked her head to one side and smiled. "Perhaps."

"I wonder why it took them so long to get together?"

"Oh, Ivy, in those days ... .it would have been scandalous!"

"Did you like him?"

"Yes, he was a dear man."

"Is he still alive?"

"Yes. He lives in New York. Still writes a play once in a while too, I've heard. Ivy, why all the questions? What are you trying to say?"

Ivy looked up at Morgana slowly. "I ... I'm sorry, I didn't mean to pry. It's just that ... " Ivy was losing her nerve.

Morgana had great respect for Ivy's intuition. But she also had her own talents. Now she felt that Ivy had some information, but was hesitant to share it. *Why? What does she know?*

Ivy felt sick. How could she reveal what she had found?

Morgana asked. "It must be something about Carl isn't it?"

Ivy looked up, then she hesitated. "Yes."

"Does it also have something to do with my mother?"

"Yes … .and you also."

"What, for heavens sake?"

Ivy told Morgana about the photograph.

"You found a photograph of my mother, me, and Carl?"

"Yes. It was hidden inside one of the carousels."

"Carousels? What are you talking about?"

"Kevin showed me your mother's carousel collection, and the other night I was looking at them."

"And?"

"Each one is different you know. Some revolved, some were music boxes."

"Yes, Ivy, I know all that … but what is this leading to?"

Ivy was feeling very uncomfortable. She hadn't realized how awkward it would be telling Morgana that she had fooled around with her mother's carousel collection. "Did you know that one of them had a tiny panel underneath … ?"

"A panel?"

"Yes, when I ran my fingers over it, a panel sprung open."

Morgana frowned.

Ivy continued. "There was a photograph inside … . It was of you and your mother and a man … but the man … was not your father."

"Really? I wasn't aware of any photograph like that."

"You were a very small child in the picture."

"I just can't imagine why the photo was hidden in the carousel." She shrugged. "But I guess if it was … she was probably hiding it from my father."

"Did your mother ever talk to you about her collection?"

"Not too much. Everybody knew about it."

Morgana looked at Ivy curiously. She could see that Ivy was having a difficult time. She reached across the table and took her hand.

"What are you trying to tell me, Ivy?"

Ivy was losing her nerve. Then for some reason she thought of the relationship she had developed with her own father, how much knowing Dru had meant to her, and how empty her life would have been if the two had never met. The feelings she had for her father gave her courage.

"There was an inscription, Morgana."

"Yes, go on. What did it say?"

Ivy could go no further. "I think it would be better if you read it yourself."

Morgana was beginning to feel nervous and vulnerable. *What was Ivy thinking of, going through my mother's things? What did she discover? It isn't like her to pry. Maybe there is a side to her that I don't know.* Morgana called for the check and paid it.

Then she spoke to Ivy a little icily, "I think we should have a look at that photograph, don't you?"

✻ ✻ ✻ ✻

CHAPTER 32

Rosemary
for Remembrance

As Morgana drove Ivy back to the house, Ivy felt guilty and depressed. Why had she pushed all this stuff with Morgana? It was none of her business, and so unlike her, but she felt something urging her on. She sat staring out of the car window at the winter scenery, but it did nothing to cheer her up.

What must Morgana think of me now? she thought. *Some shadowy figure following her around, prying into her business?* Ivy thought she'd never live it down. She regretted not listening to Dru. *Dad was absolutely right,* she thought.

They finally pulled up the driveway and silently walked to the house. Elizabeth heard them come in and started talking to Morgana

Ivy was grateful for the time. She went upstairs and into her room, into Marianne's room. Then, she slowly walked over to the cabinet. *Why do the carousels beckon me so?* For a few moments she sat in the window seat staring at the cabinet. Then she thought, *Maybe there is something else, something more.* Ivy opened the cabinet again and began to examine the ornaments.

There is a puzzle here, and it's not just about Morgana. After a while, something slowly began to take shape in Ivy's mind. *Why didn't I see it before? The horses! The carousels. The horses ... Rhiannon. There must be something here connected to Rian.*

The photograph had thrown her off the track. That wasn't the only secret. There was another one, perhaps a more important one, but Ivy couldn't figure out what it was.

She went over to her canvas handbag, pulled out her cards, and threw them on the bed. The first card was the Knight of Cups; a poet an artist, but possibly deception too ... the second card was ... another knight, this time the Knight of Swords. Whenever Ivy saw two knights fall side by side facing each other, she read them as some sort of confrontation ... .then a third card; eight of cups ... shattered emotions. She threw two more ... The other cards made little sense to her. She put them away. The rest of the answer did not lie in the cards. It lay in these carousels.

There was a knock at her door. Ivy closed the cabinet and opened the door. Morgana came in and walked over to the window. She was quiet for a moment, and then she spoke. "Ivy ... I'm sorry if I spoke harshly."

"You're sorry? Why? I'm the one who is sorry."

"No, it was an accident. If we didn't want the carousels touched we should have locked the cabinet."

"It was locked."

"Then how ... "

"The key was on top of the desk."

"Seems like somebody wanted you to open it."

"Still, I shouldn't have."

"Listen, Ivy, I'll get right to the point. I'm not one who believes in coincidences. I think things happen for reasons, the key out like that." She saw the key lying on the desk and picked it up. "This one?"

"Yes."

"Where is the photograph?"

"Still in the carousel."

"May I have it?"

Ivy took out the ornament and gave it to her.

Morgana felt for the groove and pushed on it. As before, it sprung open. She reached into the little carousel with her fingers, felt for the photograph, and pulled it out.

For a moment, she only stared at it. Then, she turned it over and read the inscription. Her face changed. At first she didn't seem to comprehend what she had read. She recognized herself as a child with her mother and Carl, but the inscription made her feel disconnected. Her head reeled.

"I think I need to sit down." Ivy helped her to the window seat. Morgana said nothing for what seemed an eternity. She just kept looking at the picture, reading the inscription. When she finally did speak, her voice was trembling.

She kept shaking her head. "This is crazy. My mother never mentioned anything like this to me."

"You had no clue?"

"No. I ... don't believe it! Mom would have told me. I know she would have. My mother was a free spirit, a true pagan. If Carl was my father she would have told me!"

"Perhaps not, Morgana. Perhaps there were reasons ... maybe she was afraid of something."

Morgana was silent for a moment, then she spoke. "The only person she feared was her father."

"That's awful."

"He tried to break her. He was a very controlling person, trying to run everyone's life. I told you he broke up their relationship in the first place."

"Why did she go along with it?"

"She was afraid of him. In those days women had no real freedom about such things. What could she do?" Morgana turned away. "He was a tough old man, lived to be nearly ninety, and even then ... I always sensed she was afraid to cross him. But this idea that my mother and Carl were my parents ... " Morgana shook her head. "It's too crazy. I don't know why she'd keep it from me."

"Maybe she was afraid if she told you it would get back to Elizabeth, or worse, to her husband?"

Morgana put the photograph back on the desk. "Maybe it was ... Elizabeth. I can see that being a powerful reason. Elizabeth would never have accepted it." Morgana got very quiet. She walked slowly towards the window and looked out. "I guess ... I'm just not ready to accept it either."

Ivy felt horrible. Why had she meddled? Why didn't she listen to her father and stay out of it?

Finally, she spoke. "I'm ... so sorry ... " She was nearly in tears. "I should never have brought it up. I guess it was because I was separated from my own father for so long."

Morgana turned and faced Ivy. "Perhaps for some reason it was meant for you to find out."

"Perhaps," said Ivy softly, looking straight into Morgana's eyes. "It was meant for you to find out."

Morgana looked startled. Suddenly, she had the feeling that there was something important here she had forgotten. She walked over to the secretary and started tapping her fingers slowly on the desk. Her brow was furrowed.

Then, after a moment or two she began pacing slowly back and forth in the room. She looked past Ivy, and started lightly tapping the knuckles of one of her hands in the palm of the other. Suddenly she turned towards Ivy and snapped her fingers.

"I remember now! When my mother died there was a will ... and she left her carousel collection ... to me."

For a moment, the room they were standing in seemed to disappear. The hush was deafening. Then, Ivy whispered, "Oh, Morgana ... and you left it here?"

"Well, yes ... I thought it belonged in this house ... in this room. I had completely forgotten about it."

"Then perhaps your mother did want you to find the photograph! She must have known you'd discover it."

Morgana was silent again. She just kept shaking her head.

Ivy watched her. "I guess you'll never understand why I opened all this up. I am truly sorry ... that I've hurt you."

"I know you meant well, Ivy. You did it for me, and I'm not angry with you. I'm just very confused at the moment. If it's true, it's a hell of a thing to find out at my age."

Ivy knew that even though Morgana couldn't admit it, she wasn't sure anymore. She also knew that there was nothing more to be gained by going on with it now. It would take time to sink in. She wanted to embrace her, to comfort her, but she was afraid.

Morgana, on the other hand, began to grow calmer.

For that Ivy was relieved. She had hoped if it were at all possible, they could pursue the other part of the riddle, the carousel itself.

It was Morgana who opened the door to that.

"I wonder why my mother collected carousels?' she said after a little while.

"I was going to ask you that. They are so beautiful, I thought you might know."

"No. Not really. They amused her I suppose. My mother collected many different things. She loved antique furniture like this." Morgana pointed to the secretary. "When she moved to New York, she took a few of her favorite pieces, but most of it was just left here. After she died, Carl sent them back to Elizabeth. He said those were her wishes."

"Morgana, do you remember that book you dreamed about, the one Rian had?"

"The Merrywells?"

"Yes."

"Last summer, the night I did the reading out in California, you said you dreamed about that book, and that it had some kind of carousel etched on the front."

"That's right. It did."

"Dad remembered that too. I think there's a connection. Yesterday, I stopped by Rian's store and bought this book. It's called *Ancient Mythology*. Ivy showed Morgana the book.

"Anyway, I looked up carousel, and here's what I found. I'll read it to you: *Fairies Wheel: descended from the Celtic Wheel of Arianrhod. Riders were pre-Christian fairy folk. Their souls were on a karmic cycle.*

"And look at this. *The carousel was, in ancient times,*

a wheel of chariots with Pagan origins. The name Carnival, which is where we find carousels, comes from the old Pagan festivals of the Goddess Carna, who is also the mother of Rein-Carnations. These are the same cycles controlled by the Hindu Goddess; Kali's wheel of karma. In other words, these carousels represented the wheel of karma; fate! They are disguised figurines representing the Old Pagan Religions."

"But what has this to do with Rian?"

"It has to do with your mother and Rian! Rian is connected to the horse. That is her power animal, her totem. My impression is that your mother followed the Old Religion, just as you do, and I think she suspected that Rian was connected to the missing Lady of Annwn ... Rhiannon."

"You seem to know almost everything," said Morgana. "It never crossed my mind that my mother could have known about Rian back then."

"But you admit she did follow the Old Religion?"

"Yes, I admit it, and Carl also. His 'Craft' name is Myrddin. But that is a very private matter. No one must ever find out."

"Then it was your parents at my father's initiation?"

"I don't know. It's possible."

"Why didn't you say anything last summer?"

"At the time, I really didn't make the connection. Myrddin is not an unusual Craft name. Many men who belong to the old Mystery Schools use it."

"That's true ... .but the woman, she was older; she was from New York!"

"Ivy, that still doesn't prove anything. Look Carl was very ... very private about this."

"How do you feel about it now?"

"I'm not sure anymore."

"Morgana, listen. When you told us about your dream of Rian and the book, you said there was something familiar about it. Do you still feel that way?"

"Yes, but I can't remember anymore than that. It was just a feeling."

"We both know that feelings and intuitions should not be dismissed that easily."

"If what you say about Carl and me is true, and I'm not saying I believe it, I don't ever want Elizabeth to find out. She would never understand. Don't you see, for the first time in our lives, we are close!"

"I understand, that you feel caught in the middle, but Elizabeth need never know. Besides, much more than moral judgments are at stake here. We may be talking about Rian's safety, her life! Don't forget what happened to your sister!"

Morgana would never forget that. She walked over to the writing desk, picked up the photograph again and stared at it. Suddenly, and without any provocation, the carousel fell off the desk, on to the floor, and shattered.

Morgana jumped. "How did that happen?"

Ivy knelt down, picked up one of the pieces of the carousel and held it in her hand for a moment. But then something very strange began to happen. A familiar scent began rising slowly from the broken ornament. Ivy noticed it first, then Morgana. There was no doubt about it, the scent of rosemary was filling the room!

Ivy looked up at Morgana and stared into her eyes. Then she spoke. "The same way it happened to Rian, when she received her athame."

Morgana looked startled.

Ivy pointed to the vial of oil. "Did that vial belong to your mother?"

"Yes."

"I think you should smell it," Ivy said gently.

Morgana opened the vial and sniffed. "Rosemary. It must have been my mother's own personal ritual oil."

For a moment she just stared down at the broken carousel. Then she knelt down next to Ivy and picked up a few of the pieces herself. "You're right, Ivy. It happened in the same way Rian received her athame. Perhaps my mother is trying to tell me something."

✻✻✻✻

CHAPTER 33

Midnight Madness

Rian was in the store very early. Tonight was the Millcott holiday party, also known as Midnight Madness. Thousands of people would be in town milling about, buying Christmas presents, and taking advantage of the many bars and restaurants. For a town as small as Millcott, thousands of people made it very crowded.

Rian and Kevin had been decorating the day before, and the shop looked terrific.

"Well, Kev, I think I've finally got the aromatherapy section the way I want it. What do you think?"

"Looks great, Ri. Those tree branches hanging over the shelves really look good."

"Coffee break. Want some?"

"Thanks."

After Rian left, Kevin continued rearranging some of the merchandise so that everything looked its best. For some, this day and night would be the most profitable of the Christmas season. It was advertised on the radio, and flyers and posters went out to the outlying neighborhoods. Aside from that, most people near the town knew of it. It had become a Millcott Christmas tradition.

Before Rian got back with the coffee, Caitlin popped in.

"Hi, Kevin. Here are the spices Rian wanted for the hot cider!" She put a bag down on a table.

"Thanks, Cat."

"Listen, don't forget to drop by tonight. I've got some special food. You'll love it! Is Viviene reading?"

"Uh-huh, later. She'll be here about six o'clock."

"Looks like snow again, don't you think?"

"Maybe. It could slow down business if it's heavy," he said. Kevin looked out the front window.

In Millcott, the streets were so hilly that when it snowed, only a four-wheel drive could adequately function. His car had been stuck on those icy streets more than once while he spent the night in the store. He kept a sleeping bag upstairs for just such an emergency. "Let's hope it holds off till after midnight."

"I hope we have just a little light, dry snow, Caitlin purred. "It would be perfect."

Just then Rian came back with the coffee. "Hi, Caitlin! Oh, you've brought the spices!"

"Yes. Everything you asked for. Cinnamon sticks, ginger, all-spice, and nutmeg."

"Great! We'll have some incredible wassail tonight! I really appreciate it," Rian said, looking into the bag.

Caitlin's family had a commercial herb farm just outside town. Often, Rian bought many oils, potpourris and herbs from her.

"Ummm ... the store smells so good!" said Caitlin. "Just like Christmas should."

"Yeah, I think so."

"You've done a great job. Everything looks terrific!"

"I wanna come down and see yours a little later," said Rian.

"O.K. I'm almost done decorating. Just a few final touches of glitter and sparkle here and there." Then Caitlin said more quietly. "Rian, how's everything .... going?

Suddenly, Rian felt annoyed with this gentle girl. She didn't want to discuss any of her rituals outside a circle. *I'm beginning to feel like Viviene now,* she thought to herself. Rian looked at her awkwardly, and Caitlin got the message.

"Well, guess I'll get back," said Caitlin. "Bye."

I hurt her feelings, thought Rian. She liked Caitlin, and that made Rian feel bad.

Rian ran towards the porch. "Cat!" Caitlin turned around.

"I'm sorry," Rian uttered. "Please try and understand."

"No problem! I do understand," Caitlin smiled and left.

Maybe she really does, Rian thought hopefully.

Morgana, Robin, and Ivy picked up Dru at the motel, and caught up with Viviene in Millcott. They had a buffet lunch in town, and Robin ordered mimosas for everybody. He had to fly back to California that day.

Dru had been feeling ill again, and Ivy was a little concerned about him.

"I just have some off days once in awhile," he told Ivy. "Stop worrying so much."

Ivy knew it was unsettling for her father to be around alcohol, even at a restaurant. That had been the most difficult addiction to break. As a result, they rarely dined out or socialized.

Ivy knew her father hadn't attended any twelve-step

programs since he had been in Millcott. She meant to ask Rian if she knew of any nearby.

At lunch, Ivy and Morgana told Dru about the carousel and the rosemary. Morgana asked, "Do you think you would recognize a picture of the woman who attended your initiation and gave you the book?

He shook his head slowly. "I don't know. It was more than twenty years ago."

Morgana took out a photograph booklet she kept in her purse and opened it to a picture of her mother. She handed it to Dru.

He looked at the photo carefully. "I just don't know Morgana. The woman I met was very quiet ... and hooded. I really didn't spend much time with her."

Morgana showed him another photograph of Marianne. It was a close up, and she was wearing a winter coat with a hood. Dru was trying. He looked at the photograph intensely. "The eyes," he said. "Something about her eyes." Then he shrugged. "Could be."

"You think it is?"

"She looks familiar, but that could be because she reminds me of you, Morgana."

"Do you think it's at all possible it was she who gave you the book?"

Dru hesitated and sighed. "It's possible, but as I told you last summer, this woman barely spoke to me. She sat very quietly with Myrddin. When the ceremony was over, she walked up to me and handed me a gift. I do remember her saying something complementary about my library, and that I might find the gift .... interesting. I put her present with all the others. By the time I got around to opening them, she was gone. I never even got a chance to thank her."

"If it was Marianne who gave you the book, then she had to know about Rian. Perhaps she gave you the book to awaken her! A kind of Initiation Quest."

Dru nodded and gestured with his hand. "It's possible."

"How did you know Myrddin?"

"I didn't know him well. Come to think of it, I think Chris introduced us."

Ivy looked up. "Were they good friends?"

"They might have been. I know Chris used to live in New York. Back in those days magickal people were very secretive about themselves."

"If Myrddin trusted Chris, he might have told him about Rian."

"That's true, and Chris might have told the ... "

"Rag Bone Man ... that's what Rian calls him now." said Morgana looking over at Viviene.

"I want to show you something" said Dru. Very carefully, he revealed part of a small doll hidden under his jacket.

Viviene looked astonished. "Dru, is that a poppet?"

He smiled. "It is. And inside it is a link from our creature's clothing."

Ivy turned pale. "Dad, what are you doing with it here?"

"It wouldn't do for the maid to find it in the hotel would it?

"No ... but ... " Ivy shook her head. What could he be thinking?

"How did you ever get the link?" asked Viviene.

Dru explained to the others about the trip to Chris's

farmhouse, and what they had found there. "I kept the piece of cloth and made a poppet," said Dru quietly.

"What are you doing with it?" asked Morgana.

"A little disarming," Dru answered.

"Do you think it's working?" asked Viviene.

"Perhaps not yet ... I feel the connection growing stronger, though."

"I really don't think we should be talking about this here," Ivy said. There was an edge in her voice.

Morgana agreed and changed the subject. "What about Rian? I wonder if she is doing anything to protect herself?"

"I believe she is," said Ivy, "but I don't know what. I do sometimes sense he's nearby."

Morgana shuddered. "I hope you're wrong."

"She rarely is," said Dru looking grim.

The group chatted a little while longer as they finished their brunch. Then, Dru asked to be taken back to his motel because he felt tired. They all left the pub. Morgana dropped off Dru at his motel. When the others got home, they met up with Rian.

She ran into the room. "Hi, everybody! Gotta make some hot cider for tonight. I'm on my way to the kitchen!"

Morgana wanted to talk to her, but Rian didn't have time. "I have to get back as soon as this stuff is ready. See you later."

Morgana went upstairs. She sat in her room thinking for a little while. She finally picked up the phone and called the railroad station. An express left for New York in less than forty minutes, so that would put her there about six. Then she looked in her little address book for

Carl's telephone number. She had seen nothing of him since her mother's death. He did send her a Christmas card every year, but that was about it. Suddenly, she felt a little guilty for not keeping in touch. After all, he had always been generous towards her when she was a child, and even if he wasn't her father, he had been a good husband to her mother.

She called. A woman answered.

"Yes?"

"Is Carl Meriden there?

"Who is calling?"

Morgana recognized the voice. It was Juliana; Carl and Marianne's housekeeper.

"Is this Juliana?"

"Yes."

"Julie. Hi! This is Morga … This is Marty. Marianne's daughter. Do you remember me?"

"Why, of course I remember you! How are you these days?"

"Oh, fine." They chatted briefly. "I know you want to talk to Mr. Meriden. Wait a minute, and I'll get him."

A moment later Carl answered the phone. He sounded very happy to hear from her. They talked for a few minutes, and then Morgana told him. "Carl, I'm coming up to New York today. I thought I might stop over and see you, if you have time."

"My dear, at my age that's all I do have! I'd like very much to see you."

The conversation was short. He was home, and he would see her. Morgana told Elizabeth that she had a million errands to run, and that she was going to visit an old friend. "I might be home very late. Rian drove in with Kevin today, and left me her car. If she calls, tell her I'll try to see her later, O.K.?"

The day wore on. Viviene came by a little earlier than expected. She hoped to catch Kevin. By the time she arrived, Rian had brought the cider back and picked up refreshments. She had already arranged the cheeses and crackers on a tray, and put the spice cake Elizabeth had made along side it. Everything was laid out on a table with spiced apples, pine branches, and red ribbons.

"The table looks delectable!" said Viviene.

"Thanks. Try the wassail."

Viviene ladled some into a hot-cup and tasted it. "Ummm."

"Hey, Viv, I have to run down to Caitlin's for a minute. Can you watch things?"

"Where's Kevin?"

"He went down to the harbor to pick up some gift items from the other store. He'll be back soon."

Rian put on her coat and started out the door. Viviene noticed the silver pin on her collar. "Like your new pin; where'd you get it?"

Rian was caught off guard. Viviene looked at her curiously. "What's the matter?"

"Nothing. Scotty gave it to me."

"Scotty?"

"I told you about him."

"Yes, he's the one you met at the ocean."

"That's right."

"So, are you two seeing each other again?

"Kind of. We've just started dating."

"When did all this happen?"

"He came in the store last week. It was the day you were here. And then he started calling. . .you know. Anyway, he gave me this pin for Christmas. It's weird too, because I dreamed he gave it to me before he did!"

"Really? Let's see." Viviene looked at the silver pin. "Three horses ... how'd he know?"

"Know what?"

"About the horses?"

"Oh, he doesn't know. I don't talk about that with him."

"Just a coincidence?"

"What are you getting at?"

"The horses, Rian! He must be very intuitive."

"Perhaps he is."

Viviene looked at Rian curiously. "So you dreamed about the pin ... ?"

"Yes, the night before he gave it to me."

Viviene reached over as if she were going to touch Rian's pin, but Rian quickly backed off. Viviene smiled. "I'd say you are definitely coming around."

"Meaning?"

"Meaning that your rituals are developing your psychic powers."

Rian smiled. "I feel that way too."

"Good. I've noticed the change."

"You have?"

"Yes, there's something different about you."

Rian smiled again, then grew more intense. For a moment, she didn't say anything, as though she were trying to make up her mind about something. "You know Viv, I think ... I might be falling in love with this guy," she said

Viviene looked at her. She wasn't really surprised. "Yes ... maybe that is part of it ... but there's something else." She hesitated, but then she said more lightly. "Hey, Rian, don't you think you should go do your errand at Caitlin's?"

Rian looked at Viviene. She'd almost forgotten. Viviene's affirmation gave her a sense of security, even pride. As she walked up toward Caitlin's store, she remembered when she could have cared less about Viviene's opinion. Now it meant a lot to her.

At Penn. Station, N.Y.C., Morgana got off the train, walked up the long flight of steps and went outside. At the curb, taxis were lined up bumper to bumper waiting for passengers. Morgana opened the door to one of them and gave him the Park Avenue address. The driver screeched away from the curb and drove off.

The impressive apartment building looked very much as she remembered it. There was building going on across the street where an older structure was being renovated.

As she walked through the door Morgana felt twinges of fear. On the train she was filled with both dread and excitement. Now, the anticipation was giving way to marked tension. What if he never wanted her to know? What if it were he who wanted the secret kept. She hadn't thought of it that way. In her mind, it was always her mother's secret. What if the whole thing were not true ... ? Then why the inscription on the photograph? Was it some cruel joke her mother wanted to play on her father? Why hide it in the carousel then? No ... Ivy was right. Something was here. This man could be her father.

She rang the doorbell. An elderly man opened the door, and invited her into the apartment. She looked around. Everything was as she remembered it. The beautiful art work, the magnificent thick oriental rugs, the Country French furniture, and the rich colored fabrics that permeated the room.

"Here, let me take your coat!" He was quite tall. His thinning, silver hair fell casually across his forehead and curled just a little long behind his ears.

Morgana felt awkward, but smiled and greeted him warmly. She suddenly realized that she hadn't seen him since her mother's funeral, which was over five years ago. *He must be nearly eighty by now,* Morgana thought, *but he doesn't look it.* She remembered how dark and thick his eyebrows were, how they matched his mustache and the tips of his neatly trimmed gray beard. Now his eyebrows were tinged with white, and his mustache and dark edges of his beard had faded to a speckle. Still, his age had not dimmed what a handsome man he once was. Then, she noticed he was using a cane.

He was very cordial, very happy to see her. They talked about old times, about Marianne. She told him about her life in California and about her family. He told her about a play he was currently working on.

In her handbag the photograph remained hidden. Morgana was waiting for the right time to bring it out. About seven o'clock, Juliana served dinner ....

Rian walked quickly down Main St. and entered Caitlin's shop.

"She's back in the house," a young clerk told her.

"Thanks."

Outside again, Rian went around through the stone passage and up the steps to Caitlin's house. She tapped on the window, and Caitlin opened the door.

"Hi, Rian."

"Hi, Cat. May I come in for a minute?"

"Sure … " Caitlin stepped aside and Rian walked into the crystal house.

She looked at this warm and generous young woman for a moment. "Cat, I owe you an apology. I'm very sorry if I seemed insensitive earlier."

"No. You were absolutely right. We should never talk about such things … out in the open."

Rian admittedly felt more protected here than in her shop, but she still didn't wish to open up a conversation about her ritual work. She smiled at Caitlin and then reached into her coat pocket and pulled out a pretty little wrapped box.

"Cat, you've been a very good friend. I hope you like this."

Caitlin looked surprised. She hesitated for a moment. Then she reached out and accepted the gift. "Thank you, Rian."

"Go ahead," Rian urged. "Open it!"

Caitlin undid the wrappings carefully, and pulled out a beautiful gold locket, and a wide smile came across her face. "Oh, Rian, it's beautiful! How did you know I wanted it?"

"Ummm..little bird."

"You bought it at Simone's place!" Caitlin was referring to the exclusive Heirloom Jewelry shop in Millcott. "Thanks so much, Rian. I love it!"

"You've given me a lot more, letting my friends stay

here and everything. That was very generous."

"I was glad I could help."

Rian gave Caitlin a little hug. "You did; you really did." Then Rian let her go. "I'd love to stay and chat a while, but I have to get back to the shop. Viviene's watching it for me. Maybe I'll see you later, O.K.?"

"Oh, Rian, I almost forgot. After the shops close, I'm having a little party! "Just a few people; try and come, will you?"

Rian hesitated. "I'd really like to … but Ivy, Dru, and Morgana are coming down later, and I might have a date, too."

"Oh, that's all right. Bring them with you!"

"Are you sure?"

She smiled. "Yes, no problem. Oh, and please bring your date. I'm dying to meet him."

Rian laughed. "He'll probably be blown away by this house. I promise, I will definitely try and stop by."

Carl and Morgana finished their dinner. Morgana thought the conversation had gone extremely well. They had reminisced about the old days and the lovely times they spent together. Carl seemed to miss Marianne very much.

Well, thought Morgana, it's now or never. She reached into her handbag and took out the photograph. For a moment she just stared down at it. Then she said, "Carl, I didn't just come up here for a friendly chat."

He smiled. "I guessed that, Marty." Carl's voice was still very rich and deep especially when he was being serious. "What's really on your mind?"

"I wanted to show you something." Not knowing

any easy way to prepare him, she simply handed him the picture.

Carl took a pair of horn-rimmed glasses out of his inside coat pocket, put them on, and looked closely at the photograph. After a long pause he looked up at Morgana and asked. "Where did you find this?"

"I didn't. A guest of ours, who is staying in Marianne's old room, found it. It was hidden in one of my mother's carousels, and ... she showed it to me."

Carl just kept shaking his head as he looked down at the photograph. It seemed like forever to Morgana before he finally spoke. "Your mother never wanted you to find out."

Morgana felt a tremor run through her body. It was true. Finally she was able to ask. "Why?"

"I think mainly it was to protect you and your family. I promised her I would never tell you. Before she died, I thought she might have a change of heart." He shook his head again. "But she died so suddenly. There wasn't time."

Morgana was speechless, but she thought, *She must have wanted me to find out sooner or later, otherwise why did she will the carousels to me?*

Carl looked at her seriously. He began speaking slowly in those deep rich tones. "I want you to know that I loved your mother ... from the beginning." He shrugged. "Circumstances kept us apart, and it was very difficult. Finally, we gave in to our feelings." He gestured towards her. "I wanted your mother to break with J.T. then, but she couldn't. I think she was afraid of hurting Elizabeth, and then, of course, there was her husband, and her father. After a lot of mental anguish, your mother decided it would be best to allow J.T. to believe that you were his child. I was against it, but in the final analysis … " He paused and looked at Morgana. "It had to be her decision … "

He looked sad for a moment. His head was cast down, his elbows resting on the table. Then, he looked up straight into her eyes and tried to smile. "Perhaps fate will be kinder … next time around, humm?"

Morgana only nodded. She was feeling as though part of her life had been turned upside down. They talked for a long time, and gradually it got easier. Finally, she could see that Carl was growing tired.

Juliana brought coffee. "Decaffeinated?" he asked, looking up at her grimly. "You bet," she answered and smiled. "And here, don't forget these." She gave him some pills. Then she left the room

Morgana couldn't help noticing the little exchange. *He's not well,* she thought. She decided to ask him one more question and then leave. "It really has nothing to do with you and me," she commented.

Car smiled and poured them both another cup of coffee. "In a way, I'm a little relieved that it doesn't. What's on your mind?"

"This question may sound a bit strange to you, but I need to ask. Do you remember my mother giving a book to a man named Dru at an Initiation ceremony a long time ago?"

"Dru?" Carl looked surprised.

"Yes, you knew him, didn't you?"

"I did. He lives in San Francisco. Do you know him, too?"

"Yes, I've known him for a long time."

Carl hesitated. "I heard he was ill. How is he?"

"Much better. He has a daughter who has helped him quite a bit."

Carl paused as though he were trying to make some connections in his mind. Then he smiled. "I had nearly forgotten he had a child. But I seem to be getting off the track. You asked me about a book of your mother's?"

"Yes, it was called 'The Merrywells.' It was kind of a … journal, written in long-hand."

Carl nodded. "I remember that book well. Your mother did give it to Dru, but not at an initiation ceremony." He gestured. "It was right here."

"Are you sure?"

Carl smiled. "I think I still have a pretty good memory, Marty."

Marty laughed. "I never thought for one minute you didn't." Then she asked, "Did you attend his initiation?"

Carl looked at his daughter curiously. "Why do you ask?"

"We've been trying to find that book for a long time. Someone stole it from Dru."

He looked at Morgana. "Perhaps it was only lost."

"No, it was definitely stolen."

"Really?" He studied Morgana's face for a moment. "Marty, why am I getting the impression that this is a little more serious than a missing book?"

Carl's statement startled Morgana. What does he know? she wondered. She wanted to ask more, but Carl seemed to be getting very tired. She noticed his hand holding the cup of coffee had begun to tremble a little.

Just then Juliana came in and told them it was time for him to go to bed. "He just got out of the hospital a few days ago," she said quietly to Morgana.

"Oh, I'm sorry. I didn't know." Then she looked over at Carl. "Why didn't you say anything?"

"No, no, no ... I'm fine!" he gestured, "I'm really O.K. Just a little tired that's all. I wouldn't have missed this meeting for anything. I'm so glad to see you again."

"I feel the same, Carl. I really do." She kissed him on the cheek. Juliana went to the closet to get Morgana's things.

"Marty," Carl said as he helped Morgana on with her coat, "Your mother gave Dru that book right here." He looked at her as if he wanted her to understand something important.

Morgana said good-bye to Carl and promised to visit him again very soon. Juliana called downstairs and had the doorman hail her a cab.

During the train ride home she kept hearing Carl's words: *Your mother gave him the book right here.*

Poor man ... he's old, Morgana thought. He forgot all about the initiation. Still, the train rumbled his words into her mind ... *gave him the book right here ... gave him the book right here.* Morgana sighed and took out a magazine to read.

Rian left Caitlin's house and hurried back down to her shop. As she went in, Viviene was holding the phone. "For you, Rian ... ."

Rian took the phone. "Hello. Hello?..Apothecary." No one answered. Then, click.

"Wrong number."

"Really? The guy asked for you."

Rian felt annoyed. She put the phone down and

walked over to pour herself some hot cider. Suddenly she froze. *Oh shit!* she thought. *It's him! What's that number? Star-something.* "Viv, what's the number you punch to get someone back?"

"You mean star 69?"

"Yeah, that's it." Rian punched in the three digits. Then she heard the whiny siren. "The number you have dialed is not in service. Please hang up and ... "

"Damn!" Rian slammed down the phone.

"Rian, what is it? Who was that?"

"It's him! Him! He never gives up, does he?"

"Has he been calling you?"

"Yes! The first night I started doing my ritual alone, he called several times. It was late at night. He kept waking me up every time I fell asleep."

"God, he knows then."

"How? I never said a word. I've been so careful!"

"I don't know, Rian, but he's picked you up."

"Viviene, remember I told you earlier that Scotty gave me this pin in a dream, the night I started the ritual?"

"Yes."

"Well, every time I'd slip into a dream, the phone would ring. Finally I dialed star 69. The recorder came on and told me it wasn't a working number. That's when I knew!"

"And it was during one of those dreams, that you received this pin?"

"Yes, just as I told you before."

Viviene was quiet for a moment. Then she said. "Remember, I told you before that performing rituals opens you up!"

"Yes."

"That pin could be a protective amulet; a gift from the Otherworld."

"Like the athame?"

"It's possible."

"I hadn't thought of it that way." Rian pushed back her hair. "It just gets me down sometimes ... he never gives up!"

"But the good part is, you're growing stronger! Your fetch is protecting you. Now the creature can't get into your dreamtime anymore, so he's trying to influence you when you're awake, which is much less effective."

"He knows when you are sleeping ... ..He knows when you're awake ... .like Santa Claus, for God's sake!" Rian remarked angrily.

The door opened. Kevin came in. Rian walked away. She knew that Viviene had wanted some time alone with him. Rian hadn't always liked Viviene, but she felt differently now. She not only liked her, but also trusted her instincts.

Rian also suspected that Kevin had a heavy 'thing' for Ivy. She wondered how it would all turn out. She believed Ivy liked Kevin, but how much she couldn't tell. To her, Ivy was a thing apart. She seemed to sort of go in and out, as though she lived in two worlds. *Perhaps she did*, Rian thought.

Though the day was busy enough, it wasn't until later that customers really started filling the streets. By eight o'clock, the town was like a zoo. Rian and Kevin could hardly check people out fast enough. An hour later Rian took a break and walked outside for a few minutes. The air was brisk and cold and a few snow-flakes had begun to fall.

Rian heard someone call her name. When she

looked around she saw a familiar face, but she couldn't put a name to it.

"My name's Rudy. I play with Scott's band."

Rian looked at him again. "You do?"

"Well, sometimes."

"Oh, I remember you ... you're the new drummer."

"Not yet. I'm still auditioning."

"Scotty said he liked the way you played."

"Yeah?" Rudy seemed pleased.

"Uh-huh. I had the impression he was definitely impressed with you," she smiled.

"I appreciate you passing that on to me. It's a great band. I hope to play in it full-time soon."

Rian backed off. Maybe it wasn't her place to say anything. "Well, I have no idea if he's made any decision yet, but he did say that you were good." She smiled.

"Well, thanks for that. Oh, bye the way, I've got a message for you from Scott."

"What's that?"

"That he'd be down to see you. He got someone to sit in for him later. Man, did I have trouble parking. I don't know why he couldn't have told you that on the phone!"

"He sent you all the way down here to tell me that?"

Rudy grinned at Rian's expression. "Hell, no. I'm playing at the Roadhouse tonight." He pointed up the street.

Rian made a face at his little joke. Then she laughed. "Do you play there regularly?"

"Only when they need a drummer. Now 'days a lot of bands use synthesizers with built-in drum machines."

"Oh. I guess that's not too good for drummers, huh?"

"No, but it's cheaper," he said wistfully. "Well, gotta go. We start soon."

"See ya!" Rian was getting cold. She rubbed her hands together and walked back into the store. Business was the best she'd ever had. Morgana was back; Scotty was coming. Things were working out. *If only that creature weren't still hanging on.*

Rian returned to the counter, and Kevin took a break. Viv had been reading cards all evening upstairs in the office.

Scotty ought to be down soon, thought Rian.

The phone rang, and Rian picked it up. It was Scott.

"I've got a slight problem."

Rian felt a touch of disappointment. "What's wrong?"

"The guy that was supposed to sit in for me just called. He's tied up and can't get here 'till the last set. Think that would be too late to come over?"

"I don't think so. You'll miss the shopping, but a friend of mine is having a little house-party up the street after, so come anyway."

"O.K. See you later then."

After Kevin came back in, Rian called home. Her mother picked up the phone.

"Hi, Mom? Have Morgana and Ivy left yet?"

"No. Morgana's been out all day, but Ivy is here."

"O.K., Let me speak to her."

"Hi!" said Ivy. "How's it going?"

"Busy. When are you all coming over?"

"Morgana's not here. She went out."

"Yeah, Mom just told me. Well, anyway, Caitlin is giving a party after the stores close. She would like you and Dru to come."

"Well, that's nice of her. Sounds like fun! I'll see what Dad wants to do."

"O.K., see you later … "

In Philadelphia, Morgana's train took a ten-minute break. She got off, used one of the telephones along the wall and called her house. The line was busy. She waited a minute and then dialed again. Ivy picked right up.

"Hello, Ivy, it's Morgana. Don't say anything. I'm on my way home from New York. I have a few minutes here in Philly, and I wanted to touch base with you. Why don't you and Dru go on to Millcott. I'll meet you there later."

" Morgana, did you see Carl?"

"Yes, but I don't have time to get into that right now."

"O.K., I understand. How will I get into Millcott?"

"Ask Elizabeth. I'm sure she wouldn't mind loaning you her car for a few hours."

She hesitated. "I guess I could ask her. By the way, Rian called. She said there's a party at Caitlin's after the stores close, so if you get back late, meet her over there."

"Are you going?"

"If Dad's up to it. Last time I talked to him, he told me he was going to take a walk in the snow."

"Oh yeah! It'll be good for him. Look, I have to go. I'll try to see you later."

Ivy hung up the phone. *So Morgana finally knows,* she thought, *and she didn't sound upset. I'm glad I told her. It was the right thing to do.*

Morgana was right. There was no problem about

the car. Elizabeth and her husband had planned to go out that night, and were taking his car. "I'll leave my keys on the dinning room table," Elizabeth told her.

Ivy went upstairs, and started to get ready. She looked forward to visiting the crystal house again. A few minutes later, Dru called.

Ivy answered it. "Hi, Dad! Did you have a nice walk?"

"Yeah, it was great out there! Been years since I've walked in the snow."

Ivy told her father about Rian's invitation to Caitlin's.

"Who's going?"

"I don't know. Probably some of the merchants and Rian. She has a date with Scotty. I think he's coming too."

"Will Morgana be there?"

"Humm, I don't know, Dad. She went somewhere."

"Oh.. where?"

"I'll tell you about it later."

"Ivy, I don't want to disappoint you, but I'm a little tired after being outside. In fact, I'm beginning to feel a little chilled."

"Dad, I'm not going then. I'll come over."

"Don't be silly. Go and have a good time."

"Are you sure?"

"I'm going to take a hot bath, and relax. I'm not sure milling about with all those people is my cup of tea."

Ivy could see her father's point.

"O.K., but if you change your mind, let me know!"

Ivy dressed warmly in jeans and a soft blue wool turtleneck sweater. She picked up the car keys and drove to Millcott. The place was even more crowded than she expected. It took her nearly half an hour to find a parking place.

Meanwhile, Dru started looking for his medication. He had been using an herbal brew which helped him, but he couldn't find the medicine bag he usually kept it in. After searching futilely, he felt chilled again. He called Rian at the store.

"Hi, Rian. Is Ivy there?" asked Dru.

"No, I haven't seen her. Is she in town?"

"She should be."

"Parking's a bitch tonight. I guess you decided not to come, huh?"

"Too much for me." Dru was feeling much worse when he hung up the phone.

Ivy finally parked the car. As she leaned over to lock the passenger door she noticed something had slipped in between the seat and the door. She reached down and pulled up her father's medicine bag.

He must have left it in the car while we were out today. Ivy knew he kept all kinds of things in there. In fact, he was hardly ever without it. Suddenly, she had an idea. She got out of the car and swung Dru's bag over her shoulder.

Ivy hit just about every store in town. She couldn't remember having so much fun Christmas shopping in a long time. The shops were so quaint, the atmosphere so charged! When she got to the end of Main Street she saw The Apothecary sign and went inside.

Upstairs, Viviene was taking a break. She was doing short mini-readings tonight. Trying to say something meaningful in ten or fifteen minutes could be trying. She poured herself some hot wassail and tried to relax, but she couldn't. Something had been bothering her since

Rian got that weird phone call. She reached down into her purse and pulled out her special cards. Then, she laid them out.

For a minute, she just studied them. Something was very odd here. She picked them up quickly and put them away, but it didn't help. She tried again. This time she shuffled them for a while, and pulled five cards. A few minutes later, Viviene went downstairs.

"Rian, I have to go out. Don't accept anymore appointments for me tonight."

"Viv? What's the matter?"

"Stay put kid. I have to talk to Dru. Where's he staying?

Rian told her.

"Thanks, see you later." As she left, she passed Ivy coming into the shop.

"Hi, Ivy," said Viviene. "You look like Santa with all those packages!" Then she was gone.

"Have some wassail." Kevin was very happy to see Ivy. He gave her a light kiss on the cheek.

"Hi, Kevin. This town is so busy!"

"Are you having a good time?"

"Can't you tell by all these packages?"

Kevin smiled. "Oh, by the way, your father called."

"He did?" Kevin offered her the phone and she rang his motel room. There was no answer. "When did he call?"

"Oh, I don't know. About an hour ago at least."

"Humm, he's not answering. I guess he fell asleep, or went for another walk." She laughed. "He loves the snow."

Ivy began looking around the shop. She went into the back room, and then, when Rian wasn't busy, she approached her.

"Rian, last summer when we were in your store my

dad saw something he really liked. I thought I'd get it for him for Christmas ... if it's still here."

Ivy went into the back room and looked around for the clay smudge pot that Dru had admired so much. Rian went back to help her.

"We've had several. Can you describe it?"

"You said a local artist made it. It was small, red clay and had little fetishes on it."

Rian smiled. "You mean this one?" She took a small bowl off the shelf.

Ivy recognized it. "Yes, that's it!"

"It must have been waiting just for you!"

"I'd like to buy it."

Rian discounted the price. Ivy was relieved. She had carefully put aside just enough money for her father's present, and now she'd have a little left over.

It was getting close to midnight. The town started to thin out. The streets were getting quieter, and some shops were already closing.

"It's almost twelve," Rian said to Ivy. "But I think I'll stay open just a little longer. Why not go up to Caitlin's? I'll meet you there in a little while."

"O.K." Before she left, Ivy told Kevin where she was going. He said he'd be along soon.

Ivy walked up to Caitlin's crystal shop. She was open. Up at this end of the town there were still many people on the streets.

"Hi, Caitlin!"

"Ivy. Hi!"

"Thanks for inviting me."

"I'm so glad you could make it."

"Rian and Kevin will be down in a little while. It's

not as busy down at her end of the street." She started browsing around. "You certainly have some beautiful crystals." Ivy purchased a small piece of blue celestite for Elizabeth.

"Listen, if you like, you can wait in the house. It's a lot warmer there. I'll be up soon."

"Thanks. Can I help with anything?"

Caitlin thought for a minute. "You could heat up some of the hors d'oeuvres. They're in the frig."

"O.K."

Ivy went through the stone passage way, up the steps, and around to the back. She noticed the little herb garden. It was all frozen now, and there was a light snow covering it. But when she went into the house she found many little pots of herbs sitting all around where they had been transplanted for the winter.

Ivy milled about in the kitchen for a while, setting things out. She put out the sodas and beer, but decided to wait a little longer before heating up the hors d'oeuvres. Then she sat down cross-legged on the floor. This place brought back many memories.

She took the little smudge pot out of the Apothecary bag and wrapped it up with some Christmas paper she had bought in town. Then she pulled out Dru's medicine bag.

I think Dad celebrates the Winter Solstice too, and that's tomorrow, she thought. So, when I give it back to him he'll just happen to find a little surprise!

She opened the buckle of the medicine bag, and noticed a bag of herbs on top. *I hope these are not the ones he bought earlier today; the ones he needed. I wonder if that's why he called?*

She considered the idea, but decided that if that were the case, he would have certainly left a message. *Oh well,* she thought, *maybe he started feeling lonely, and decided he wanted to come down after all.*

She pushed and pried at some of the stuff he had packed down in his bag trying to make room for the package she had wrapped. Then she smiled to herself. "And they talk about women's handbags. What is all this stuff?"

Her fingers felt globs of tissue paper. She thought that could go. She pulled it all out, and put it aside. *Now, that's better.* She put the tissue paper aside on the floor, and something fell out.

Ivy leaned over and picked up a piece of black cloth. What is this … .? After a moment, Ivy realized it was the same piece of torn cloth they had found at the farmhouse. *Why did he tell us he put it in the poppet?* Ivy wondered. *I guess he still gets confused sometimes. Was he just trying to show off?* She did not want to think her father was losing his grip. *I'm not going to confront him about this until we get back to California,* she decided.

She was careful not to touch the cloth as she rewrapped it, and put it in her pocketbook. Then she tried to push the little bowl down into the pouch again, but it still didn't fit. Something seemed to be stopping it. Down near the bottom her fingers felt something hard. She removed her hand. *I shouldn't be doing this,* she thought. *I'll just give it to him.*

Ivy put the package back in her shopping bag, but the weight tipped it over.

"Well, I guess this present doesn't want to go in there either." She decided to try one more time, without the excess wrapping paper and ribbon. *Now,* she thought, *this will just fit.* It didn't. There was still something at the bottom stopping it. Frustrated, she reached far inside to shift whatever it was in there, around.

Her hand grasped a little book. She pulled on it, pushing it to the side. *Dad's not going to like this,* she thought. She moved the book to the side, and pushed the smudge pot down. "There now. Finally!" She tried to buckle the medicine bag, but the book bulged out of the top. "Oh, no! Why does this have to be so difficult?"

She took out the book and looked at it. "He probably doesn't even know it's in here." Then she turned it over and her heart nearly stopped!

She just stared at it for a moment, too stunned to think. *How ... I don't ... understand ...* Ivy held the book in her hands. There was no mistake. It was a small, hand-bound and blue, with a carousel etched on the cover.

Ivy's mind had stopped functioning. Then it started racing. A thousand questions ran through her mind. She didn't get it. *Why does my father have this book? Why didn't he told me? Had somebody planted it there? No, of course not. What is happening?* Ivy began to shake. *Is it possible that all this time, my father knew? That he knew about everything? That he'd deceived me?* Her mind immediately rejected such an idea. *Was he trying to hide it to protect me from something?*

She began looking further into the bag, but it was as if all of her psychic ability had suddenly disappeared. She wasn't a psychic now, she was a daughter. He must have been much sicker than she ever realized. She went to the phone, and dialed the motel. Still no answer. Then she sat back on the floor, confused and numb.

Suddenly, Ivy was jolted by a knock on the door. *Oh no! People are here already*, she thought. She tried to get a grip on herself.

She put her shopping bag aside, and the medicine bag next to it. Then she took the wrapped cloth, and the book, and stuffed it in her handbag, and put it next to a chair. Dazed, she walked over to the door slowly and opened it. In the doorway stood Dru.

❀ ❀ ❀

CHAPTER 34

The Rag Bone Man

"Dad! What are you doing here?"

Dru looked bad. He pushed his way in. "Where are the keys to the car?"

"What?"

"I'm sick. Where are the keys? I think I left my medicine bag in there. I need some of my herbs."

"I have your medicine bag right here." Ivy picked it up.

"Dru looked at her strangely. "What are you doing with it?"

"I found it in the car. I was afraid to leave it in there. There were so many people in town. I thought it would be safer with me."

"I need it ... now."

"Dad, what's the matter with you?"

"Just give me the bag."

Ivy gave her father his medicine bag. He groped down into the bag looking for the herbs. His hand found the smudge pot. "What's this?"

"It was a gift I bought you. Oh, Dad, you spoiled my surprise. It was for Winter Solstice."

"You were in my bag?"

"Yes. I'm sorry. It was for a good cause."

Dru was looking sicker by the minute. He put his hand down into the bag, pulled out the smudge pot, and threw it on a chair.

For a moment, he said nothing. Then he began looking for his herbs again. As he searched around inside the bag, he became alarmed and frowned at Ivy. "Ivy, when you tried putting that smudge pot into my bag, did you … take anything out?"

"Yes."

"Why did you do that?"

Ivy felt awkward. "It … " Then she laughed nervously. "The pot wouldn't fit."

"Ivy … " he sounded strange. "You found that book didn't you?"

Ivy felt trapped. Then she answered "Yes … and I'm very confused. How on earth did you get it, and why didn't you tell me?"

"It's a long story." Dru seemed anxious.

"Dad, sit down. You don't look well."

He groaned. "I feel terrible."

"Why did you come down here?"

"I needed my medicine … I couldn't reach you."

"I'll get it."

"No, Ivy. I'd really prefer it if you didn't go through my things. Haven't you done enough of that with Morgana?"

Ivy raised her head. "I think I did the right thing in her case."

"Where is Morgana tonight?"

"I guess she couldn't make it.

Dru began sifting though his medicine bag for his

herbs again. "I need those herbs Ivy."

Ivy didn't know what to do. She was afraid to help him with his bag. He seemed so protective of it.

After a minute, he found what he was looking for, but as he tried to get them out of the bag, his hands were shaking so much, he dropped the pouch. The herbs scattered all over the floor.

Viviene drove her car out of the traffic in Millcott onto a nearby highway. In less than ten minutes, she pulled into a motel driveway, parked as fast as she could, ran into the motel office and up to the desk clerk.

"Excuse me," she said. "What room is Dru Parkington in?"

The bored clerk checked his book. "Room 116."

"Thanks." Viviene ran down the walkway. Room 100, 102, 104 … ..she kept going. Finally she came to 116, and knocked on the door. No one answered. She knocked again harder. Still no answer. "Shit!" She ran back to the clerk.

"I need a key," she smiled. "I'm Mrs. Parkington."

"Oh." The clerk looked in his book. "No, he's only paying for a single."

"Well, he wasn't expecting me until tomorrow, but I got away early because of the holidays. I'll be glad to pay the extra fee." Viviene took out a twenty dollar bill and waved it at the desk clerk.

"Well, I guess it's O.K. then," he said taking the money. "Here's your key."

"Thanks."

Viviene hurried back to room 116. Once again she knocked. Still no answer. She unlocked the door and opened it slowly. The room was dark. Her hands searched for the light-switch.

A few minutes later at The Apothecary, Rian got a phone call. Trembling, she hung up the phone and began to lock up.

At the crystal house, Dru began pacing unsteadily around the room. He saw Ivy's canvas handbag on the floor and picked it up. It was not buckled securely and the contents tumbled out all over the floor. Among Ivy's things were the book and the tissue with the piece of dark cloth. He stared down at the items stunned for a moment. He didn't move or say a word. Then, he moved backwards a step and knocked over Ivy's shopping bag. All of the presents fell out.

He stared strangely at the floor, and his face looked very weird to Ivy. He said he was sorry.

Dru kept staggering about. Then he tried to pick up the herbs again. They were scattered everywhere. He tried to gather them up with his hands, but they stuck to Caitlin's colorful Indian rug.

"Dad, stop this. Stop right now!" She went over to her father and tried to get him up on the couch.

He shrugged her away. As he tried to pick up the herbs, Ivy thought, *He's still addicted! Those herbs must be some kind of drugs or something.*

Ivy inched her way towards her father. "Come on, Dad, sit down. I'll find you some herbs here. What do you need? Caitlin has lots of them. Look around." She gestured to the potted plants.

Dru sat down.

"Now, what can I get you?"

"Just sit here, Ivy." He took her hand and pulled her down. With the other hand he began to lick the tiny leaves off his fingers. "There, see? I'll be all right ... We'll be able to leave in a minute."

The whole episode was making Ivy sick and dizzy. When she looked at her father, his face seemed to blur.

Rian hurried up the street, through the passage, and up the steps to the back door, but she was not prepared for what she saw when she looked through the window-pane. The place was a mess, with things strewed all about. She could see Ivy's open handbag, and Christmas presents scattered all over the floor.

Dru heard someone at the door, and as it slowly opened, he turned around.

Rian didn't move. She just stood there staring at Ivy, who was sitting on the couch ... ..and holding the hand of the Rag Bone Man!

"Ivy, what are you doing? Get away! Get away!" Rian screamed.

Ivy looked around. "Rian, what's the matter with you?"

"Look who you are sitting with!"

Ivy looked at Dru and blinked. She started shaking her head ... "What are you talking about?"

"Don't you see?"

Ivy looked at Dru again, and turned a puzzled look at Rian. *What's the matter with her,* she thought. *Has everyone lost their senses tonight?*

Rian didn't move. At first she couldn't understand Ivy's situation. But as she watched the bewildered look on Ivy's face, she began to realize with horror that Ivy wasn't seeing what she was seeing. "Ivy, please, just move away from the couch ...carefully," she said softly.

Ivy looked at the man sitting next to her, her eyes straining to see what Rian was seeing. Then, she nervously got up and slowly backed away from the couch. Still puzzled, Ivy began to laugh nervously again as though she hoped this whole insane evening was some kind of Midnight Madness joke, and she was too stupid to catch on. But that thought was fleeting, and the queer smile left her face almost as quickly as it had come.

She heard Rian's voice encouraging her. "That's it." Rian stood near the door. "Now, come on over here, Ivy."

But Ivy couldn't. She just kept staring at her father on the couch with that mystified look on her face. For a moment, the room was totally silent. Ivy barely breathed. She pulled some of her hair away from her face and around to the back of her head, as if to help her focus better. And then slowly ... very slowly ... her vision began to clear. Yet, in truth, it wasn't her vision that was finally clearing ... it was her mind.

"Oh my God" she whispered. "My God ... What is going on here. What is happening?"

The man rose slowly from the couch. "Shouldn't have spilled my herbs, Ivy."

Instinctively, Rian started to move towards her, but the creature whirled around. "Don't even try, you bitch!"

Ivy jumped back. She was petrified.

Still keeping an eye on Rian, the man stooped over and tried to pick up more herbs off the floor.

"Help me here!" he ordered Ivy. "Hurry up!"

In her confusion, Ivy began to try to gather up tiny flakes of herb. But as she watched him, she grew more panicky. He seemed to be changing. His face grew harder, his eyes narrower, his silver hair was turning dark, and all around him a smoky haze seemed to be gathering.

Oh my God, she thought, her hand coming slowly to her mouth in horror ... *what is happening to my father?*

She began to crawl around on the floor like a trapped animal. *Where is my father? What happened? He was here ... just before!*

She turned her head slowly and looked up at her father. Screaming in revulsion, Ivy got up off the floor and scrambled to her feet. She ran by him towards the door as fast as she could, but he blocked her way and hit her hard. Ivy fell, stunned. When she saw he wouldn't let her out, she ran up the spiral staircase, stopped at the landing, turned and looked down. And then what she saw, what she finally saw ... finally had to accept ... completely paralyzed her!

He grinned up at her and hissed through missing teeth. Then he started up the stairs. "I'm going to kill you, you smart-ass little bitch!"

Rian moved towards him. "Stop it!"

The creature turned around. For a moment he forgot about Ivy and began to advance towards his real enemy ... Rian.

Rian was terrified. Inside herself, she tried to reach for her sense of power.

She knew that the time had come. Closing her eyes, she tried to think of the rune, but he was on her before she could utter a word.

"So, you found my book?" The creature grabbed her arm.

Rian pulled away. "Stop it!"

"Took my book!"

"Let me go!" Rian screamed. She tried to shake loose, but he only gripped her tighter. Then he threw her to the floor. She was totally immobile.

The creature started looking around the room and at the things on the floor. He noticed the tissue paper crumpled under Ivy's purse. By now the creature was totally crazed. He looked up the stairs and saw Ivy looking back, her face as pale as a ghost.

"You liar … ..you thief! You stole my things!"

Rian saw him move towards the stairs again. She screamed to divert his attention. "It was you who stole my things, creature!" Rian was trying hard. The creature stopped and turned. Rian lunged for his back foot, which was on the step, and pulled as hard as she could. He fell down and hit his chin on the staircase. For a moment, he was dazed.

Rian needed that moment. She thanked God for that moment. *Now*, she thought … *Now!* She closed her eyes and said the rune over and over, visualizing the familiar spirit, the fetch, she had created. She felt something move on her shoulder. From the silver disk came an eerie sound. It got louder and louder, and then it laughed like a horse.

The creature was up. He began coming towards her. Rian backed away. She continued saying the rune, calling for Mora. She repeated it to herself over and over.

"You think you can best me, little girl?" he whispered.

"You think?" He sneered. "You're only a novice. Who taught you those little tricks, huh..?"

Rian backed away. She was losing her courage.

The creature laughed at her. "So, bitch, you think you can destroy me with your little spells, huh?"

Rian tripped over Ivy's purse, and fell backwards. The creature laughed at her. "So, I'm curious. Who else knows about me, huh? Tell me, or I'll kill you, and your friend upstairs!"

Rian was lying back on her elbows, slowly pulling back as the creature advanced towards her. "I'm the only one who knows."

"Liar! Liar! Who else?" The creature lunged for her and grabbed her throat. Rian was terrified. Nothing was working. She was going to cry. Where was Mora? Was there a Mora? She began to doubt the whole thing.

"What's the matter little girl? Doesn't your magick work?"

Suddenly, he released the grip on her throat. Somebody was coming in the door. He turned and saw Viviene.

She wasted no time. "Rian! Rian! Listen to me! You have more power than he could ever dream of. Use your power Rian. Use it! Call *Mora*! Call ... Call ... I can't do it for you!"

The creature turned and faced Viviene. He hissed. "Get out of here!"

"You wish," she smiled cruelly.

He lunged for her. She was ready for him. Her athame was already out and she drew a blazing blue pentagram in front of him in the air. It stopped him cold. He turned towards Rian, then back towards Viviene. Then he sneered. "She can't do anything. She's a beginner."

"I wouldn't be too sure, creature."

Rian saw the Elemental coming towards her again.

"Call!" Viviene urged her on!

Rian said the words out loud this time.

"Mora! Hear my words; Heed the spell!
"If danger threatens; Serve me well!"

The creature kept on coming. Rian moved across the room and picked up a large crystal.

The creature laughed at her. "So … you're gonna use some of that crystal magick on me, huh?" he taunted. He jumped across the room at her. Rian hurled the crystal at him and missed. It shattered into a million pieces. Rian froze. The creature looked over at where the crystal had smashed, and then gleefully recognized his medicine bag lying under the debris. He swooped it up, shook it, and threw it over his shoulder. Then quickly turning his attention back to Rian, he grinned and advanced towards her again.

"Well, well, well. You can't even throw a rock, much less a spell, little girl, so I think I'm gonna kill you!"

Rian backed away. She was terrified. Why had she come down here? She couldn't remember any more. Suddenly, the creature was on her again. He grabbed her shoulders and started shaking her till she thought she would break. Then, he threw her to the floor. She crashed so hard, she believed every bone in her body was broken.

"Rian, don't give up!" It was Viviene. "Rian, see it! See your totem! Don't just say the words. … Think it … Think it in your mind!"

The creature turned again towards Viviene. He couldn't touch her as long as she held the athame. Viviene knew she could keep him away from her, but Rian was the only one who held the power to destroy him.

Rian staggered up, but fell again. She thought she was going to pass out. Strange images passed through her mind. The man in her dreams giving her the herbs and then her rescue by the ladies in the boat. They once saved her before from this demon.

She tried to say the words, but they wouldn't come. All she could think of were the ladies in the boat ... the lake. Were they the same? One of them was saying softly. "Say the words, Rian, and think of us. We are your kin. Try!"

The faery women continued to urge her softly ... gently, and finally Rian in her altered state began to say the words again in her mind and whisper them softly. She wondered if this is what it felt like to die. Everything was getting darker and darker, and Rian felt as though she were sinking down ... down into the waters down ... down ... and then ... nothing.

But Rian did not die in the lake. She was revived. And the process enabled Rhiannon to emerge! As the magickal waters soothed and healed Rian, they also opened the current for Rhiannon to come through. The words gave Rhiannon and her power animal shape and form, and so, while Viviene and the creature looked on in awe, Rian was at long last awakened! And as she was, she slowly rose to her feet.

This time it was the creature's turn to back up. He heard the horse again. It grew louder and louder. He saw Rian change, transform! Her long black hair sparkled, and her clothes seemed ablaze with fire. Her face became strong and radiant, and next to her stood the ghostly white shadow of a horse.

Rian saw the creature staring at her. But now she was not only Rian, she was also the powerful Rhiannon; Queen of the Otherworld, with Mora, the terrifying night-mare.

"So," said Rhiannon softly, "We meet again."

The Rag Bone Man was visibly horrified. His sort of magick was limited, and he was certainly no match for Rhiannon and Mora. Now, there could be no trickery. He realized that she knew everything, and was ready for him. Rian had been awakened, not by death, but in life. The creature had no choice. He could not escape. He made a stupid lunge for her, but a black raven came forth and plucked at his eyes. He screamed.

"You have come to the end of the road, demon. You are finished!" Rhiannon held out her hand. "I am Rhiannon, Queen of the Otherworld, and your wicked days on this plane are done."

The creature backed up slowly. "No! Wait! … No..!" He held out one hand in front of her, as if somehow he could push her away. With the other, he groped inside his medicine bag and found his small sharp knife. Then, with every last effort in his body, he lunged towards Rhiannon. Mora shrieked out and rose up on her hind legs. The creature dropped his knife and moved back in terror.

Rhiannon removed the silver disk from her collar and held it towards him. He moved back.

Then she said:

"By the art of the lake,
By the well and the sidhe,
By the magick of nine,

And the rule of three.
From the lake and the pond,
From air, earth, fire and sea,
To the Unseelie Court,
I do banish thee!"

As Rhiannon held out the silver shield, an electric-blue light began to emit from it. Like a vapor, the light encircled the smoky aura of the Rag Bone Man as he fought to escape.

Then, very slowly, Ivy began to descend the stairs. From her vantage point at the top, she had watched incredulously as this extraordinary scene took place below. On the occasions that she wanted to go to Rian's aid, something firmly held her back. But after the Elemental was incapacitated, that hold was released. With each step she felt her emotions rising up in her. No more the psychic, only the daughter, she cried out, "Where is my father?"

The creature could barely move now. He hissed at Ivy, "Dead!"

Ivy collapsed on the staircase. Then she began to weep. Rian wanted to go to her, but she had to keep an eye on the Elemental. The blue light became brighter and brighter.

Finally, the creature fell to the ground, and began to disintegrate.

When it was all over, the only thing left of the creature and his possessions was a small charred bone. She picked up the bone and broke it. Half of it in she placed in the smudge-pot Ivy had brought, and burned it up with the powerful blue light. The other half she put away to keep as a link to the creature. Once the bone was broken, he could never appear as a human again.

No one had noticed that Caitlin and Kevin were standing dumb-struck in the doorway, watching. Slowly they came in. No one knew what to say. Kevin went over to Ivy who was completely wiped out. Her body ached, and her eye was swollen.

But then everyone turned and watched Rhiannon as she slowly returned to Rian and to herself.

"Are you all right?" said Kevin when he finally felt the time was right to approach his sister.

"I'm … yes, I think I am. I'm O.K … " And in fact she was. She didn't hurt or ache. She felt completely healed after her terrible ordeal.

"What happened here?" said Kevin. "When I came to the door, you were standing there looking, I don't know, like something on fire! And this blue light was coming out of your hand."

"I'm not entirely sure myself, Kev," said Rian slowly. "But I guess you're both entitled to hear what happened." Viviene and Rian told them the whole story.

Still stunned by what they had seen and heard, the group quietly began picking things up. Morgana arrived soon after. By then, most of the room had been put back together.

Morgana was amazed when she heard the story of Dru. "I just can't believe that he fooled us all this time!" she said. "It's incredible."

Rian gave her aunt the book. "Ivy found it in his medicine bag," she said.

Morgana took the book, and leafed through it. "I remember it now," she said. "It did once belong to my mother … so, that is what Carl was talking about." Morgana told the others she had just learned that her mother did not give Dru the book at an initiation ceremony. It was given to him at her home in New York City.

Ivy sat silently. She was too numb to say anything.

"Where is the creature now?" asked Kevin.

Rian thought it curious that Kevin addressed the question to her; as though she were an authority.

"I don't know. When I … threw that blue light, I seemed to be in a dream, as though I were someone else … somewhere else. I suppose he went back to wherever he came from … or maybe he is dead. One thing I know, he will not be bothering any of us again." She looked at Viviene.

Viviene looked over at the ashes in the smudge pot.

"But what is death to an Elemental?" asked Viviene. "They don't really stop existing. They are part of the elements. If you freeze water, it becomes ice … if you burn fire, it becomes smoke … .It doesn't stop, it transforms. What you did as Rhiannon was to banish him from this plane. I heard you send him to the Unseelie Court."

"What's that?" asked Rian.

"An Elemental Plane for nasty's is the only way I can describe it. It's probably where he came from."

"And escaped from," added Morgana.

There was no party, of course. On the way back to the crystal house Viviene had rushed into Caitlin's store and told her to call it off. Caitlin could tell by Viviene's behavior that something very serious was going on.

Rian had completely forgotten about Scott. When she did think of him later, she sighed in relief. "I guess his replacement never made it. After what happened here, I can't say that I'm sorry. Can you imagine … what he would have thought?"

Just then, Kevin remembered. "Rian, Scott did call just before I left. He wanted me to apologize to you. He said his stand-in never showed." Kevin reached into his pocket and pulled out a piece of paper. "Here is his number. He wanted you to call him."

Rian sighed. "Thanks, Kev. It's so late, he's probably left by now." But Rian wanted to hear his voice.

While Rian was using the phone, Kevin and Morgana were trying to comfort Ivy. She was still too dazed to say much of anything.

"I think you should see a doctor about that eye," said Kevin touching it gently. Caitlin had already given her ice to put on it.

"No. I think I'll call my mom in the morning. I don't know how to explain this to her. She'll think I've lost my mind." Then she laughed a little ironically. "Maybe I have."

"Perhaps, you shouldn't try to explain … just yet," said Morgana. "If you like, when you go back to California, you can stay with Robin and me for a while."

"I don't want to go back to California."

Morgana nodded. She felt so sorry for the young woman.

"I just can't accept the fact that my father is dead."

"I'm so sorry," said Morgana. She put her arm around her.

"Is it possible … he was lying?" said Ivy.

Viviene answered. "It's very possible he doesn't know. Elementals are very one-dimensional. What I think happened here is that when the Rag Bone Man got through to this plane, he decided to work on your father to get to Rian. His idea was to incapacitate Dru, or possibly kill him and slowly take his place. It probably took him a long time to get the hang of looking human, much less acting that way."

"And he had friends who worked with him," said Ivy.

"He must have promised them a lot, the fools. I always said that getting involved with magick makes some people crazy."

Rian remembered Viviene saying that. Now she understood what she meant.

"What did those herbs have to do with it?" asked Ivy.

"I'm not sure about that. I can only assume that he must have devised some magical concoction that helped him take on Dru's appearance."

"Yes, and when they wore off, he would start to change back." said Ivy. "That's why he was so anxious to get them."

For a moment no one said anything. Everyone was lost in their own thoughts.

"You know," said Ivy. "I used to wonder if that creature transformed himself for short periods of time. I even mentioned it to my fath … to him. Now I understand why he told me he was going to those so-called treatment centers."

"It must have been a strain just maintaining his disguise," said Viviene. He probably went off to be alone and gather power again."

"Yes, and I bet I know where he stayed," Ivy remarked, her voice filled with resentment.

"It also explains why he looked so different to me," said Morgana. "I hardly recognized him. What a perfect disguise … a recovering addict."

Ivy went on. She needed to talk. "I thought when he first got here tonight that he was on drugs again. I just couldn't understand why he was acting so crazy! But finding the book is what really threw me. And even then … I made excuses." She stopped for a minute. "What I really can't understand … .is why I never saw it? Why I never knew?"

"That was planned from the beginning, I'm sure," said Viviene. "As soon as he heard of you, he probably threw a veil over himself to prevent you from seeing through him. Then he decided to use you as a sort of psychic go-between. You could always tell him things he couldn't quite figure out himself."

"You were also an excellent cover," said Morgana. "You gave his story credibility. He completely tricked me."

Rian looked over at Viviene. "Viv, how did you know?"

"At first it was just a hunch. I felt that something was wrong. I threw the cards, and saw the Magician again. But this time I saw him crossing Ivy. I couldn't figure that out at first, so I put the cards away. But then something kept nagging at me, and I threw them again. Now, all along, during this whole scenario, I've connected certain cards with certain people The Magician was the Rag Bone Man; Rian was the Queen of Cups; Morgana, the Queen of Wands … etc. Ivy, I always saw in the Major Arcana as the Star card and Dru I saw as the King of Cups. When I threw the cards the second time, I only threw five. The Star card fell again, but when I crossed it, the King of Cups came up … Dru. I thought that was very odd, so I threw the third card and it was the

Moon inverted … secrets; deception, then the three of swords; sorrow, and finally the Death card … transformation. But, of course, even then I had no idea what was really going on."

"Is that why you asked me for Dru's address?" asked Rian.

"Yes, and no. I'm leaving out one more thing. When I went to gather up the cards, one fell on the floor. It was the King of Cups … Dru's card. Now my personal cards are very old, and when I went to pick it up, I noticed another card was sticking to it."

"Which one?" asked Rian.

Viviene looked over at Ivy.

"The Magician," Ivy said, resignation in her voice.

Viviene nodded. "When I got to the motel, Dru was gone, but the desk clerk gave me a key to his room, and I got inside. It was quite a revelation. Books on black magic laying around, notes on shape-shifting. But the one thing that finally grabbed me was this. She opened her pocketbook and pulled out a doll."

Ivy gasped. "The poppet!"

"That's right, but remember when he showed it to us it was partially concealed? That's because the poppet was you," she said to Ivy. "It had your picture attached to it with a blindfold around your eyes. Looks like he had some of your hair too," Viviene said as she flipped up a lock of red hair stitched to the doll's head. Just another little precautionary measure to keep you blinded to his identity."

Ivy noticed the clothes on the doll. "This is too much. It's dressed in an old tee-shirt I threw out."

"But this was the clincher." Viviene pulled out one

more thing from her tote-bag and held it up. "Remember this?" Viviene looked at Rian.

"Oh God, his beret!" said Rian. "I'd know it anywhere. Remember those red and black clothes ?"

"They were there, too. But you have to understand, that even though I had come to the conclusion that there was a connection between Dru and the Rag Bone Man, and that Ivy was in some kind of danger, I never dreamed that Dru and the creature were the same person! In fact, my first impression was that Dru had been kidnapped or something. Nothing made sense."

"And that's when you called and said the Rag Bone Man was nearby, and to keep an eye on Ivy."

"Yes."

Ivy shook her head wearily. "I feel so betrayed, so stupid. I guess the chances of finding my father alive are pretty slim."

"Try not to be too hard on yourself," Viviene said softly. "You were up against a powerhouse! To me the Star card means 'hope' and it's your tarot card. Anything is possible."

The group talked for a long time, but finally they grew exhausted, and everybody wanted to leave. After they did, Caitlin burned sage for hours.

Morgana stayed with Ivy. The next morning they had a long talk. Ivy told Morgana that she decided to return to California after all. "If there's even the slightest chance my father's still alive, I want to try and find him."

Morgana agreed to do whatever she could to help, but, inside, she felt Dru was lost forever.

❈❈❈❈

Epilogue

Rian was so burned out when she got home, she fell asleep on the sofa downstairs. The memory of Rhiannon had dimmed already, and, in fact, the whole sequence of events seemed almost illusionary to her now.

As soon as she dozed off, she had a brief dream. In a dark, shadowy place, vague images were seated in a circle. For a while, there was only silence. Then she heard a bitter voice say. *"It's been much too long; we'll never get him back."* After that the scene faded, Rian fell into a deep, restful sleep.

Her handbag was lying on a nearby chair. Just before dawn, Starlight went over to it, sniffed, growled and aggressively chewed her way through the leather. Her tail wagging with anticipation, she strutted out to the kitchen, went through the little doggie door and laid out under her favorite tree. Then, with a sense of tremendous satisfaction she chewed up the other half of the bone.

❈❈❈❈

STAY IN TOUCH

On the following pages you will find some of the books now available on related subjects. Your book dealer stocks most of these and will stock new titles in the Llewellyn series as they become available. We urge your patronage.

To obtain our full catalog write for our bimonthly news magazine/catalog, *Llewellyn's New Worlds of Mind and Spirit*. A sample copy is free, and it will continue coming to you at no cost as long as you are an active mail customer. Or you may subscribe for just $10.00 in the U.S.A. and Canada ($20.00 overseas, first class mail). Many bookstores also have *New Worlds* available to their customers. Ask for it.

Llewellyn's New Worlds of Mind and Spirit
P.O. Box 64383-412, St. Paul, MN 55164-0383, U.S.A.

TO ORDER BOOKS AND TAPES

If your book dealer does not have the books described, you may order them directly from the publisher by sending full price in U.S. funds, plus $3.00 for postage and handling for orders *under* $10.00; $4.00 for orders *over* $10.00. There are no postage and handling charges for orders over $50.00. Postage and handling rates are subject to change. We ship UPS whenever possible. Delivery guaranteed. Provide your street address as UPS does not deliver to P.O. Boxes. UPS to Canada requires a $50.00 minimum order. Allow 4-6 weeks for delivery. Orders outside the U.S.A. and Canada: Airmail—add retail price of book; add $5.00 for each non-book item (tapes, etc.); add $1.00 per item for surface mail. Mail orders to:

LLEWELLYN PUBLICATIONS
P.O. Box 64383-412, St. Paul, MN 55164-0383, U.S.A.
Prices subject to change without notice.

Prices subject to change without notice

THE COMMITTEE
by Raymond Buckland

"Duncan's eyes were glued to the destruct button. He saw that the colonel's hand never did get to it. Yet, even as he watched, he saw the red button move downwards, apparently of its own volition. The rocket blew into a million pieces, and the button came back up. No one, Duncan would swear, had physically touched the button, yet it had been depressed."

The Cold War is back in this psi-techno suspense thriller where international aggressors use psychokinesis, astral projection and other psychic means to circumvent the U.S. intelligence network. When two routine communications satellite launches are inexplicably aborted at Vandenberg Air Force Base in California, one senator suspects paranormal influences. He calls in a writer, two parapsychologists and a psychic housewife—and The Committee is formed. Together, they piece together a sinister occult plot against the United States. The Committee then embarks on a supernatural adventure of a lifetime as they attempt to beat the enemy at its own game.

Llewellyn Psi-Fi Fiction Series
1-56718-100-7, 240 pgs., mass market   **$4.99**

THE MESSENGER
by Donald Tyson

"She went to the doorway and took Eliza by her shoulders. 'But you mind what I tell you. Something in this house is watching us, and its thoughts are not kindly. It's all twisted up and bitter inside. It means to make us suffer. Then it means to kill us, one by one.'"

Sealed inside a secret room of an old mansion in Nova Scotia is a cruel and uncontrollable entity, created years earlier by an evil magician. When the new owner of the mansion unknowingly releases the entity, it renews its malicious and murderous rampage. Called on to investigate the strange phenomena are three women and four men—each with their own occult talents. As their investigation proceeds, the group members enter into a world of mystery and horror as they encounter astral battles, spirit possession—even death. In their efforts to battle the evil spirit, they use seance, hypnotic trance and magical rituals, the details of which are presented in fascinating and accurate detail.

Llewellyn Psi-Fi Fiction Series
0-87542-836-3, 240 pgs., mass market   **$4.99**

HOW TO MEET & WORK WITH SPIRIT GUIDES
by Ted Andrews

We often experience spirit contact in our lives but fail to recognize it for what it is. Now you can learn to access and attune to beings such as guardian angels, nature spirits and elementals, spirit totems, archangels, gods and goddesses—as well as family and friends after their physical death.

Contact with higher soul energies strengthens the will and enlightens the mind. Through a series of simple exercises, you can safely and gradually increase your awareness of spirits and your ability to identify them. You will learn to develop an intentional and directed contact with any number of spirit beings. Discover meditations to open up your subconscious. Learn which acupressure points effectively stimulate your intuitive faculties. Find out how to form a group for spirit work, use crystal balls, perform automatic writing, attune your aura for spirit contact, use sigils to contact the great archangels and much more! Read *How to Meet and Work with Spirit Guides* and take your first steps through the corridors of life beyond the physical.

0-87542-008-7, 192 pgs., mass market, illus.   **$3.95**

HOW TO SEE AND READ THE AURA
by Ted Andrews

Everyone has an aura—the three-dimensional, shape-and-color-changing energy field that surrounds all matter. And anyone can learn to see and experience the aura more effectively. There is nothing magical about the process. It simply involves a little understanding, time, practice and perseverance.

Do some people make you feel drained? Do you find some rooms more comfortable and enjoyable to be in? Have you ever been able to sense the presence of other people before you actually heard or saw them? If so, you have experienced another person's aura. In this practical, easy-to-read manual, you receive a variety of exercises to practice alone and with partners to build your skills in aura reading and interpretation. Also, you will learn to balance your aura each day to keep it vibrant and strong so others cannot drain your vital force.

Learning to see the aura not only breaks down old barriers—it also increases sensitivity. As we develop the ability to see and feel the more subtle aspects of life, our intuition unfolds and increases, and the childlike joy and wonder of life returns.

0-87542-013-3, 160 pgs., mass market, illus.   **$3.95**

GHOSTS, HAUNTINGS & POSSESSIONS
The Best of Hans Holzer, Book I
Edited by Raymond Buckland

Now, a collection of the best stories from best-selling author and psychic investigator Hans Holzer—in mass market format! Accounts in *Ghosts, Hauntings & Possessions* include:

- A 37-year-old housewife from Nebraska was tormented by a ghost that drove phantom cars and grabbed her foot while she lay in bed at night. Even after moving to a different state, she could still hear heavy breathing.

- A psychic visited with the spirit of Thomas Jefferson at Monticello. What scandals surrounded his life that the history books don't tell us?

- Here is the exact transcript of what transpired in a seance confrontation with Elvis Presley—almost a year after his death!

- Ordinary people from all over the country had premonitions about the murders of John and Robert Kennedy. Here are their stories.

- What happened to the middle-aged woman who played with the Ouija board and ended up tormented and possessed by the spirit of a former boyfriend?

- Here is the report of Abraham Lincoln's prophetic dream of his own funeral. Does his ghost still roam the White House because of unfinished business?

These stories and many more will intrigue, spook and entertain readers of all ages.

0-87542-367-1, 288 pgs., mass market   **$4.95**

DOORS TO OTHER WORLDS
A Practical Guide to Communicating with Spirits
by Raymond Buckland

There has been a revival of spiritualism in recent years, with more and more people attempting to communicate with disembodied spirits via talking boards, séances, and all forms of mediumship (e.g., allowing another spirit to make use of your vocal chords, hand muscles, etc., while you remain in control of your body). The movement, which began in 1848 with the Fox sisters of New York, has attracted the likes of Abraham Lincoln and Queen Victoria, and even blossomed into a full-scale religion with regular services of hymns, prayers, Bible-reading and sermons along with spirit communication.

Doors to Other Worlds is for *anyone* who wishes to communicate with spirits, as well as for the less adventurous who simply wish to satisfy their curiosity about the subject. Explore the nature of the Spiritual Body, learn how to prepare yourself to become a medium, experience for yourself the trance state, clairvoyance, psychometry, table tipping and levitation, talking boards, automatic writing, spiritual photography, spiritual healing, distant healing, channeling, development circles, and also learn how to avoid spiritual fraud.

0-87542-061-3, 272 pgs., 5 1/4 x 8, illus., softcover

$10.00

POLTERGEIST
A Study in Destructive Haunting
by Colin Wilson

Objects flying through the air, furniture waltzing around the room, dishes crashing to the floor. These are the hallmarks of the poltergeist phenomena. Now Colin Wilson, the renowned authority on the paranormal, investigates these mysterious forces in this fascinating and provocative work.

A middle-aged businessman and his wife rented a house on Cape Cod for the summer. They were, for some reason, its first occupants in nine years. Neither paid much attention to the first disturbance—a tapping near the front door. But then they heard a clicking noise—followed by a deafening crash from the garage . . . What happened next is revealed only in *Poltergeist!*

Countless similar cases of poltergeist mischief have been recorded from the days of ancient Greece and Rome to the present. But what are poltergeists? Where do they come from? Why do they appear and how do they interact in our world? In this comprehensive study, Colin Wilson examines the evidence regarding poltergeists and develops a masterful and definitive theory of the forces that surround us and are contained within each one of us.

0-87542-883-5, 448 pgs., mass market   **$5.95**

HOW TO UNCOVER YOUR PAST LIVES
by Ted Andrews

Knowledge of your past lives can be extremely reward-ing. It can assist you in opening to new depths within your own psychological makeup. It can provide greater insight into present circumstances with loved ones, career and health. It is also a lot of fun.

Now Ted Andrews shares with you nine different tech-niques that you can use to access your past lives. Between techniques, Andrews discusses issues such as karma and how it is expressed in your present life; the source of past life information; soul mates and twin souls; proving past lives; the mysteries of birth and death; animals and reincarnation; abortion and pre-mature death; and the role of reincarnation in Christian-ity.

To explore your past lives, you need only use one or more of the techniques offered. Complete instructions are provided for a safe and easy regression. Learn to dowse to pinpoint the years and places of your lives with great accuracy, make your own self-hypnosis tape, attune to the incoming child during pregnancy, use the tarot and the cabala in past life meditations, keep a past life journal and more.

0-87542-022-2, 240 pgs., mass market, illus.   **$3.95**

THE COMPLETE BOOK OF AMULETS & TALISMANS
by Migene González-Wippler
The Pentagram, Star of David, Crucifix, rabbit's foot,
painted pebble, or Hand of Fatima ... they all provide
feelings of comfort and protection, attracting good while
dispelling evil.

Spanning the world through the diverse cultures of
Sumeria, Babylonia, Greece, Italy, India, Western Europe
and North America, González-Wippler proves that
amulets and talismans are anything but mere supersti-
tion—they are part of each man's and woman's search
for spiritual connection. This book presents the entire
history of these tools, their geography, and shows how
anyone can create amulets and talismans to empower his
or her life. Loaded with hundreds of photographs, this is
the ultimate reference and how-to guide for their use.

0-87542-287-X, 304 pgs., 6 x 9, photos, softcover

$12.95

THE CELTIC HEART
Kathryn Marie Cocquyt

The Celtic Heart tells the adventurous, epic tale of spirit, love, loss, and the difficult choices made by three generations of the Celtic Brigantes tribe, who once lived off the coast of North Wales on an island they named *Mona mam Cymru* ("Mother of Wales," or Anglesey).

Follow the passionate lives of the Brigantes clan and the tumultuous events during the years leading up to the Roman Invasion in A.D. 61, when Anglesey was a refuge for Celts struggling to preserve their inner truths and goddess-based culture against the encroachment of the Roman Empire and Christianity. As their tribal way of life is threatened, the courageous natures of the Chieftain Solomon, the Druidess Saturnalia, and the young warriors Kordelina and Aonghus are tested by the same questions of good and evil that face us today.

Filled with ritual, dream images, romance, and intrigue, *The Celtic Heart* will take you on an authentic and absorbing journey into the history, lives, and hearts of the legendary Celts.

ISBN: 1-56718-156-2, 6 x 9. est. 592 pp., softbound   **$14.95**

COMPANY OF PROPHETS
African American Psychics, Healers & Visionaries
by Joyce Elaine Noll

This is a unique and significant collection of supernatural and ethnic materials never before arranged in one volume! *Company of Prophets* describes African Americans born in the United States who have extrasensory perception, psychic abilities and spiritual gifts, in a time frame from the 17th century to the present.

This book adds to the historical data not previously available on African Americans, unearthed through recent nationwide interviews and research. It features people from all ages and walks of life, including contemporary and historical leaders in education, business, theology and the arts. They share their experiences with astral projection, soul travel, levitation, healing, past lives, channeling and divination. In their own words, gifted subjects provide practical advice and workable techniques to assist readers in increasing their own psychic awareness.

Discover how Harriet Tubman used her ESP to bring slaves safely North to freedom; how an internationally known sculptor astral projects to perfect his work; how a child learned to gather, cook and use herbs from disembodied Indian spirits. These are just a few of the amazing reports in *Company of Prophets*.

0-87542-583-6, 272 pgs., 6 x 9, photos, softcover $12.95

THE LLEWELLYN PRACTICAL GUIDE TO ASTRAL PROJECTION
The Out-of-Body Experience
by Denning & Phillips

Yes, your consciousness can be sent forth, out of the body, with full awareness and return with full memory. You can travel through time and space, converse with nonphysical entities, obtain knowledge by nonmaterial means, and experience higher dimensions.

Is there life after death? Are we forever shackled by time and space? The ability to go forth by means of the Astral Body, or Body of Light, gives the personal assurance of consciousness (and life) beyond the limitations of the physical body. No other answer to these ageless questions is as meaningful as experienced reality.

The reader is led through the essential stages for the inner growth and development that will culminate in fully conscious projection and return. Not only are the requisite practices set forth in step-by-step procedures, augmented with photographs and visualization aids, but the vital reasons for undertaking them are clearly explained. Beyond this, the great benefits from the various practices themselves are demonstrated in renewed physical and emotional health, mental discipline, spiritual attainment, and the development of extra faculties.

Guidance is also given to the Astral World itself: what to expect, what can be done—including the ecstatic experience of Astral Sex between two people who project together into this higher world where true union is consummated free of the barriers of physical bodies.

0-87542-181-4, 266 pgs., 5 1/4 x 8, illus., softcover

$8.95